Call On Me

a novel

Katie Edward

VALLEY LILY PRESS

ISBN: 978-1-7370994-1-3

To the KC fandom.
This one is for you.

Author Note

First of all, thank you for supporting my first novel! I really appreciate it. You've supported a small woman-owned business, and that's awesome.

I've always been a fan of stories that involve call girls. *Pretty Woman, Breakfast at Tiffany's, Sweet Charity* are some of my favorite movies. While writing the original version of this story, I was obsessed with the show *Secret Diary of a Call Girl*, which if you haven't seen I HIGHLY recommend.

There's a line in the movie *Pretty Woman* when Julia Roberts reveals that she became a sex worker after she met her friend, Kit, who made it sound so great (Kit is obviously one of the coolest rom-com sidekicks in cinema, and it's a true shame she's not in the movie more). The confidence and freedom evoked by the women in these stories was something I admired when I was younger and still admire today.

However, the fact remains that the escort business—and sex work in general—is not the glamourous life we see depicted in movies and books. Unfortunately, sex workers lack many basic protections and rights that most working people enjoy. My ask is that if you enjoy this story, that you'll look into ways you can help support sex workers and ensure that they can do their work without fear of harassment, violence or prosecution. Reach out to your lawmakers to decriminalize sex work. Check out ACLU.org or other human rights' organizations to learn more about how decriminalization can help sex workers and what you can do to make that need a reality.

xoxo,
Katie

Chapter 1

"What a total jerk!"

"Yeah! We will totally kick his ass!"

Lacey Hollis gave her two best friends a grateful look. It was the first smile she'd cracked in almost four days, the grey clouds over her life being chased away by Chloe and Willa describing the emotional and physical ways they would make Lacey's ex feel pain. After all, it was what a girl's two best friends since childhood were supposed to say when the boyfriend she'd been with for the better part of a decade was caught with another woman.

That day of reckoning had started out perfectly mundane. Grant had kissed her on the head as she'd finished her toast and coffee and told her to have fun shopping, before he headed out to the office. She should have seen it as a bad omen, when the heel on her favorite pair of shoes snapped and cut her shopping trip short.

After just an hour, she was forced to cab it home, rather than hobble around like a weirdo down Rush Street. She'd been walking through her front door, lamenting the damaged pair of lilac chunkyheels hanging from her hands, when she'd noticed a pair of maroon lace-up pumps by the entrance that definitely didn't belong to her.

Tiptoeing further into their apartment, she'd found Grant on the living room couch, pants down and a bleach blonde head bobbing up and down between his thighs. Lacey was still having trouble getting the image and Grant's accompanying "oh yeah baby" moans out of her brain. In retrospect, there were many things she wished she would have done and said the moment Grant's eyes bulged out of his head in surprise when he'd noticed her in the doorway. She'd been so shocked; she hadn't even had the ability to work up a dignified screech. All she managed were a few high-pitched stutters and then a slam of the front door as she left behind Grant, their relationship, and their beautiful Lincoln Park loft apartment.

That had been on Friday.

Willa and Chloe couldn't believe it had taken her three days to come to them with the news. It was hard to admit that she'd spent the weekend crying over pints of ice cream and hiding in a hotel room. Room service and a spa package had done wonders for her spirits. As did binge watching television and ignoring all of Grant's lame apology texts and voicemails.

After a lonely weekend of wallowing, Lacey was happy it was Monday and she was with her girls. Between the boxes of tissues and the bouts of self-pity, she'd been looking forward to the new week all weekend. Their Monday breakfast was a tradition they'd started after college, when work began to take over their lives, and Mondays always felt like a drag. At the start of every week, Lacey, Willa, and Chloe gathered at the same central café, just off the train stop and near the Chicago River, and exchanged stories about work, boyfriends, and whatever else came up over lattes and scones. That day's topic had of course shaken things up and as soon as Lacey broke the news, her friends had gone into full on revenge planning mode.

"So what are you going to do?" Chloe asked sipping her latte, her tongue darting out to catch the foam on her lip. The absent-minded move managed to be both flirtatious and refined. Even the most ordinary things Chloe did were usually a combination of the two, like drinking coffee, or even running track freshman year of high school. Lacey always figured it must have been a product of a French mother and a childhood spent in Europe that made her so effortlessly sophisticated.

Lacey shrugged, curving a piece of blonde hair behind her ear. "I don't know. My mom said that I could come home for a while, but I really don't want to go back to Virginia." She shuddered at the thought. Her mom was great, but they'd never gotten along. Their relationship had improved once Lacey moved out of her childhood home and into her own life.

Virginia was the place the three of them called home. Even Chloe, who'd grown up in France, and moved to the little town known as Crystal Creek the summer before high school. Their friendship had a rocky start, but they'd been thick as thieves since the ninth grade. Even the big move to Chicago after college was a decision they'd made together, along with Willa. Almost twelve years of friendship and nothing could break them apart.

"Of course you can't. Your life is here," Willa agreed. The petite girl gave Lacey's hand a small pat. Willa had changed her hair again since last week. It was dark brown and streaked with teal, matching the ring in her nose. The shade was beautiful against her warm, brown skin.

"I guess I need to get a place." Lacey exhaled, twirling her spoon around her coffee. Now that she was down a boyfriend, she was down an apartment as well.

"To get a place you'll need money," Chloe noted.

"I have money," Lacey replied, a little indignant "I still have

3

some savings from the trust my dad left me. And then...I guess...I'll get a job."

Willa and Chloe traded a significant look and burst into a fit of laughter.

"You? Lacey Hollis? A job?" Chloe was still snickering behind her hand. "You've never worked a day in your life!"

"I waitressed at the Grill!"

"You quit after a day," Willa reminded her.

It was true. But it had been hard to remember all those orders and to constantly have to check on people and run around and refill drinks. Her feet had been killing her by the end of that first shift and she'd missed their friend Tucker's party that Saturday. It so was not worth the twenty bucks she'd made in tips that night.

Lacey frowned. Their teasing was harsh but true. Work was just not her thing. She'd also discovered college hadn't been her thing either after a year and a half. When she'd discussed dropping out with Grant, he'd had the perfect solution at the time.

"I'll support you," he'd promised with a sweet kiss.

They'd been dating for over two years by then, wedding bells had already begun to ring in Lacey's ears at that point, so dropping out and letting him take care of her seemed like a viable option.

From that moment, Grant had become the primary source of Lacey's financial support. His parents were rich and once he'd graduated law school, he started making his own money. He had never minded fronting the cost on anything they did or anything she'd wanted. He paid all their bills, their rent, Lacey's credit cards...everything.

Lacey sat up straighter, squaring her shoulders, and flipping her curls. The teasing from her friends, no matter how gentle, had struck an indignant chord within her. It wasn't that Lacey couldn't be responsible and take care of herself; she'd just never tried because she never had to before. But the good news was Lacey had never been met with a problem she couldn't fix.

"How hard can it be? I can get a job and a new place and I won't need Grant or anyone else. Let's brainstorm job ideas," said Lacey, fully positive that together they could solve her problems.

"I can't imagine you flipping burgers or working retail," Willa began.

Lacey scrunched up her face. "Ew. No. Gross. I was thinking something that involved less tacky uniforms and more Joan Holloway."

"So like an office job?" Willa clarified. Lacey nodded. "I don't know if that's possible."

"Why not?" Lacey could just see herself in cute, retro looking pencils skirts, pen tucked into her bun, strutting around in a sleek pair of pumps.

Chloe interjected. "What Willa is trying to say is that you don't have any skills."

Willa elbowed her in the ribs. "Yeah, but I was trying to be nice about it."

"I can do things," Lacey insisted, "I have skills."

The girls waited for her to elaborate.

"I was…I was head cheerleader in high school," Lacey said with pride to an unconvinced Chloe, "I'm athletic! I could work in a gym!"

Chloe shook her head. "You have to have certifications for that."

"Then I'll get them!"

"You have to study," Willa explained. "A lot. And then you'll need money to pay for the tests."

Both of them were looking at her like two parents telling their five year old she can't be a unicorn princess when she grows up because they didn't exist.

Lacey stomped her feet under the table. "Well what am I supposed to do? Isn't that what America is all about? Making sure everyone is taken care of?"

"Not exactly," Willa gently replied with another sympathetic smile.

Lacey felt tears start to build behind her eyes. She promised herself she wouldn't cry anymore. She gave herself one weekend to cry all of her tears over Grant and the entire situation and then no more. She would not be one of those girls who agonized over being cheated on or let it make her feel bad about herself. It was his decision to be an asshole and sleep with another girl. It had nothing to do with her.

Lacey twisted the napkin in her lap as the finer details of the situation started to crash over her. She hadn't realized before that his act of infidelity would cause her entire life to crumble. If she had, she might have given herself another few days to wallow. Or maybe an entire month.

No boyfriend.

No home.

No income.

She literally had nothing.

Seeing her oncoming panic attack, Chloe reached over and took her hand, giving it a comforting squeezed. "I'm sorry. We aren't being very supportive."

Lacey sighed, calming down just a little. She didn't have nothing. She still had her friends and that was something. "No, you are. You're being honest and that's more important. I'm just— I'm in over my head here."

"Look," Willa said, "why don't you come back to the office with Chloe and me. We'll help you make a resume and see if we can find something that will work for you."

"And in the meantime, I'll see if I can track down a few apartments for you to go check out," Chloe added brightly.

Lacey smiled, grateful to have the two of them in her corner. "Thanks guys. I really don't know what I would do without you."

"That's what friends are for," Chloe declared.

"And we'll still totally kick Grant's ass if you want us to," Willa added with a wink.

"Like when you shoved Davey Chappell into the sandbox for

yanking my pigtail in the third grade?" Lacey laughed.

"Exactly like that," her best friend replied.

Willa was sweet as apple pie, but she had a temper that was a force to be reckoned with, especially when it came to those she loved. She even had a black belt to back up her ass-kicking threat.

Willa continued to describe various scenarios of seeing Grant on the street and kicking him into traffic, while Chloe picked up the bill for their meals. By the end of breakfast, Lacey was starting to feel much better. She wouldn't end up homeless, on the street, with no one to love or take care of her. Her friends were coming to the rescue and she would be fine.

With no other plans for the day—other than getting her life together—Lacey headed downtown with Willa and Chloe to their office. The two business owners and partners rented a loft space in a tall skyscraper that stretched up high into the Chicago skyline and overlooked the river.

She'd been to their office before, but walking into the space, Lacey wished for the first time that she were a little more like her friends when it came to work and career. She wanted to be smarter, like Willa, and more independent, like Chloe. The two women had started their own business together four years ago, a few months after they'd all moved to Chicago. She remembered when things started to take off and they'd scoped out the office space. The previous tenant had used it as an art studio and gallery, and with a few changes the women had renovated it into their own workspace. Lacey had had such a great time helping them design and decorate.

All the walls were exposed brick painted white except in the very back, which was floor to ceiling windows. Long, gauzy curtains hung from the high gold rods attached to their ceiling, sweeping delicately against the hardwood floor. Rarely were the curtains ever actually closed, allowing for an excellent view of the river and the city below.

Giant canvases adorned the walls, splashed with gold, blush, and silver. Toward the front of the room was a sitting area, complete with a comfy couch and textured throw pillows, perfect for entertaining prospective clients. Further back were Chloe and Willa's desks, each adorned with hints of the girl's personality.

Chloe paused at the large, gilded mirror in the front of the office, smoothing down her raven hair, before gliding to her desk. She favored minimal and chic, her area neatly organized. Her white desk was free from even a single speck of dust, sleek black pens organized in a small cup by her computer. The only hint of color was the red ledger in front of her computer screen. On the wall were simple framed black and white photographs of the Eiffel tower, a little girl with an umbrella, a vase of roses. Lacey remembered Chloe once mentioning that her father had taken them. The little girl with the umbrella was a very young Chloe.

Across the room, facing Chloe's desk was Willa's. A string of purple lights stretched up and down the wall beside Willa's desk, a pair of gold noise-cancelling headphones hanging on a hook attached to the edge. Her pen cup was filled with colors as various as the dyes she used for her hair, little absently sketched doodles decorated the giant calendar on her desktop.

Willa made her way to the sound system and turned on some music.

Harsh guitar sounds filled the room and Chloe lifted a brow to Willa. She shrugged and grinned at Lacey, flipping to something more "work appropriate." Neither Chloe nor Lacey had any love for the hard rock Willa chose to listen to when working late nights.

Lacey left her bag on the couch and strolled over to Willa's desk, taking a seat in the mint-green padded guest chair. She daydreamed what her own workspace might look like if she had an office like her friends. Pink would be the dominating color, with maybe a few hints of gold.

"You don't have anyone coming in today?" Lacey inquired.

Chloe shook her head, opening her red ledger. "Just a meeting with the girls later on. Maybe a call-in or two, but the schedule is free today."

The girls got right to work on the job hunt. Willa helped Lacey type up a disappointingly thin resume, while Chloe searched for apartments.

"Here's a good one," Chloe said, red polished finger pointing at her screen. Lacey leaned over to take a look.

"A studio? In Rogers Park?" Lacey frowned. "Nothing in River North? Gold Coast?"

"Not in a realistic price range," Chloe remarked.

Lacey groaned, but decided that maybe they should switch priorities and find her a job before looking for an apartment. Perhaps, if she were making enough money, her price range could be adjusted, and she wouldn't have to settle for a crappy studio in a shady part of the city.

A couple of hours later, her high hopes for a glamorous life as a newly single and independent girl were quickly fading. Willa had scoured every job listing website she could think of but couldn't find anything for her friend. There wasn't anything available that didn't require experience, a college degree, or — much to her dislike — physical labor.

The same went for apartments. Everything was too expensive or so far away that she wouldn't even be able to say she lived in Chicago anymore.

"Great, so now we're back to square one," Lacey grumbled, slouching in her chair. "And even if I do get a job, it'll be something minimum wage and I'll get to come home every night to my crappy, south-side apartment trying not to get caught in a drive-by."

"What about your trust? How much do you have saved up?" Willa reminded. "Can it get you by for a few months at least?"

Lacey looked down at her hands, catching her bottom lip between her teeth. "Three hundred dollars," she mumbled.

"Three hundred dollars?!" Willa exclaimed. Lacey jumped at the volume of her usually soft-spoken friend's voice. "Lacey! When you inherited that trust it had $40,000 in it! How do you blow through $40,000 in two years? I bet you didn't even have enough sense to invest any of it."

Willa bit off her reprimand, shaking her head in disappointment.

"Geez Willa, I know! I screwed up! I'm a crappy adult! I'm sorry I didn't think that my boyfriend would cheat on me and result in me having to be able to support myself out of freakin' nowhere!"

"Damn it," Chloe muttered, returning to the conversation after having stepped away to take an urgent phone call.

"What is it?" Willa asked. Judgment toward Lacey's fiscal irresponsibility still colored her tone.

"I just got a text from Scarlett," she said to Willa. "She's got the flu and can't make it to her appointment."

"What about Victoria? She's usually up for extra work."

Chloe shook her head. "Victoria's already booked. Everyone is booked," Chloe ran her fingers through her long hair. "I hate cancelling on new clients. It only results in bad word-of-mouth."

"I'd fill in," Willa offered. "But Tristen would kill me."

Chloe gave her a grateful look. "I appreciate the offer Wills, but you and I are off the books for appointments. We agreed remember?"

A light bulb flickered inside Lacey's mind and she jumped up from her seat, excitement dancing in her eyes. "I can fill in."

"What?" Willa blinked at her.

"Let me fill in for Scarlett tonight," Lacey urged. "I can do it."

Willa sighed and started shaking her head. "Lacey..."

"I need a job. I need the money," Lacey urged, plowing right over Willa's attempted reasoning and denials and toward a new idea rapidly forming inside her mind. "Why can't I just work for you guys?"

"I don't know if you're cut out for this, Lace," replied Chloe. "There's more to it than you might realize."

"Oh, come on, it's not waitressing at The Crystal Creek Grill. It's dressing up and going out to fancy dinners. Apparently, those are the only two things I'm good at." The last part was added a bit harshly. They'd never said as much, but over the past two hours, Lacey could feel her friends slowly judging the trophy-girl lifestyle to which she'd become accustomed.

Willa and Chloe exchanged looks from across the room, while Lacey held her breath and silently pleaded with them to let her take the job.

"Okay, fine," Chloe agreed, ignoring the way Willa's jaw dropped to the floor. "But tonight is just a trial. If it goes well, then we'll think about hiring you full time."

Lacey couldn't help but jump up and clap her hands together. "Oh my gosh! I promise you guys won't regret this!"

The two business owners winced at one another as she rushed forward and gave them both a grateful hug, squeezing them tight. The look said that they hoped Lacey was right and that they wouldn't regret the crazy decision they'd just made. Both women, ignoring their better judgment, had just signed their best friend up to be the newest addition to their high-class escort service.

Asher Knight rolled into the office late after a long weekend, aviators covering half his face and the obvious lack of sleep sagging his features. It wasn't that he was still hung over; it was just that the bright sun was bothering his eyes and doing nothing for the slight headache drilling into the bridge of his nose.

It had been his oldest brother's stag weekend. On the suggestion of their younger brother, they had taken a "manly bonding trip" to Vegas to celebrate Duncan's last weekend as an unmarried man. At the time it had seemed like a good idea to— put it in Jaime's words—"take Duncan's poncy arse to Sin City," but the ache in his head was suggesting otherwise. His brothers and their friends spent three days gambling, drinking, and wreaking havoc in ways they hadn't since before he could remember.

The perks of being the boss meant that no one would say anything if he chose to hide out in his office all day, slamming water and paracetamol. Well, almost no one.

"Made it in today I see." A dark haired man moved along side him, extending a cup of coffee in his direction. Asher was grateful for the caffeine, but not the comment, or the knowing smirk that accompanied it.

"Barely," he admitted. Delaney Sawyer, the namesake Sawyer listed next to the second Knight in steel-colored letters just beside the front desk, looked fresh and crisp as ever. Surprising, when one considered that the man had been on the same red-eye return flight as Asher, and had been the same amount of still drunk during said flight.

Delaney followed Asher into his office, taking a seat as Asher shrugged off his messenger bag and hung it on the coat rack behind his desk. He groaned, finally daring to slip off his sunglasses, thankful the large windows of his corner office faced west. "I don't think I've been drunk for 72 hours straight since university."

Delaney chuckled. "Well, that's how we do it across the pond."

Asher rolled his eyes. "I've lived here for five years, Del," he reminded his partner, taking a large gulp of coffee. "How'd your brother fare?"

"He's wrecked," Delaney laughed, mischievous pride sparkling in his crystal blue eyes. "He won't be coming in today."

The younger Sawyer had definitely had more than his share of fun on their weekend trip. So much fun, in fact, that he'd missed their return flight. Gabriel Sawyer had disappeared on their last night in Vegas, but was in touch enough for them to know that he hadn't gotten into *too* much trouble. Delaney explained that he'd arrived home just after dawn, glassy eyed with flecks of glitter still in his hair, and headed straight to the toilet.

"Your little brother can be quite…indulgent," Asher remarked.

"He *acts* like the moral brother," Delaney reminded him, "but he has his vices. Don't let the angelic look fool you. He's worse than I am."

Asher chuckled to himself, remembering a few key moments of the weekend that involved Gabriel and a few girls that they had met at one of the casinos. Given their history, he needed no reminder of Gabriel's tendency to sometimes get a little out of hand. Asher had known the Sawyer brothers as colleagues and friends for a few years. Sometimes they were different as night and day, with Delaney usually playing bad boy to Gabriel's chivalrous charm. But knowing them better, it was often Delaney who was cleaning up the messes of his younger brother.

"Good morning Mr. Knight, Mr. Sawyer. How was your weekend?" One of their associates poked his head into the doorway. A young man fresh out of law school, bright eyed and nervous, like a tail wagging dog waiting for admission into the master's domain.

"Good," Asher replied, not particularly wanting to engage the lad. "Fine."

"Was there something you needed, Lucas?" Delaney was less inclined as usual to feign politeness.

"Um, no… I just—no." The younger man tucked tail and retreated at the obvious dismissal.

"I hate that kid," Delaney muttered, taking a sip from his coffee. "Such a fucking suck up."

"I agree," Asher said. The young boy was quick witted and eager, but in the way of a person who was used to being liked and accepted and handed rewards for very little work. A big fish from a small pond, who was floundering now that he'd moved into a larger body of water.

"Why did you guys even hire such a tool like that?"

"Duncan's the one who hired him," Asher replied, "but he is

intelligent. I'm sure if he figures things out, he'll move up to junior partner within a few years."

"I hope not," Delaney muttered, stretching out his legs. "Have you ever seen his girlfriend though?"

"No."

"Well, let me just say, *damn*! The new associates went to O'Toole's about a month ago and I stopped by and she was there with him—"

Asher shot him a look and interrupted. "Why on Earth would you go to O'Toole's?"

O'Toole's was a pub downtown where all the associates and legal assistants in their office liked to hang out after work. It wasn't the type of establishment the partners of a law firm would find themselves in.

"If you buddy up to the new associates and pretend to be their friend, they're comfortable talking shit in front of you," Delaney explained, with a sly arch of his brow, "then you know who to get rid of right out of the gate."

"That explains why you wanted to get rid of that new legal assistant out of nowhere last month," Asher inferred.

Delaney ignored him. "As I was saying, the girlfriend. Hot, blonde, with a perfect body," he described, swiping his hand through the air in the shape of feminine curves. "Not the brightest crayon in the box, but you know, nice and perky." His dark brows wiggled up and down.

Asher chuckled as he scrolled through his emails, sparing a glance in his friend's direction. "Sounds to me like someone has a crush."

"I'm just saying. A girl can do better than a tool box like Grant Lucas."

Asher's lip curved, his mouse clicking. "And you're the bloke to show her that?"

"Maybe I will the next time he brings her around to an event or down to O'Toole's," Delaney answered. He wouldn't admit it out loud, but Asher had no doubt that it was possible that Delaney could successfully hit on Lucas's girlfriend. The man was gifted with the sort of crystal blue eyes women often found themselves lost in and that usually distracted from the smarmy words tumbling from his smirking mouth. Asher had witnessed it on more than a few occasions and even more frequently that past weekend in Vegas.

"Sawyer, get out of my office. Some of us have work to do."

Delaney chuckled as he stood up from his seat. "Or hangovers to secretly sleep off behind a closed office door," he jabbed. "Hey, maybe Lucas's girlfriend will be at that charity thing tomorrow night."

"Out!" Asher demanded, having had enough of Delaney and his nonsense.

The sound of Delaney's laughter could be heard down the hall until Asher got up and shut his office door.

It was unfortunate that no one in their lives knew about Vamp. In any other instance, Chloe and Willa's level of success at such a young age would normally be admired and celebrated. However, given the nature of their controversial industry, Vamp remained a closely guarded secret that only their innermost circle of friends was privy to.

The two young women had gone into the escort business not long after moving to Chicago. It wasn't as if the girls had grown up dreaming that one day they would be hookers or call girls. The three friends had always possessed rather modern views on sexuality, in spite of being from rural Virginia where religion and abstinence were king. Part of their shared point of view came from Chloe's twenty-something aunt, who'd been a grad student when she'd been named guardian of her newly orphaned niece and nephew. Chloe, Willa, and Lacey spent many of their teenage years going to Aunt Jessa whenever they had a question that was too embarrassing to ask other adults or their parents. Her approach to parenting had always been about openness and honesty.

The girls had been fresh out of college, stumbling unhappily through internships and job hunts until a one night stand had accidentally paid Chloe for sex. She had been mortified, and slightly insulted, but then an idea came to business minded Willa.

"What if we actually did this for a living?" she'd suggested.

Lacey and Chloe had almost spit out their lattes on that particular Monday morning breakfast.

"Are you crazy?" Lacey had wondered.

"Have sex for money?" Chloe wanted to clarify.

"Well, no," Willa explained, "but we could get other girls to do it and take commissions."

At the time, Chloe was already a junior talent scout at a PR agency. She knew how to find talent and how to brand their business. Willa had gone to business school and was good with accounting and numbers and all the boring stuff.

"Wait, isn't it kind of illegal?" Lacey had asked.

Willa had smiled conspiratorially. "There are always ways around the legal part."

Soon after, Vamp Escorts was born, officially known to outsiders as Vamp. After doing some research on the escort industry, Willa had the idea to front their business as an interior design planning and consulting firm. It was smart, considering that a lot of their clients would likely be men and women with disposable incomes, who would believably have money to burn on interior designers. The name Vamp came from "revamp" which to anyone who asked is exactly what they did.

Only instead of revamping people's homes, they revamped their sex lives.

Chloe managed to find a few girls and gather a few regular clients. Soon working girls across the windy city were begging to become a Vamp. Chloe and Willa had built the best business to work for, because they actually cared about their girls and protected them. Unlike seedy website listings, who catered to any John with an Internet connection, Vamp took their clients on an exclusive by recommendation basis. Their girls didn't have to worry about being met by a serial killer, a pervert, or an undercover cop.

"The girls always come first," was Chloe's mantra.

They were high class, meaning they didn't take clients out of a certain pay bracket and they charged *a lot*.

Chloe and Willa had been out as escorts themselves a few times in the beginning. They felt like they should try it, just so they could actually experience what their employees experienced. But now Willa was in a serious relationship and Chloe had chosen to abstain to exist solely as the madam and pass along the clients to her girls.

To Lacey, it had always seemed like such a glamorous and easy life. Every girl was her own boss, flitting effortlessly in and out of the office when she visited, telling stories of trips to Paris or extravagant gifts or hot sex. Sometimes she wished for similar attention and adventures. The trade off seemed simple.

However, as her day of Escort 101 crawled by, she'd slowly been finding out that being an escort meant a lot more than just sitting across from a guy, sipping wine, and fulfilling his sexual fantasies. The girls had spent the rest of the morning educating her on the finer points of being a high class call girl.

"Okay, so we've covered dress and dinner behavior, and you know the rules," Chloe checked off their accomplishments on her note pad.

Lacey nodded, ticking each rule off on her fingers. "Call when I arrive at the hotel after dinner to check in, then check in again once I leave. Bring extra condoms and lube. Don't drink any alcohol."

"Right," Willa replied, beaming. "Now your client tonight

17

has paid for an over-nighter, so you'll just call us in the morning when you are on your way home. Don't forget to accept the money before anything happens."

Willa had explained the delicate dance of clients leaving an envelope on a table for the escort to pick up. Some clients found it awkward to just hand over cash and Lacey should never ask for it, but might need to cleverly remind him if he forgot to pay.

"What's his name again?" Lacey asked.

"Asher Knight," Chloe read from the ledger.

"God, *Asher*. He sounds like he's gonna be a hundred years old. Do you know him?"

Chloe shook her head. "No, I only spoke to him over the phone. He's a new client, looking for a new agency to work with after a disagreement with his last."

"Disagreement?" Willa questioned. It was the first time she was hearing of a problem.

"A girl with Diamond Elite got a little too attached." The two madams exchanged a 'been-there-seen that' type look.

"You make it sound like he's picking out an escort the way someone picks out a dentist," Lacey remarked.

"It is similar," Chloe replied. "Repeat customers are our greatest assets, just like any other service-based business. That's why it's important for us to make a good impression and keep appointments."

"So, what do you know about him?" Lacey wondered.

"He's 35 and ex-pat from London with a delicious accent," she told her with a grin. Chloe knew Lacey had always had a thing for accents. Orlando Bloom had been the only reason she'd let Willa drag her to see Lord of the Rings. "And he's a lawyer."

Lacey made a face. "Ugh, I've had enough lawyers in my life."

"Well, this isn't about you," Willa reminded her, "It's about him."

"I know," Lacey replied, starting to get a little sick of all the lectures. "But what if he's like, totally gross? Like back hair and pimples? I don't know if I could sleep with someone who's just completely...*ew*."

Her skin crawled at the idea of being bedded by someone completely repulsive. She knew her college acting skills would come in handy when pretending to be turned on by a veritable stranger, but she wasn't sure if she could do all that well with someone who wasn't at least a little attractive to her.

"It doesn't matter," Willa insisted, in a rare moment of bluntness. She sat down next to Lacey, who recognized a serious note in her friend's brown eyes that made her sit up and listen. "Look, one time I was with this client... he was a middle-aged, balding, hedge fund manager. He was completely boring and awkward. But he was really sweet. And I made him feel good about himself and gave him something that no one else ever bothered to give him." Lacey's confusion must have shown on her face because Willa clarified. "I gave him *affection* and intimacy, which are two things everyone needs. In the end I felt good because he felt good. *That's* what matters." Willa reached up and smoothed Lacey's hair, the way Lacey's mom used to do to comfort her. "Lace, you're beautiful and nice, and even when you're at your most shallow, you do the right thing and make people feel great."

It was hard to imagine punky Willa with a boring suit type of guy, but Lacey supposed that was the point. They weren't really themselves when they were with their clients. She wouldn't be Lacey Hollis. She would be an escort and Asher Knight—35-year-old British lawyer—would be her client. She would be whatever he needed her to be.

Chloe took a seat on her other side. "Don't worry. Everything will be okay."

"I'm not worried, I can do this," Lacey took a deep breath and smiled. "Well, I guess I should go. I have some shopping to do for my date tonight."

Lacey stood and shouldered her purse.

"Okay, so just take a cab to this address," Chloe instructed, scribbling the information down on a piece of paper and handing it to her. "You're meeting him at eight. Don't be late."

Lacey looked at the address of the restaurant on the paper and then up at Chloe, her best friend and new boss. She'd prove to them and herself that she could do this and stand on her own. She wouldn't let them or herself down.

By some grace from a higher power, Asher had made it through the day. Even with a headache from hell. Thankfully, the stabbing between his eyes was finally going away. As planned, he got to spend most of the day at his desk, answering emails and going through contracts; mindless work that he could do in his sleep. Delaney popped his head in just before six to invite him out for a drink.

"How can you possibly think about alcohol after this weekend?"

Delaney shrugged. "Sawyers can hold their liquor."

"I know," Asher replied thinking of the amount of alcohol both Sawyer men had imbibed that weekend, "but I can't tonight. I have a date."

"A date, or a *date*?"

Asher threw Delaney an annoyed look. He knew the significance in the emphasis on the word. Even though Delaney was someone Asher considered a close friend, he still hated that Delaney knew one of his biggest secrets. "The latter," he answered begrudgingly.

The dark haired man looked left and right down the hall before stepping further into the office. Asher shut off his computer and began packing up his messenger bag.

"Seriously, I will never understand why you go out with

escorts. I'm sure you wouldn't have any trouble scoring women," Delaney said.

Asher laughed, giving him a cocky smirk. "I know I wouldn't." They'd been through it before, when Delaney had first found out about Asher's preference for call girls. "The escort route is a much easier path. No fuss. No complication. None of the responsibility of a girlfriend or wife."

"Hmm, you do make an excellent point," Delaney considered, tapping his chin. "I might have to try it sometime."

Delaney was the only person who knew of Asher's habit. Not even his brothers knew. It wasn't that he was some sort of sex addict. He was a busy man that didn't have time for relationships. Women could be demanding. He was committed to his career, to providing for his siblings. He didn't need the added drama of a relationship in his life; there was enough drama already.

Just then Asher's phone chimed with a text alert.

"Speaking of…" he said opening the text, "hmmm."

"Hmmm?" Delaney mimicked.

"It seems the girl I originally selected is ill. They're sending a replacement instead. Someone called Lacey."

"What's the problem?" Delaney asked, noticing Asher's disappointment.

"I'm very specific about who I select. I don't want just anyone." It was only a couple hours until their schedule date. Shrewd of the agency to wait until the last minute to let him know of the change, leaving him little room to back out.

"It's not like whoever they send is going to turn out to be a dog."

"True," Asher agreed, "I suppose if it goes badly I can always cut the night short."

He quickly typed in his reply to the escort agency and then dropped his phone into his pocket, locking his office behind him and following Delaney over to the lifts.

"If it goes well, will you bring her to the charity event

tomorrow?" Delaney asked, stepping into the lift beside him.

"Del, she's an escort, not a girlfriend," Asher replied pushing the button marked "L". "We'll enjoy the evening together and then we'll part ways."

"So?" Del pressed. "Can't hurt to have a date to something like that."

"I don't see escorts more than once. It's a rule I have." Admittedly it was a new rule, after his latest escort experience. Aurora had been beautiful and charming, but it soon became clear that she was hoping for more out of her career as an escort than Asher was willing to give.

Delaney nudged him on the shoulder. "Lighten up. What happened to the Asher that we saw in Vegas?"

His mouth curved, a wicked look in his eye. "You know what they say, mate. What happens in Vegas stays in Vegas."

Chapter 2

A slender leg, wearing a very precarious and expensive looking heel, appeared from a cab door in front of Red 77 at eight sharp just as instructed. The valet at the door let out a whistle, nudging his buddy and pointing toward the street as Lacey stepped from the car and onto the sidewalk. She rolled her lips together, to hide the delight she felt at the boys' reactions. Spray tanned, waxed, buffed, polished, she'd worked all day on her appearance. She had to look like absolute perfection. Tonight, she stepped into a world of sexual fantasy. To be an escort, she had to shed her usual flower dress, bubbly self and slip into the role of sensual, mysterious dream girl.

She smoothed her silken curls and tucked her clutch purse under her arm, walking toward the large, crimson door of the restaurant. When Lacey had been out shopping, she tried to pick something based on the alter ego she'd assume for the night, and not what she would have normally selected. Long sleeved, short, and tight, it looked like a demure cocktail dress until she turned a revealed a considerable lack of fabric at her back. The evening breeze whispered across her bare skin, tickling her, adding to the edginess unfurling in each notch of her spine.

The valet boy managed to pick his jaw up off the ground and rushed over to open the door for her.

Chloe and Willa had explained that different clients liked different types of girls; some liked the sweet, normal girl next door while others preferred the provocative temptress. Asher hadn't specified what kind of girl he wanted, only that she be beautiful, well mannered, and high class, so the girls had encouraged her to play whatever character she liked.

Lacey had chosen to go with temptress. She thought it would be much easier to get through the night if she was anyone but herself. The pampering and prepping had been fun, but her nerves started to get the better of her the closer it got to the date's time. It was the idea of the sex that was getting to her the most. Would she be able to go through with it? That was really the key element to the whole job. Willa had told her it was okay to fake orgasms if she needed to—and she probably would need to—it was just part of the deal. Lacey didn't mind that. Admittedly, she'd had to fake a time or two for Grant's sake.

At first, when she had been picking out some new lingerie, she realized that she was a little intrigued by the opportunity of getting laid. She was on the rebound, after all. It would be rebound sex. Meaningless and hot—assuming that Asher was attractive and not into anything creepy—and it would be just the thing to get her over Grant.

Nerves struck her again as she stepped through the restaurant door. Could she have sex with a stranger? Thanks to her long-term relationship with Grant, she hadn't even had a one-night stand. All of her crazy sexual experiences had been vicarious through stories mostly told by Chloe. She didn't count the odd boy here or there in high school, before her and Grant had started dating. Those encounters had been less sexual and more experimental, nothing but hormones and awkward fumbling in the backseats of cars. She'd never had the opportunity to develop the sexual confidence of Chloe. She'd wasn't the woman who could go out to a bar, pick up a guy, screw him, and never see him again. Even Willa had experience a couple of nameless hookups before she started dating Tristen.

Maybe she could be that woman, though, now that she was single and being given the chance. Maybe if she hadn't had a boyfriend for the better part of a decade she would have been flitting around all over the city, having a sex life that was worthy of Carrie Bradshaw.

"Good Evening." A chic, young girl in black greeted her at the host stand. "How can I help you?"

"I'm meeting someone at the bar," Lacey told her. The hostess smiled and pointed in the direction of the long bar behind her.

The clacking of her heels on the wood floors gave her confidence and she let her hips swing a little more with every step, keeping her chin high and her eyes forward. She remembered what Willa and Chloe kept telling her all afternoon, this wasn't about her, it was about *him*; tending to *his* needs, making *him* feel good. She could do this.

The swanky, dark atmosphere of the restaurant helped her slip further into character. A few travelling businessmen sat in the tables around the room, chatting over Heinekens and expensive scotch. A couple of them paused their conversations to check her out, shooting her appreciative glances as she glided past. She coolly ignored them and scanned the lonely bachelors seated at the bar, trying to pick out which of them was her date for the evening. She had no idea what Asher looked like, but Willa assured her that she would know him when she saw him.

25

Her eyes fell upon a man seated near the end of the line, his body positioned in his seat to face anyone walking by. He was staring more deliberately at her than any of the other men had, expectation in his eyes unlike the others who'd turned her way. Lacey clamped down on her sudden excitement. He was *absolutely* gorgeous. Obviously tall even though he was sitting, with dark blonde curls that looked like they would be soft to the touch, sexy if rumpled. She may have been the dream girl that evening, but this man was a romance novel fantasy come true. He wore a grey suit that managed to look sexy instead of stuffy and his gaze held promise, danger, and excitement.

He raised both of his eyebrows at her and Lacey realized she had been staring.

Giving her curls a coy toss, she walked toward the man, hoping that he turned out to be the one she was looking for.

"Asher?" she inquired, approaching him with her best flirty smile. "Lacey." He greeted and took her hand, placing a kiss over her knuckles.

Lacey exhaled, relief replacing all the anxiousness she'd been feeling about the date, the sex, everything. Asher was good-looking and charming. The night was going to be a piece of cake.

Asher couldn't believe his eyes when Lacey had walked into the restaurant. She was—in a word—breathtaking. Physically, she was everything he could have hoped for in an escort. She was blonde and lithe and she carried herself with confidence and grace. He was suddenly glad for the change in his original date.

They had just enough time for introductions before the hostess was whisking them away to the table Asher had reserved. Lacey sauntered in front of him, a teasing sway in her hips that was no doubt added for his benefit. He took the time to study his date, enjoying the expanse of smooth skin revealed at her back.

Asher grinned. The dress she wore left very little to the imagination and he was already imagining the fun he would have taking it off after dinner.

Their table was tucked into a dim, intimate corner. Seduction wasn't exactly part of the equation when it came to dating escorts, Asher knew this, but it still kept things interesting. Lacey slid into the black leather booth first, and Asher followed. Candlelight flickered between them on the table, maroon curtained walls enveloping them into their own private world. They were handed menus and assured that their server would be with them soon.

Asher watched as Lacey assessed her surroundings. He'd brought escorts to Red 77 a time or two, enjoying the privacy it allowed.

"This is an interesting place," Lacey remarked, her fingertips touching the brass of the candleholder. "Kind of gothic chic. Were you a secret goth when you were a teenager?" Her lips curved up playfully.

"I have to admit I did have a penchant for black eyeliner when I was fifteen," Asher answered.

"Really? I was actually kidding," she laughed. He liked the sound. "I wouldn't have guessed." She looked him over, head cocking slightly to one side, clearly trying to imagine him with the makeup.

"Oh really? What would you have pegged me for then?"

Lacey's mouth twisted in consideration, her blue eyes appraising him once more. "Sci-fi nerd."

His brows shot up. "Science fiction?" It was an unusual answer.

She shrugged. "Or something else spacey. I bet you were like that guy who was really dorky in high school and then grew up to be hot."

"And got his revenge on those who scorned him in his teen years?"

"Exactly," she beamed, eyes flicking back to her menu. Asher had to laugh at her teen soap opera account of his life, if only because he wished his childhood had been that simple.

The waiter arrived to introduce herself and take their drink orders. Asher requested a bottle of red wine.

"A glass of water, too," Lacey interjected, "please."

The server nodded and left to get their drinks. They were alone once again. The brief interruption, however, had been enough to put an end to the easy banter from before.

Lacey drummed her fingers lightly against the damasked table cloth. "Do you come here often?"

"Is that a line?" He remarked with a grin.

"I think we're past lines, don't you?" A more sultry smile, different from her previous, stretched across her lips. She batted her long lashes a couple of times. The overzealous flirting amused him. Asher was starting to see the way she vacillated between sexy and sweet, the sweetness being her obvious default.

The waiter returned with their wine, uncorking the bottle and allowing it to breath, before artfully pouring the red liquid into two, long-stemmed glasses.

"I'll be back with your water, miss." The waiter turned and left.

"I like that this place is quiet and private," Asher said, finally answering her question. "I'm a private man."

The waiter returned a third time to take their orders.

"I haven't had time to even look," Lacey said, attempting to quickly pick something from the menu.

"May I?" Asher asked, "I know exactly what you should have."

Lacey smiled and nodded, allowing Asher to order for her. The waiter departed again and Asher was relieved that their time would finally be uninterrupted until their dinner arrived.

"So, you're a lawyer?" Lacey prompted.

Asher nodded, taking a sip from his glass. "Yes, corporate law. Mergers, acquisitions..." He waved his hand dismissively.

"Quite boring really."

"Sounds like it," she agreed. "My ex is a lawyer. He always talked about what he did but I never understood a word of it to be honest." The comment came absently and she tensed, startled by her own honesty. "Sorry," she said, turning sheepish. "I guess I shouldn't talk about exes to you. That's against the rules, right?"

"No apology needed, love," he replied, curious about the mention of rules.

She smiled and took a few gulps from her water, eyes flicking away across the restaurant.

Asher noticed that Lacey didn't touch the wine throughout the meal and only picked at her food. There were a few awkward conversation moments, but it was clear she was on guard after the mention of her ex-boyfriend. The earlier confidence and lightness she had shown disappeared. Asher frowned. Maybe the night wasn't going to go as well as he hoped.

Lacey knew she was failing. Badly. It turned out that she didn't actually know how to play the role of mysterious temptress. She didn't know how to talk to Asher without revealing facts about herself or getting too emotional. Chloe advised her against providing clients with too many details about her personal life. Reason one being, most clients weren't interested, and secondly, there was always the potential of being stalked or harassed if a client got too attached. Even though Vamp did reference checks on all potential clients, there was always a possibility for crazies to slip through.

Asher didn't seem like one of the crazies. He actually seemed nice. Lacey wondered why a man like him went out with escorts in the first place, as opposed to just taking out regular women. There was no denying he was hot. Certainly he was good-looking enough to get any woman he wanted. In addition to being incredibly attractive, Asher was smart, successful, and had a sly-dimpled smile that could charm the habit off of a nun. She understood the hedge fund guy from Willa's story, and why he might hire escorts, but Asher didn't make sense to her.

After her faux pas of mentioning Grant, Lacey's guard was up in full force. The nerves from the beginning of the evening were back and she was mindful of every little thing she did. She was so lost in her hyper vigilance that she barely noticed when Asher paid and it was time to leave.

They walked out of the restaurant, his hand hovering near her lower back, and she managed a smile when the hostess wished them a pleasant evening.

Asher walked over to the curb and stretched out his arm to hail a cab. There was a physical distance Lacey was beginning to pick up on and she realized that she hadn't been doing very well with the seduction part of the evening.

"Yes, the sex is inevitable," Willa had explained, *"but you still should tease it. Dangle a carrot, build the anticipation, make it seem as real of a date as you can."*

Recalling Willa's words made her realize the thing that had been bothering her most since first clamping eyes on Asher. The thing stopping her was the thing that stopped anyone in the whole of history from making a move on a person they were attracted to: rejection. Lacey had been out of the dating game a long time and hadn't had to worry about a guy not liking her since she was a teenager. She honestly couldn't remember how to deal with the possibility. But she didn't need to be afraid of rejection, did she? The night was already a sealed deal.

She glanced over her shoulder, to see the two valet boys from earlier checking out her ass. One jumped and looked away, embarrassed to be caught. The other however, had the audacity to wink. Offensive as it might have been, she channeled that wink and let it guide her next moves.

Lacey stepped over to Asher and—in a bold move—ran a

hand down his arm. He looked down at her, his grey-blue eyes meeting hers, as she slid her hand into his. She flashed him a demure little smile.

"Why don't we walk a little bit?" She purred near his ear. "It's a nice night out."

Asher's mouth curved. "Sounds like an excellent idea, love."

He kept hold of her hand and led them away from the street and down the sidewalk, toward one of the bridges set over the Chicago River. The hotel Asher had mentioned during dinner was on the other side of the water, a few blocks away. They strolled along the walkway over the river, lights from the buildings twinkling in myriad colors against the choppy waves.

"This bridge is haunted you know," Lacey blurted. "A boat sank in the river and all these people drowned. Apparently if you look closely, you can see the faces of ghosts in the water."

Asher glanced down into the river, seeing nothing but water, and then back at her. "Where did you hear that?"

"Willa and I went on a ghost tour thing back when we first moved here. She's really into that stuff." Lacey replied. Then she groaned, covering her face with her hand. "I'm sorry. I did it *again*. First ex-boyfriends and now dead people." She huffed out a laugh, shaking her head, and mentally kicking herself. "I promise I'm usually not so depressing."

Lucky for her, Asher offered a reassuring smile. "It's alright. It's an interesting fact, even if it is depressing." He leaned in close, almost whispering. "Do you believe in ghosts?"

Lacey shrugged as they made it across the bridge to the street again and waited for the signal to change so they could cross the street. "I don't know. I guess I believe that there is probably more out there in the world than I have the ability to understand."

Asher nodded thoughtfully. "I agree."

"How long have you lived here?" She asked.

"Five years," Asher replied as they stepped onto the crosswalk. "Give or take a few days. I moved here from London with my two brothers and my sister."

"You all moved together?"

"Not all at once," he said. Lacey waited for him to continue, but he didn't. "Do you have any siblings?"

Lacey shook her head. "Nope. Just grew up with my mom. My parents are divorced."

"I'm sorry to hear that," Asher offered.

"It's okay. They divorced when I was a little kid, because my dad was gay. Trust me, it made everyone a *lot* happier." There she was again, going on about herself, but she couldn't seem to help it. In effort to stop her unstoppable personal sharing, she shifted the conversation back to Asher. "What's London like? I've always wanted to go there."

A hint of a smile touched Asher's face, his eyes staring into vacant space as he recalled his home. "It's beautiful, truly. Full of life and history and culture. There's a sense of anonymity that I really appreciate."

Lacey could hear the note of longing in his voice. "When was the last time you were there?"

"Five years ago."

He was quiet then. Lacey noted that his time away from London was the same as the time he told her he'd lived in America. "You seem like you miss it. Why don't you ever visit?"

"There isn't much for me there." He answered in a clipped sort of way.

Lacey studied his profile; his jaw twitched and she realized the way he danced around answers to personal questions. "You really do like your privacy, don't you?"

"I do," Asher affirmed, not unkindly, swinging their joined hands between them. "That's why I like Chicago so much. It's not pretentious or flashy like New York or LA. You can enjoy the benefits of living in a large city and just be."

Lacey gave him a warm smile. "I agree."

They reached the hotel and Asher led her toward the

elevator. The opulent lobby was vacant, except for the woman at the front desk speaking to a couple of bellboys. The three of them turned their heads in her direction and Lacey gulped. A nervous feeling fluttered in her stomach and she tried her best to smother it. They didn't know she was an escort. There was no way they could tell, right? The woman eyed her—maybe with judgment or maybe it was cool observation—but continued her conversation with her co-workers.

The elevator doors slid open as she and Asher approached and they walked through. Asher pressed the button to take them up and Lacey let out a relieved breath, thankful they made it past the front desk.

"Everything alright?" Asher asked. Lacey gave him a reassuring smile and nodded.

The elevator doors opened once more. Asher released his grip on her hand to allow her to step out first. Recalling her chosen role, she moved away from him and once again did her best snake like temptress walk.

He directed her down the quiet hallway to the last room, sliding his key card into the knob and unlocking it. The sconce just above Asher's head caught the secret anticipation flickering in his eyes. The room door opened to a small foyer and beyond that a living area. Lacey walked in and took a look around at the luxury suite. She was impressed. The hotel room was almost like an apartment, meant for long stays or special occasions. It seemed like a lot for one night. A lounge area and mini bar took up most of the front. The bedroom and its king-sized bed could be seen through the open French doors at the back. She walked through and took notice of the bathroom, complete with Jacuzzi tub and rainfall shower.

"Wow," Lacey exclaimed after her short, self-led tour. She rejoined Asher in the lounge area. "This is nice."

"Would you like some champagne?" Asher asked. "I could call for some room service."

Lacey shook her head. "No, thank you."

"Do you not drink? I noticed you didn't touch your wine at dinner."

"Are you a lawyer or a detective?" Lacey teased, quirking her eyebrow.

"I suppose I'm a bit of both," he replied, slipping off his gray suit jacket and placing it over one of the white easy chairs.

She smiled at the remark, her eyes trailing down to the envelope on the decorative side table. Asher must have dropped it there while she'd been admiring the bathroom. She knew what was in it. The girls had told her that it was important to take the money before anything beyond dinner occurred.

Willa's instructions rang in her ear.

Take it, count it, and then…

Lacey lifted her eyes to Asher. She knew that it was time.

No more dinner or drinks or talk. He wanted her. The expectation in his eyes made her shiver. She wasn't sure if it was from nerves or anticipation.

"I'm just going to freshen up," Asher said, seeming to remember the rules better than she did.

Her skin felt tight. Prickly. All Lacey could do was nod as he passed her and made his way into the bathroom. The door clicked shut and she waited for the sound of the shower until she walked over to the envelope. She picked it up and flipped it open.

"Holy crap," she whispered at the shocking amount of bills tucked inside.

Her hands were shaking as she attempted to flip through the bills and count out the amount, having to restart twice. A few minutes later the water shut off and she quickly shoved the money into her small purse, setting her things down on the table. Asher would be out of the bathroom and ready to go at any second. Frantically she ran to the mirror hanging by the room door and fluffed up her hair, smoothing her lips and eye makeup. The rabbit beat of her heart refused to slow no matter how many deep breaths she took. She could only hope that he took her rapid breaths and heaving chest for excitement instead of anxiety.

The door to the bathroom clicked open and she spun, seeing Asher in nothing but a towel, slung low around his lean hips. She licked her lips and moved toward him. The lights in the room dimmed as he twisted the switch, casting shadows across his body as he strolled forward, his eyes raking over her. Lacey pushed aside the twisting in her stomach.

Temptress, temptress, temptress, she recited in her head.

Slowly she bent forward, sliding her fingers down her legs, until she reached the straps of her shoes. She flicked open the buckles around her ankles and stepped out of her heels, rising back up just as slow as before and stepping to close the distance between them. Her fingers brushed against the knot of his towels, nails lightly scraping his slender stomach.

Asher reached for her hips and tugged her closer. Lacey gasped.

Then his lips were on hers.

She inhaled his fresh, steamy scent and slid her arms around his neck, his curls damp between her fingers. His kiss was expert, each swipe of his tongue and turn of his lips sending fissures of electricity to her chest. Asher was the first guy she'd kissed besides Grant since high school. It was a surprise to hear herself moan in earnest, the sound causing him to pull her in even tighter.

His hands traveled down her bare back and over her ass, squeezing it briefly, before his fingers were sliding down to the hem of her dress and tugging it upward. The movement of fabric, the feel of nothing covering her but the thin strip of lace underwear, set off an alarm inside Lacey's head. Panic took over and she pushed away from him, backing up a few feet and tugging her dress down.

"No, no, no, no, no," she repeated shaking her head frantically. Needing more distance, she continued to back away to the opposite side of the room and turned away from him. She gripped the ends of a table against the wall; the giant white and gold vase perched in the center shaking at the sudden force. "What the hell was I thinking? I can't do this. *I can't do this*," she whispered to herself.

Asher reached out and touched her shoulder. She jumped and spun around, not realizing he'd come closer. The confusion in his eyes immediately made her feel bad. Chloe and Willa were going to murder her for backing out. Hopefully, Asher would be nice enough not to take away his business just because she was the ultimate idiot. Who had she been kidding? She couldn't be an escort!

"Look, I have to be honest." She exhaled loudly, scooping her hair away from her face. "This is my first time."

Asher's eyes widened and he seemed to go a few shades paler. "Having sex?"

"No!" Lacey shouted, startling him. "I've had sex! Plenty of times!" Asher smirked and her cheeks flushed. The reasons to be embarrassed were piling up. "I meant, this is my first time as an escort. Getting paid for sex. I've never done this before."

His expression softened in relief. "I suppose I should have known," he remarked, "you *are* different from any other of the working girls I've met."

Lacey's mouth twisted and crossed her arms. "I'm not sure if that's a compliment."

"I assure you, it is," he smiled.

Her shoulders relaxed and her heartbeat was starting to calm down to a pace not resembling a coronary. It didn't seem like he was too mad at her for rejecting his pre-paid advances.

"Well, I am sorry for misleading you," she offered walking back to the table with her purse. She pulled out the envelope of cash and handed it to him. "You deserve a full refund."

Asher waved her off. "Not necessary."

Lacey stared at him for a moment, waiting for him to reconsider and take back the money, but he simply stared back without moving or changing his mind. "I hope you won't take your business away from Willa and Chloe," she said, tucking the money back into her purse. "They were just trying to be good friends, that's all. There are other girls who work for them who have tons of experience."

"Don't worry, sweetheart. There's no harm done."

Lacey smiled, grateful. Asher was being surprisingly understanding. After settling the fact that they weren't going to be having sex that night, Lacey realized there was no point in lingering in the hotel room with him. She walked back to where she had left her shoes and picked them up.

"Thanks for the nice dinner. It was really great," she said, turning to tell Asher goodbye.

"Wait, Lacey," Asher stopped her as she headed for the room door. "Why don't you stay? The room is paid for overnight, it might as well get some use."

"I couldn't—"

"Please," Asher said, "I insist."

"Well, I did want to take a swim in that Jacuzzi tub," Lacey bit her lip, considering. "Okay, I'll stay. On the condition that you stay as well."

His head tilted to the side. "A negotiation?"

"Mhmm," she nodded once. "I'd feel bad taking your money and using the room you paid for when you don't even get anything to enjoy. Besides we were having fun talking before. We'll hang out."

"I don't think I've ever just *hung out* with an escort before," Asher admitted.

"Well, technically I'm not an escort, since I just sort of retired, " she giggled. "Please. *I* insist."

Asher nodded. "Very well, it's a deal." He looked down and both of them realized he was still in just a towel. Lacey averted her eyes as he looked back up. "I should go change."

"I'll call room service," Lacey suggested. "I don't know about you but I could *definitely* use a drink."

"How about that champagne?"

Lacey grinned. "Sounds perfect."

Instead of inevitable sex there were strawberries dipped in dark chocolate and bubbly, sweet champagne. Asher had changed into a pair of sleep pants and a t-shirt and Lacey had ditched her sexy dress to wrap herself in one of the fluffy robes hanging in the bathroom. A couple of *Keeping Up with the Kardashians* reruns were watched at her request, and then Asher tried to teach her how to play chess, at *his* request. They'd settled across at the small dining table on the far side of the suite.

"No, the rook can only move horizontally or vertically. It's the bishop that can move diagonally," Asher instructed, for what seemed like the eighteenth time.

"Who invents a game that has so many rules about where pieces can go?" Lacey complained twirling her white queen in her hand.

Asher plucked the piece from her finger and set it back into place. "Well, it was believed to have originated in India sometime around the 6th century A.D."

"Well, well Mister Wikipedia, aren't we smart," she teased and picked up her glass of champagne. The bubbles ticked her nose as she sipped.

"I didn't read it on Wikipedia," he protested, as if the knowledge of the internet was beneath him, "I read it in a book."

"Which book?"

"*The Game of Kings* by Stewart Gordon."

"Impressive," Lacey replied, finally making her move.

Asher shrugged, finishing off his glass. The crystal clinked against the table as he set it back down to take his turn. "I like history. I like knowing where things came from."

38

Lacey frowned as Asher stole yet another pawn, his black pieces dominating the board. She wasn't very good at the whole thinking-two-moves-ahead thing.

Asher reached for the bottle of champagne to refill his glass, but found it empty. He frowned. It had to be the champagne buzz, coupled with the whiskey he'd had at the restaurant bar, and the wine he'd had a dinner, but he was definitely feeling more loquacious than usual.

The gorgeous creature across the table from him was a mystery to him and he found himself intrigued by the small facts about her life she'd accidentally revealed throughout the night. He wondered how a girl like her ended up as an escort, considering she had no skill or experience for the job. Asher cleared his throat. "So, you mentioned before that Willa and Chloe were just trying to be good friends?"

"Mhmm," Lacey murmured, studying the board, her finger tapping against her lips in deep concentration. Though it had been brief, he'd very much enjoyed kissing those lips.

"What did you mean by that?"

She touched the tip of her bishop with her index finger, but then snatched her hand back, going for the knight instead. As soon as she moved the piece, Asher shifted his queen and captured it from her. Lacey groaned.

"Do you really want to know?" He nodded. "I broke up with my boyfriend recently."

"The lawyer you mentioned? What happened?"

"He cheated on me," Lacey admitted, her eyes fixed to the game board. Her embarrassment was clear. "We lived together and he supported me financially, and now I don't have a job or a place to live. I never went to college, I just sort of thought I would marry him and be a house wife and a mom and not have to worry about anything like that." Lacey peeked up at him through her eyelashes. "It was a really stupid mistake. I was stupid."

Asher reached across the table and tucked his hand under

her chin, lifting it so that he could look her in the eyes. He thought of his past, his sister, his brothers, his entire family history. "I suppose we all make mistakes when it comes to love."

Lacey rewarded his sympathy with a half smile. "Yeah," she sighed. "But no one expects prince charming to cheat after eight years together."

"Eight?" Asher was incredulous. He couldn't imagine a relationship that lasted that long for someone as young as Lacey. He did a quick mental calculation and realized the pair must have been dating since high school.

"Yep, since we graduated high school," she confirmed. "And you know the worst part? The excuse he gave me for cheating was because he wanted to experience *something else* before he committed to me. He wanted to know for sure that I was *the one*." Hurt and irritation filled her tone. "He even tried to propose to me that night. Telling me that he did in fact realize he wanted to marry me."

On one hand, Asher understood her ex's point of view. If they'd been together since childhood, without experiencing life and all its possibilities as two independent and free people, perhaps jumping into life long commitment was an ill-conceived prospect. But on the other, the man was a bastard for cheating. Asher knew enough about women to keep the first opinion to himself. "This man, whoever he is, sounds like a complete fool."

"He is," she agreed, "it just sucks that I didn't realize it sooner."

Lacey moved a pawn and swiped one of Asher's from the board. He chuckled when she did a small victory dance in her chair.

His buzzed chattiness took over once again. "I was engaged once," he admitted. Lacey shot him a look, clearly surprised at the confession. "I was young. There was a girl back in London, called Bianca."

"What happened?"

"School, ambition, career," he listed. "Among *other* complications. She didn't enjoy coming in second to everything else."

"I guess no one does," Lacey observed. "Do you regret it? Giving up love for career and all that?"

"No," Asher affirmed without hesitation, "I made my decisions. I don't regret anything. I did what was right at the right time."

It wasn't just career and ambition that forced his hand, but Asher would never go into that story, no matter how much alcohol he had consumed.

They were silent for the rest of their turns until Asher called out "checkmate" for the third time that night.

"So is that why...the escorts?" Lacey ventured. Asher regarded her curiously. She was clearly following some line of thought he'd not been privy to. "I have to ask. I mean you're a nice, good-looking guy. You shouldn't have any trouble getting women in bed on your own."

Asher grinned at the compliment. "You think I'm good looking?" Her answering blush entertained him, as did the accompanying eye roll. "To be perfectly honest, my past is exactly the reason I see only escorts. I don't want a relationship. Being engaged, and then being with the women I dated after her, showed me that those sorts of relationships aren't something I desire for my life. I'm happy being who I am, doing what I want to do, without having to answer to anyone."

"That makes sense," Lacey replied, rearranging the pieces on the board.

It was more than Asher could ever remember sharing with another person. A piece of him wanted to take back the words, to lock them back inside his mind and heart where they would be safe, but then he reckoned after this night they would part ways and never again see one another. Where was the harm in sharing a little more than normal?

"Another game?" she asked.

Asher shook his head. "I think I'm ready to turn in. I've got work in the morning."

"Okay," Lacey said, rising from the table, "I can take the couch—"

"Absolutely not," Asher interrupted, "the bed is yours. I'll take the couch."

"No argument here." A smile tugged at her lips and Asher realized that he might have just been swindled out of a comfortable sleep.

He watched her grab her purse and lock herself in the bathroom to wash up. Asher took a water bottle from the mini fridge, gulping it down, wanting to avoid any chance of a champagne-induced headache in the morning.

By the time Lacey emerged, Asher had arranged himself on the couch and turned out the light. His eyes were closed as he listened to her quiet footsteps against the carpet. He opened them again when he felt her hovering over him.

"I just wanted to apologize again," she whispered in the darkness. "I know you were expecting..."

Her fingers twisted in the tie of her robe.

"Lacey, it's fine." Truly, Asher wasn't all that disappointed, in spite of how much he'd enjoyed kissing her. He'd had a long, vice-filled weekend with his friends and brothers. It was actually nice to relax for a change. "Just go to bed."

He closed his eyes, signaling that the issue was settled. A few moments later, Asher felt her move away and heard the bedroom light click off.

Chapter 3

The annoying whine of his phone's alarm pulled Asher from sleep. Growling, he grasped blindly for it, finding it on the carpet. Fighting the urge to throw it against the wall, he smashed his finger against the button, silencing the damn thing and sighing in relief at the return to quiet. The bright light of the new day trickled in through the gauzy, white hotel curtains. For a moment, he'd forgotten where he'd fallen asleep, until he realized how cramped he felt in the space where he'd slept.

He sat up and stretched, wincing at the slight ache in his back from spending his night on the sofa. His eyes flicked up and he chuckled to himself, glancing at the gorgeous blonde resting comfortably on the lush king-sized bed in the other part of the room. Wasn't this why he only went out with escorts? To avoid being forced to sleep on the couch?

Asher stood and walked toward Lacey. His alarm hadn't disturbed her in the slightest. She was still stretched out on her back right in the middle of the mattress, surrounded by fluffy feather pillows, the down comforter pooled at her waist. The robe she'd worn to bed had fallen open just a bit, revealing the supple curve between her breasts. Asher shook his head ruefully at the glimpse of her body. It was a damn shame that he hadn't had the chance to bed this beautiful girl. From the warmth of her laugh to the allure of her figure, she had been a truly fantastic companion for the evening. Even without the sex.

He strolled into the bathroom and turned on the sink, splashing some water on his face and brushing his teeth. Planning ahead the night before, he'd brought a change of clothes so he could leave the hotel and go directly to the office.

A loud ringing broke into the quiet of the hotel room once again and Asher darted from the bathroom to answer his mobile.

"Hello," Asher answered in a whisper. He looked over his shoulder at Lacey, checking to see if the noise had woken her, and saw she hadn't even stirred.

"Good morning," the familiar voice of his older brother, Duncan, greeted him. Unlike the rest of their family, Duncan no longer affected the accent Asher and the rest of their siblings did. There was much speculation as to the reason behind its disappearance, but regardless, Duncan still managed to sound just as pompous without it. "I wanted to catch you before you went into work. Why are you whispering?"

"I'm not whispering," Asher replied, clearing his throat. He spared a glance at Lacey. It seemed that she slept like the dead; she hadn't moved an inch from when he'd first awoken. He spoke again, attempting a neutral volume. "What do you need?"

"Aleksandra," Duncan's tongue rolled over the name, "is

double checking our seating arrangements and she noted you are listed as plus one."

"Yes. And?"

"And she insists it is too late to change anything. She's changed the seating chart five damn times already." Asher smirked. Duncan rarely swore unless he was very irritated. Duncan's fiancé made him swear quite a lot. It was one of the reasons Asher liked her so much. "You'd better be bringing someone."

Asher rolled his eyes at the not too subtle chastisement. He didn't understand why it mattered whether or not he brought a date. He reached up and flipped back one of the curtains, allowing more sunlight spill into the room and admiring the view. Lake Michigan stretched out and glittered in the early light as a few small boats meandered out across the water for a morning sail. Duncan had certainly become more concerned with Asher's relationships ever since he himself had proposed. Asher could recall a time, in the not too distant past, when Duncan had been just as much of a cynic as he was about love and life. Asher liked to think of it as a Knight family trait.

"Can't darling Aleksa cope with the fact there will simply be an empty chair by my side?" The thought sounded a little more depressing once he said it out loud.

"No," replied Duncan. "My lovely bride-to-be is a perfectionist and if there is a gaping hole in her reception seating...suffice it to say my honeymoon won't be very fun."

"Doesn't sound like my problem," Asher retorted.

"I'm serious, Asher. Bring a date, a *nice* woman."

Asher chuckled. "I think you're giving that warning to the wrong brother, Duncan. I only ever date nice women." Their youngest brother, Jaime, was less judicious when it came to female partners. If a girl was attractive and willing, Jaime wasn't much bothered about anything else.

Duncan was not privy to Asher's little vice for escorts. No one

45

in his family was in on that secret. He could only imagine the epic temper tantrum his sister would throw if she ever found out.

"I'm sure Gwen has a friend or two," Duncan suggested, referring to their baby sister.

Asher rolled his eyes, annoyed at Duncan's attempt to be the concerned older brother as he launched into an insufferable lecture on the reasons why Asher needed to seek out more stability in his life. It was a tired speech that Asher had been hearing in bits and pieces for the past few months as Duncan slowly descended into his role as husband. As if falling in love and getting engaged had suddenly given Duncan a new, more enlightened vision of the world.

Before Aleksa, their lives had finally begun to stabilize. Between the move from London, their father, and Gwen's little predicament, he and Duncan had finally been able to carve out a new future for their family. Throwing a new woman into the mix had shaken things up once more, no matter how well Aleksa seemed to fit with them. The wedding would no doubt bring a fresh new wave of soap opera worthy events that Asher would rather avoid.

A twinge of loneliness seized him. Though it was a constant companion, it wasn't an emotion he ever allowed himself to feel; nevertheless, it came in full force at the idea of facing what may come that weekend without someone by his side.

The covers on the bed rustled as Lacey shifted slightly, turning her head away from the bright windows, her robe falling open a bit more to reveal her stomach. Asher turned from the window to watch her, his melancholy thoughts shifting to fantasies of what it would be like to run his hands underneath that robe to touch her creamy skin.

An idea formed in his mind. A cliché one, he would admit, but the old tricks were the best tricks.

"I'll have a date Duncan," he grinned into the phone, "don't you worry."

Lacey blinked, stretching her arms up over her head, a feminine groan of satisfaction bubbling from her throat. The delicious smells of bacon, fresh orange juice, and maple syrup wafted through the hotel room. Her robe had fallen open while she'd slept and she tucked it back together as Asher appeared from the bathroom freshly showered. She smiled at him and he smiled back. The damp look was sexy on him; dirty blonde curls sticking to his dewy skin.

"I ordered some breakfast," Asher said, gesturing at the table in the outer room, "room service just dropped it off a few minutes ago."

"Thanks." She climbed out of bed and joined him at the small table where they had played chess the night before. Her fingers went for a piece of bacon first, sliding it into her mouth while she helped herself to the silver pot of coffee. Asher flipped open the morning newspaper that he'd requested along with their breakfast.

"I didn't think I'd be able to wake you," he remarked as she dumped sugar into her cup, " you slept through two phone calls and the arrival of room service."

"Yeah," Lacey replied, testing her coffee to make sure it was just right. "I've always been a heavy sleeper."

She grabbed a plate and added a couple pancakes to it, pouring some maple syrup on top. It wasn't the healthiest way to start her day but she figured she earned the treat.

"What do you think you'll do now that your career as a call girl is over?" Asher inquired, eyeing her from behind his paper.

"It's not over," she corrected. "Actually, I wanted to ask you about that."

"Oh? What about it?"

"Well," she began, tracing her fingers along the silverware in front of her, unable to look him directly in the eye, "I was wondering if you could possibly not tell Willa or Chloe that we didn't have sex last night."

Asher set down his newspaper and folded his hands under his chin, giving her his full attention. "And why would I do that?"

She fought not to roll her eyes, trying to remain sweet. He was toying with her.

"Because," Lacey continued, "last night was basically supposed to be a try out and they said they wouldn't hire me unless I did well."

He turned a bit more serious. "Lacey, you do realize that someone will have to pop that cherry at some point? So to speak."

"I know. And I can do this. I *will* do this," she affirmed, her hand clenching into a fist on the table. "I need the job. I don't have much of a choice." Lacey hated how desperate she sounded.

"Actually, I have a better proposition for you," Asher said, a sparkle in his sea colored eyes.

She tilted her head. Curious. "What are you talking about?"

A smile played at the corners of his mouth. "I want to pay you to be my girlfriend for a week."

Lacey almost spit out her coffee. Was he serious? He couldn't be serious. "Pay me to be your girlfriend?"

"I have a couple of social functions throughout the week as well as my brother's wedding this weekend. I would like to hire you to accompany me to those events," Asher explained.

He had thought about just taking her to the wedding, but reasoned that he needed to be more convincing. Spending time together that week and getting to know each other a bit more, might make the ruse more believable in front of his family. Perhaps, if his brother thought he was attempting an actual adult relationship, he might give the lectures a rest. "I told you why I don't want relationships in my life. My family doesn't seem to be able to grasp my reasoning."

"I'm sure they just want to see you happy."

"I'd be happy if they left me alone about the subject," Asher complained.

Lacey sipped her coffee, considering his offer. She was confused but still intrigued. "How much are we talking?"

"We could handle all the business through your agency. Have your friends dictate the terms and negotiate the price. I'm sure we can work out something reasonable."

"Pay me to be your girlfriend," Lacey repeated his offer. It seemed unbelievable. "I'm just—sorry, I'm confused. I'm not exactly sure what you're asking."

Asher was quick to read her unspoken questions. "I'm not hiring you for sex," he assured her. "It would just be keeping up appearances. For example, I have a charity event tonight. You would come as my date."

Lacey fell silent, eyes searching the table for advice. Asher tensed at the other end of the table. Without saying anything or looking at him, she pushed her plate away and stood, walking into the bathroom and shutting the door. She turned the tap, letting the rush of water fill the silence to give her some privacy, and stared at herself in the mirror.

She wanted to say yes. She really did. She needed the money. It was impractical to refuse his generous offer. She couldn't afford to have any qualms about pretending to be someone's girlfriend if she was planning on becoming a full-time escort . . . and Asher had said no sex. Simply going to a party and a wedding and whatever else he had planned. No sex. If nothing else, it would give her more time to adjust to the idea of sleeping with a stranger.

Her teeth pulled at her lip. It probably wouldn't be horrible. They had fun together the night before just hanging out. Asher was a nice guy, and not terrible looking. Lacey grinned to her reflection in the mirror. Okay, he was to die for handsome. She could admit that. It wouldn't be hard to pretend to be his girlfriend.

She cupped her hands under the running water and splashed

some water on her face, running her hands behind her neck and letting the coolness soothe her. Asher was probably the best choice in the world for this kind of arrangement. He had been nothing but nice to her since the moment she walked into the bar the night before. Nice *and* understanding.

"Okay," Lacey said to herself, taking a deep breath and shutting off the water. Decision made, she pulled open the door and jumped when she saw Asher hovering just in front of the doorway.

"I hope I haven't offended you," he apologized, his eyes cast toward the floor. The concern etched on his face tugged at her heartstrings.

"No, it's fine. I was surprised. I just needed a minute," she assured him. "I'll do it. I'll pretend to be your girlfriend for a week."

Asher's eyes lifted. "You accept?" It was like he expected her to say no.

"I accept," Lacey said, sticking out her hand for him to shake.

Asher chuckled in relief and took her hand, shaking on the deal.

After breakfast with Asher and discussing a few more details of their arrangement, Lacey headed straight for the Vamp office. It took a leer from her cab driver to remember that she was still in last night's dress. Ironically, she was doing the walk of shame, but hadn't actually done anything considered shameful.

The only shame she felt was in not being able to go through with sleeping with Asher last night. Based solely on the way his kisses made her toes curl there was no doubt it would have been some top-notch sex. She could have been doing the walk of satisfied—as Aunt Jessa used to tell them, there wasn't anything shameful in sex. Instead, she was feeling frustration at herself for not getting the job done. She hated failing and she had failed epically on her first night as an escort.

She didn't want to see the looks of disappointment in Willa and Chloe's eyes. Well, disappointment mixed with not being surprised that she wasn't able to go through with the sex. They had been right to be skeptical about her capability as an escort, and she hated that. She wanted so badly to prove them wrong. There was nothing she loved better than besting anyone who thought she wasn't capable of something.

The cab dropped her off in front of Vamp Escorts' office building and she took the elevator up to the suite. Tossing her hair back, she pushed open the door and breezed into the office. Willa and Chloe were already there, each seated at their desks.

"Hey Lace—Whoa!" Willa gaped at her as she strutted in, noticing last night's dress and heels. "Have you been home yet?"

"Nope," Lacey twirled and dropped onto the couch with a provocative smile.

The two madams exchanged looks and rushed over from their desks to grill her on the details.

"How'd it go last night?" Chloe asked, sitting in the decorative white chair across from her and leaning in over her crossed legs. Willa took the spot on the couch next to Lacey.

The satisfaction she felt at their surprise and attention was blurred by the fact that she couldn't feel totally smug about proving to them that she could succeed. It was a big, fat lie after all.

"It was great. Not nearly as bad of a time as I worried it might be." It was a half-truth. She didn't have to specify that the easiness of the night was largely due to Asher's saint like understanding and the fact that they watched bad TV played chess instead of having sex.

"That's great Lace," said Chloe. "Asher already called this morning to give you a rave review. He said you were excellent company."

51

Lacey grinned at the compliment; glad to hear he was a man of his word. "Speaking of Asher, that's why I came straight here. He made me a proposition before I left the hotel this morning."

"What kind of proposition?"

Lacey looked away from Chloe's pinched eyebrows and smoothed the grey fabric of the sofa with her palms, her eyes dropping to the fluffy rug covering the floor. She wasn't quite sure how Chloe and Willa would take the idea of his deal. "He wants to pay me to be his girlfriend for a week."

"Damn girl, you must have done a great job last night!" Willa exclaimed.

Chloe seemed less enthused, so Lacey quickly went on. "He said that we could do everything through the agency. So, you guys will still get commission." She explained the offer, going into detail about the brief terms that she and Asher had discussed over breakfast, leaving out the part where sex was not an official requirement.

"Hold on," Chloe interrupted, "does this mean you've already said yes to this?" Lacey nodded. She could see a little bit of irritation in the purse of her friend's lips. Chloe would never admit it, but she was a control freak, just like Lacey. If a plan wasn't discussed with her first for her approval, she often became frustrated. It didn't matter if it was a business deal or a trip to the movies. "Well," she looked at Willa, "we did agree that we'd hire you on if you did well last night. And you definitely held up your end of that bargain so...Willa, help her figure out what to charge for a week as a full time girlfriend."

The sum for a week's worth of Lacey's services came out to be quite a large number, even in spite of the fact that Willa charged a lower rate for Lacey because she was new. Lacey hoped that Asher wouldn't change his mind after seeing the price.

"You're worth it," Willa winked at her.

"There's no precedent for this," Chloe noted, "but I'd rather him actually come in and sign a contract before everything goes down. It's important that you and our business are protected."

"He's a lawyer, I'm sure he'll understand," Lacey assured.

The Vamp contracts were unique in the escort business. Willa, genius that she was, was able to craft a standard document that protected their business, the girls, and also allowed the client to avoid the legal entanglements of paying for sex. It was her super power.

Willa called Asher and left him a voicemail with a request to visit their office to finalize the particulars and expectations.

"Here," Chloe said, handing Lacey a cellphone. It was small and silver, an inexpensive flip phone that didn't require a phone plan. "Every Vamp girl has one. It's so you don't have to give out your personal number to clients. Use this for anything that's work related." Chloe wrote down Lacey's new number and input the contacts of the other girls and Asher. "Now, we'll need to create a profile for you on the website, which means a photo shoot as soon as possible. How about Thursday?"

Lacey clapped her hands at the idea of a photo shoot. It sounded so glamorous. But Chloe was wearing her serious business expression, so Lacey stopped her delighted squeals and attempted to remain professional.

"I got an email back from Asher," Willa announced from her computer. "He's coming here tonight to pick you up for the Brunswick Charity Gala and sign whatever we need."

"Oh my gosh!" Lacey exclaimed. "I should go shopping! I don't have anything to wear."

"Maybe you should go home first and change out of the slutty piece of work you have on now," Willa teased, tongue poking between her teeth.

"It's not slutty," Lacey retorted. "Besides it got the job done didn't it?" Lacey waggled her eyebrows and skipped out the door.

53

Asher smiled as he wrote his reply email to Willa. Lacey hadn't changed her mind about their deal and her friends-come-employers hadn't refused. He hoped that his shining review of their evening had something to do with that.

As he clicked send, Gabriel Sawyer appeared in his doorway and dropped some files onto his desk.

"Here are those contracts your assistant dropped off. I finished reading them." He lowered himself into one of the leather chairs in front of Asher's desk.

Asher smirked at the brown haired man. The last time he'd seen him had been at a Blackjack table in Vegas, a glass of whiskey in his hand and a fetching blonde woman at his side, purring into his ear. "Gabriel, glad to see you at work today my friend. I feared you might have reconsidered your options and decided to become a full time gambler."

"I need to work so I can pay off my outrageous gambling debts," Gabriel replied, only half joking.

"Maybe you should think twice before going to Sin City again," Asher replied. He didn't judge the younger man too much for his indulgences, but sometimes it was difficult not to considering the circumstances of their friendship.

"Maybe I should think three times," Gabriel sighed, tugging at his tie.

"Good morning, little brother," Delaney sang, entering Asher's office and taking the second chair in front of his desk. "Good to see you alive again."

"Yeah, thanks," Gabriel grumbled. "Did you bring me coffee?"

"Get your own coffee," Delaney replied, moving his large white cup out of Gabriel's reach. "So, bossman, how'd last night go?"

"What happened last night?" Gabriel asked.

Asher threw Delaney a warning look. Gabriel didn't know about his escort secret and he didn't *want* him knowing either. It was bad enough that Delaney knew.

"Nothing. Just a date."

"How was it?" Delaney repeated.

"Fine," Asher relented, knowing Delaney wouldn't drop it and Gabriel would be suspicious if he kept up with the cagey behavior. "I'm bringing her to the charity gala tonight."

"You are?" Delaney was incredulous. The statement went against everything Asher had explained about his rules for seeing escorts.

"Yes."

Asher tried to ignore Delaney's prying look and focused on his computer, reading the same email subject line over and over again. Thankfully, Grant Lucas walked by at that moment. Asher had never been so thankful to see anyone in his life.

"Grant, mate, can you come in here please?" Asher called out to him. The younger man stepped into his office.

"What's up, boss?"

Asher ignored the twin looks of confusion from the Sawyer brothers. "Delaney here was just telling me that he was interested in the work you did on the Brockman, Inc. contracts last week. I thought perhaps you could give him a quick run-through."

"Sure! Yes! Whatever you want." Lucas looked so excited about the attention to his run of the mill contract that Asher almost felt bad about the lie. *Almost.*

Delaney stood from the chair, glaring. Asher bit back his smile as he watched his annoyed partner follow their least favorite associate out of his office and down the hall. That would keep him busy for at least two hours and teach him not to pry into Asher's business.

"He's going to kill you for that you know," Gabriel remarked.

Asher shrugged. "If he kills me, at least he'll be able to represent himself in the murder trial."

Lacey spent the entire day pampering herself and getting ready for the charity gala that night. It was her second day in a row of nothing but beauty treatments. She could definitely get used to the escort life.

Grant had taken her to networking related functions a couple times so she was no stranger to these types of events. Arm candy was not a role she was unfamiliar with. She tried to ignore the slight feeling of guilt that went through her when she slapped down her credit card to buy a new dress and heels. It was almost a third of what Asher had paid her for the previous night, but with full time employment on the horizon she figured she could afford it.

Someone is going to have to pop that cherry sometime.

Asher's earlier words rang inside her head, reminding her that her escort status wasn't exactly set in stone. It was crass statement, but true. Not every client she went out with would be as understanding about the sex thing. If she was going to live life as a call-girl, she was going to have to have sex with strange men, and possibly even women.

Lacey straightened her shoulders and tossed back her blonde waves. She would worry about all of her hang-ups next week. This week she belonged to Asher, and she didn't have to worry about anything else.

For the evening, she chose a royal blue cocktail dress. The flirty, peplum ruffle accented her waist and made her look curvier. She matched the dress with silver heels and a small silver clutch. Her hair was styled into an elegant French twist; with a few loose curls to frame her face and shoulders. Her makeup remained light, preferring something less bold like the previous night and more like herself.

Asher was meeting Willa and Chloe at seven to discuss and sign his contract. Lacey was scheduled to meet him at seven-thirty to head to the gala. She arrived at the Vamp office door at seven-thirty, but Asher was nowhere to be found.

"He's late," Willa informed her.

Asher breezed through the door not two minutes later, an attractive looking dark-haired man strolling in behind him.

"My apologies," he greeted. "I was held up at work. This is my colleague, Delaney Sawyer." Asher made introductions.

Delaney shook hands with Willa and Lacey, lingering in front of Lacey, his eyes making her feel a little bit like a juicy steak that he was dying to eat. "Great to meet you, Lacey. I've heard so much about you."

Asher made an annoyed noise as Lacey reached out to return Delaney's smarmy grin and handshake with a polite smile, holding back the urge she had to stomp on his foot.

Delaney stared at her a moment longer, his leer turning into a look of concentration. "Have we met before?"

Lacey rolled her eyes. "I'm sure you say that to all the girls."

Asher sat at Willa's desk to read over the contract, while Delaney strolled around the office, examining the decorative pillows and the vacant desk across from Willa's. It was a straightforward and simple document, no fine print, just an agreement that Asher would play by the rules and accept the invoice billed to him for Lacey's "interior design consultation services." The one stipulation was that he paid up front.

"This is quite a brilliant contract you've drawn up, Miss Ross," Asher praised, scratching his signature onto the paper.

"Thank you," Willa replied, accepting the compliment. Lacey shot her a proud thumbs up so the boys wouldn't see.

"Hey, sorry, I'm back." Chloe swept into the office, slightly winded. "I had to refresh my parking meter."

"No worries, we're just finishing up," Willa said.

Delaney looked over at Chloe as she entered, the double take not escaping Lacey's notice. His eyes widened in appreciation, far beyond the admiring look he had given Lacey herself.

"Hi," he said, striding into Chloe's path and holding his hand out to her, "Delaney Sawyer."

Chloe gave him a passive glance; most of her attention focused on her client and shook his hand politely. "Chloe."

"Lovely to meet you," he smirked, eyes roaming over her. "Are you an escort as well?"

"No," Chloe replied flatly, pulling her hand from his grasp.

"Well, that's a shame," he purred. "I'd love to spend some time together."

"Delaney. Mate." Asher cautioned through gritted teeth. Lacey put a hand to her mouth to stifle her laugh. Between Chloe's obvious rejection and Asher's annoyance, she was about to explode.

Chloe stepped over to Willa and Asher and took the contract, double checking his signature. "Did you have any questions, Mr. Knight?"

"I think we're clear," he replied, eyes flicking to Lacey for the first time since he entered the office.

"Then everything is settled," Chloe affirmed. "Enjoy your week, Mr. Knight." She stepped away with Willa, allowing Asher to finally move toward Lacey.

Asher shifted his wrist to reveal the watch under his sleeve and checked the time. "We'd better get going or we'll be late."

Lacey nodded and grabbed her purse.

Delaney's eyes lingered on Chloe until Asher pulled him away. Lacey gave the girls a quick wave before following the men into the elevator, standing between the two.

"I apologize for my friend's behavior," Asher said, leaning toward her. "He insisted on coming along."

"Consider it payback for sticking me with that asshat associate this morning," Delaney retorted. He smiled at Lacey. "So, Lace, is your friend Chloe single?"

"Yes," Lacey answered. "But you're not really her type."

Lacey had seen guys far better than Delaney turned down by her friend. Guys like him who oozed fake charm and made fake promises weren't at all on Chloe's radar.

Delaney smirked, undaunted by Lacey's assessment. "You never know what could happen."

The three of them took a town car to the gala. The Metronome Museum, a modern art gallery where the gala was being held, had been closed to the public and dressed up for the night's event. The white walls of the gallery were accented by a blue glow, setting the mood. It was less stuffy than Lacey had imagined a charity event with a bunch of rich businessmen would be.

The crowd was mostly younger executives and Chicago business types. Champagne poured from fountains dotted around the room. Soft, dreamy music filled the air beyond the din of chatter. The guests mingled, sipping cocktails, and viewing the exhibits on display.

Asher put a hand on Lacey's back. She glanced over at him and smiled. "Shall we?"

He ushered her down the marble steps. Delaney separated from them, making his way over to some other acquaintances while Asher led Lacey toward the bar.

"I didn't realize anyone else knew about our arrangement," Lacey mentioned as they took the vacant area at the bar.

"Does it make you angry?" Asher signaled to the bartender with a flick of his finger.

"No, not at all," she answered. "But no one else knows that I'm an escort, right?"

Asher shook his head. "Delaney tends to stick his nose in places where it doesn't belong."

"Somehow, that's not surprising," Lacey snickered, as the bartender approached them.

"Scotch rocks and a sparkling water," Asher ordered. The bartender prepared the drinks and set them on top of the glowing bar. Asher passed Lacey the water. "If I recall correctly, you prefer not to drink while working."

Lacey smiled, appreciating his attentiveness. They toasted

and she sipped her water as Asher led her through the museum. He seemed to know a lot about the pieces hanging on the walls. As they walked along, he explained the origins of the artists, the meaning of each painting or sculpture, and the significance and skills that made each work unique.

"You really know a lot about art," Lacey pointed out as she observed a canvas, much taller than her, with red and orange splashed across it.

"I minored in art history at university," Asher shrugged. "I used to paint when I was younger. I wanted to be an artist."

"What changed your mind?" she asked, wondering why the leap from art to law.

"It was never a true possibility. My father…" The way he trailed off spoke to volumes of regret.

Lacey reached down and grasped his hand, giving it a squeeze. "Parents dictating your life. Sounds like a tale as old as time."

Asher smirked and laced his fingers with hers, taking a sip of his scotch. They stood in front of the painting, silent, observing each energetic stroke and flash of color. Their shoulders bumped lightly together, and Lacey opened her mouth to ask him about his own art when a voice from behind interrupted.

"Good evening, Mr. Knight. How—oh, shit!"

Lacey froze when she registered the familiar voice and turned to see the last person in the world she'd expected or wanted to see. The last time she'd seen his face, she'd been slamming the door on it as he'd tried to stop her from leaving with useless, stuttered apologies.

It was Grant, her ex.

Chapter 4

Asher rolled his eyes and cursed at Grant's interruption of their quiet moment. He was enjoying his evening with Lacey: explaining all of the rich history to her, answering her questions, watching her reactions. He relished seeing her head tilt in confusion at the artistic value of some pieces. She never pretended to be interested. If a piece of work bored her or she disagreed with a critical assessment she simply went on and asked about the next painting or sculpture. They'd been mostly alone throughout the galleries, only a few other couples or small groups strolling along, most of the guests preferring to stay in the main room of the museum.

A feeling of easiness swept through him while sharing this passion of his with her, and his guard had dropped long enough to mention his father in spite of the fact that she was still a stranger to him. For a moment he had toyed with the idea of telling her more, of giving a better explanation for the reason art remained a forgotten hobby while law became his career. It was more complicated than she could possibly assume.

When he turned to face Grant, he noticed the associate stood with a gorgeous, waif-like brunette girl attached to his arm. This must have been the girlfriend Delaney had raved about. Only he thought Delaney had described her as blonde?

"What are you doing here? Are you with him?" Grant demanded.

It took Asher a moment to register the angry surprise on Grant's brow as well as the fact that he was addressing Lacey as if they'd met before. Asher glanced over at her. Even under the dimmed lighting of the gallery he could see that the color and brightness had drained from her pretty face. She stood there, still as the marble statues they'd viewed in the gardens earlier, gaping at his associate.

"Grant, I—" Lacey stuttered.

"It's been less than a week and already you're out with some other guy?"

Asher looked back and forth between the two, slowly catching up to the situation. The girl on Grant's arm wasn't the girlfriend Delaney had told him about. The hot blonde that Delaney had described was, in fact, Lacey.

And the cheating ex Lacey had mentioned was none other than his overly enthusiastic associate.

"*Me*? Who's this?" Lacey shot back, finally finding her voice. She waved her hands frantically in the direction of the brunette. "What you couldn't even manage to stay with the same skank for more than a week? Already onto the next?"

The brunette finally reacted to being deemed a skank and Asher winced at the level of Lacey's voice, which was becoming a bit to loud for their current setting.

"Mallory is just a friend," Grant explained, but Lacey held up a hand and cut him off.

"You know what, Grant, it doesn't even matter." Unwilling to hear anymore, Lacey stalked away, leaving Asher alone with Grant and Mallory.

Grant moved forward to follow her but Asher caught him by the arm, preventing his pursuit.

"I wouldn't if I were you," Asher glowered.

"She's my girlfriend," Grant protested. It was more forceful than the younger man had ever been with him. If it were under any other circumstance, Asher might have been impressed to see the kiss-ass finally show a little backbone.

"Not anymore, the way I understand it," said Asher. His eyes flicked around the room. A few guests that had come into gallery, possibly because they'd heard the raised voices, were beginning to stare in their direction and whisper. "Now, how about you go back to your date and I'll go back to mine, and we'll enjoy our evening, hm?"

Grant jerked out of Asher's grasp and straightened his tie, grabbing his date's hand and leading her away. Asher looked around and everyone who'd been hovering nearby reluctantly turned away to continue their own activities now that the opportunity to witness a little drama had passed. He turned in the direction Lacey had taken, but hadn't made it more than ten steps before Delaney appeared and intercepted him.

"What the hell was that?"

"Apparently Lacey is Lucas's former girlfriend," Asher told him, "haven't you met her before? Why didn't you say anything?"

"That's why she looked familiar," Delaney snapped his fingers, "honestly, I only met her once and I wasn't really focusing on her face, if you know what I mean?"

Asher glared at Delaney's suggestive comment. "Watch it Sawyer," he warned brushing past him.

"Hey," Delaney called out to him and Asher turned back. "I saw her head upstairs and out to the bridge."

Asher nodded and headed in that direction. He saw Lacey through the glass door, standing alone on the bridge walkway. A gentle, warm breeze swept through as he stepped outside and walked carefully to where Lacey stood, looking out at the night skyline. The bridge overlooked the massive green park and the city beyond. The honking of cabs and sounds of the Chicago night echoed under them in the distance. Lacey turned toward him, sniffing and wiping at her eyes, her arms crossing defensively across her chest.

"Thank god you aren't Grant," she sniffed as he approached her. "I promised myself I wouldn't cry anymore." She sounded disappointed in herself. "Is my mascara running?"

Asher snorted in amusement, reaching up to wipe a tear from her cheek with his thumb. "No, you look perfect," he said. "So, Grant Lucas is the prat responsible for your current situation."

Lacey nodded. "How do you know him?"

"He's an associate at my firm."

"Oh," Lacey said, realizing what that meant for their arrangement. "How's this going to work then?"

"What do you mean?"

"I mean us. Our pretend relationship. Like Grant said, he and I broke up less than a week ago. He knows me Asher. He knows that I wouldn't just date another man at the drop of a hat and…" She bit her lip. "He knows about Willa and Chloe's business."

That did complicate things. Grant may have been a pain in the ass, but he wasn't stupid. It wouldn't take much to put together the real nature of his and Lacey's relationship, which could bring a world of trouble for them both. But he wasn't going to give up just because of a slight bump in the road.

Asher put his hands on Lacey's shoulders, running his thumbs across her skin. "Don't worry. It will work. We just might have to put in a bit more face time to be really convincing. And…"

"And…" Lacey urged.

"He'll be jealous. In fact, I think he is already jealous. You should have seen the look on his face when you left the room."

Lacey let out a small laugh. "What girl doesn't want to make her cheating ex-boyfriend green with envy?"

"Exactly," Asher replied, glad to see a hint of humor in her expression. He pulled her into a hug, wrapping his arms around her shoulders. Lacey tucked her head under his chin and enjoyed the comfort of his embrace.

"Thank you," she sighed into his chest. "This really isn't fair, you know. I'm supposed to be fulfilling all your needs, not the other way around."

"Don't worry. I'm sure you can pay me back later."

Lacey tensed in his arms and took a step back. Asher mentally cursed himself. He hadn't meant the comment to sound the way it came out, like one of Delaney's cheap innuendos.

"I didn't…" he faltered.

"It's fine…" she said, waving it off.

"I only meant that, it's a shame all of my ex-girlfriends live outside the States," he explained, trying to make the point that he wasn't suggesting she could pay him back in bed. He really hadn't meant it that way.

That was a lie. A part of him meant it exactly that way. In spite of their deal, Asher wanted to sleep with Lacey. She was attractive and he was a man and the taste he'd had of her the night before was more than enough to tempt him into wishing for more. If she gave him any indication…

No.

Despite their circumstances, Lacey wasn't a conquest. The girl had just had her heart broken less than a week ago, evidence of her vulnerability still drying on her cheeks. She wasn't the type who went for meaningless sex and Asher wanted no part in adding to her hurt. Asher stepped back to give them both space as she away any sign of tears, cleaning her face of any ruined makeup.

"How do I look?" Lacey asked.

Asher examined the way she threw back her shoulders and held her chin high in the air. All trace of the sad girl from moments before had vanished. "Positively gorgeous," he replied, impressed, "have I not mentioned that this evening?"

"I don't believe you have." She flashed him a bright smile and slipped her arm around his elbow. Asher opened the glass door at the end of the walkway and escorted her back inside.

He did his best to keep Grant out of her eyeline for most of the evening, while making sure Lacey stayed in view of his. Asher pulled her close on the small on the dance floor a time or two, mingled with other guests, and Lacey even dropped her no alcohol rule and downed a couple glasses of champagne.

She charmed practically everyone he introduced her to, which was no surprise. Lacey was warm, friendly, and full of energy. Her ability to genuinely engage with every person with whom she spoke would have made her an excellent politician. It was unlike the overly seductive act she'd put on at moments the night before. Lacey didn't have to try and seduce anyone, she only had to be herself and the people around her were eating from the palm of her hand.

Later in the evening, Asher caught Grant staring over at them, glowering. Asher hadn't given much thought to the younger man in the past. He'd never been as annoyed with him as Delaney tended to be on an almost daily basis. Given the new details Asher had learned of Grant's personal life, he was beginning to feel something akin to loathing for the young associate simmering just under his skin. He'd probably fire him if it wouldn't land him in an irritating lawsuit. Maybe Asher couldn't fire him, but he could prevent Grant from any further advancement while employed at *his* firm.

Asher caught Grant's stare with a cocky grin and slipped an arm around Lacey's waist, pulling her in close and kissing her hair: a clichéd alpha male challenge that a boy like Grant was sure to respond to. Lacey gave Asher a questioning look.

"We're being watched," Asher whispered into her hair.

Understanding blossomed over her features, melting slowly into something a little more devious, making Asher curious as to the thought running through her pretty brain. He didn't have to wait long to find out. She reached up and wrapped her hand around his chin, tugging him down for a not so chaste kiss. The bold move caught him off guard and it took another pass from her lips before his mind caught up with his mouth and he started playing along. Lacey slipped her tongue between his lips momentarily and Asher thought he would lose his battle with temptation right then and there. She tasted sweet, like strawberries and the champagne she had been drinking. Asher was doing everything he could not to get caught up in the showy kiss and let his hands slip to places they shouldn't in public.

After only a few seconds, she pulled away and smiled up at him. He smiled back, the urge to suggest that they leave the museum for somewhere more private overwhelming him. At that point, Asher was mentally considering a few dark corners in one of the smaller galleries where they could lose themselves.

"Did he see?" Lacey asked, reminding Asher why she'd kissed him in the first place.

Asher's eyes flicked up in time to see Grant grab his date and storm out of the party, throwing a sulky look over his shoulder in their direction.

Asher smirked down at her. "Well done, sweetheart."

She snickered, victorious, and kissed him again, surprising him once more. It was another slow kiss, Lacey trailing her tongue over his lips, teasing him. Asher held his breath, trying to control the lust that her continued kissing brought forth. If she didn't stop doing things like that, he was going to have to find a way to convince her that they should amend their "no sex" rule a bit.

When she pulled back, he asked her, "What was that for?"

Lacey smirked. "Consider it part of your payment."

Oh, she was going to be the death of him.

It had been a truly fabulous evening for Lacey. As they were leaving the party, she felt like doing cartwheels down the large concrete steps of the entrance to the museum. Aside from seeing Grant and her aching feet, she'd had a perfect evening being Asher's date. Especially during the parts when they made Grant jealous. Sure, it was a little adolescent and immature, but damn, it was fun. Making out with Asher again had certainly been a good time, too.

She didn't know where the courage had come from to steal his lips that second time. Maybe it was an adrenaline rush she'd gotten from the green-eyed game they'd been playing, but she hadn't the slightest notion of self-doubt before as she'd pulled Asher in for another delicious kiss.

The town car they'd arrived in was waiting outside the museum, parked on the curb. Asher opened the door for her, and she climbed in, sighing in relief to be off her feet. She immediately started to remove her shoes, eager to massage her sore arches.

"Where to, miss?" The chauffeur asked.

She opened her mouth to give him her address but stopped as Asher settled in next to her and shut the door. "What's your address, Lacey?"

She bit her lip. "I can't give it to you," Lacey explained, "it's against the rules."

"Lacey, I think you know by now I'm not a stalker or a serial killer," he replied with a wink.

"I know that," she laughed, "but it's just...I'm staying with

Chloe until I find a place and she'd flip out if I showed you where she lives. It's agency rules not to bring clients to your home."

"I see," Asher said, considering his alternatives, "well, if I can't take you to your current place of residence, you'll just have to come to mine."

He nodded at the driver, who had been politely not listening to their conversation, and the car pulled away from the curb. Lacey gave him a look. "Asher, I thought we agreed..."

"We agreed that you are my fake girlfriend for a week. It makes perfect sense for you to come to my apartment." He hit her with an innocent look. "There's an extra room you can stay in. Large bed, Jacuzzi bath, not unlike the one that was at the hotel last night."

Damn, he had her figured out. Jacuzzi tubs were her weakness and she hadn't gotten the chance to take a swim in the hotel's the night before.

"I guess so," Lacey relented, crossing her arms. She was trying her best to pretend like it didn't make her completely excited that he had invited her over.

The car brought them to a tall sky rise apartment on the Gold Coast, a brand new, swanky type building complete with a security system and a doorman. The glass structure gleamed in the moonlight. Asher lived near the top floor in a two-level apartment, twice the size of the one she had shared with Grant. It screamed bachelor pad, of course, complete with a big screen television and state-of-the-art entertainment center, and black leather furniture. It was minimal and modern. Lacey noticed a few paintings hung on the walls and she wondered if Asher had done any of them himself.

He gave her the grand tour. The kitchen, dining, and lounge area were on the lower level. Upstairs there were three bedrooms, two bathrooms, and a study. He had a corner apartment; two of his bedroom walls were floor-to-ceiling windows offering a fantastic view of Lake Michigan. A large balcony wrapped around the room and extended toward the second living room.

They ended up back in the lower lounge room, standing in front of Asher's giant screen TV. Lacey ran her hand over the soft black leather of the couch.

"Feel like watching a movie?" She asked, turning into fake girlfriend mode even though they were alone.

"Why not. Shall we get changed into something more comfortable first?"

Lacey nodded.

Asher provided her with a spare shirt and pair of sweats to wear to bed and showed her which guest room she could use, pointing out that the bathroom was en suite. Thankfully, there was an extra toothbrush and some toothpaste in the cabinet. Lacey brushed her teeth and washed the makeup off her face. She slipped out of her dress, laying it out on the dresser against the wall, and into Asher's clothes. Unfortunately, the sweats refused to stay on her hips. She sighed and stepped out of them. At least the t-shirt was long enough to cover the essentials.

Lacey walked out of the bathroom and down the hall, back to the living room. Asher had already returned, wearing his own in a V-neck shirt and sweats, and was just turning on the television. She announced her presence with a tiny clearing of her throat and he turned toward her.

The look on his face was absolutely priceless when he saw her in nothing but the shirt and Lacey realized that she'd secretly been planning for the exact reaction she got. It was probably a little mean of her, but she flashed him an innocent grin and walked over to the couch, pulling the afghan off the back and wrapping it around her shoulders.

"So, what are we watching," Lacey asked, settling into the couch.

Asher managed to pick his jaw up off the floor and answer her. "Well love, if you were my *real* girlfriend, I would let you choose, but since you're only my *fake* girlfriend, I'll be making the film selection."

"What's the matter? Afraid I'd pick something sappy and romantic?"

Asher lowered himself on the couch and slung his arm around her pulling her in to his chest. "Exactly," he replied, hitting play on the DVD controller. Lacey was beginning to realize that Asher never did anything coy. He was direct when it came to flirting and it was a hell of a turn on.

"I like action movies every now and then," she said poking him in the ribs. It wasn't a lie. She and Willa usually went out to see them together, gorging themselves on popcorn and nachos. Even if Lacey wasn't into all the fighting and explosions there were plenty of hot guys on screen to ogle.

"Then you'll love this if you haven't already seen it."

The movie began and the title came on. It was, in fact, a movie Lacey had seen.

"Kill Bill?" She said looking up at him. He grinned down at her.

"That's right, darling. Equal parts action movie and tragic romance."

Lacey laughed, "I don't remember Kill Bill being a romance movie."

"It is if you pay attention," Asher argued.

Lacey shrugged and snuggled up into his chest, enjoying the warmth and comfort of cuddling. Asher picked up another controller and the lamps around them dimmed, leaving only the light from the screen flickering around the room. Lacey soon became captivated as Uma Thurman twirled through the air and kicked ass on screen.

"I took karate classes a few years ago," said Lacey as the movie began to draw to a close. The Bride was making her way through the Crazy-88, slashing through each suited villain like butter. Lacey's legs were stretched out along the sofa and she was leaning into Asher, who'd kept his arm around her throughout the entirety of the movie.

"Really?"

"Don't sound so surprised," she countered. Asher chuckled. "I'm athletic! I was a cheerleader in high school. " Lacey insisted.

"High kicks are a little different than roundhouse kicks, I'm afraid."

Lacey scrunched her face at him and continued. "Willa and Chloe pay for all the escorts to take self-defense. They let me tag along for a few classes. I was actually pretty good," she told him with pride, "I managed to take out our instructor a couple times." Asher shook his head, still grinning. "What? You don't believe me? I flipped him right over onto his back."

"I'm sorry, sweetheart," Asher said squeezing her shoulder, "I'm just having a difficult time picturing it."

Lacey pushed up and away from him, the blanket that had been covering her legs dropping to the floor. "Come on, stand up, I'll show you."

Asher laughed out right and held up his hands. "Fine I believe you—"

"Oh come on, Asher, what's the matter? Afraid I'll hurt you?"

"I'm not an insecure, adolescent boy, Lacey. Your emasculating taunts have no effect on me."

Lacey put her hands on her hips and continued to stare down at him, daring him to stand up.

One of his brows arched at her challenging stance. Finally, he gave in and slowly lifted himself off the couch, pushing the coffee table back a bit to give them room. Lacey adjusted her position, spreading her feet to shoulder width and shifting from foot to foot.

"Attack me," she urged. Asher chuckled again, hesitating. They were in his living room, not a dojo, and in just a t-shirt she wasn't dressed for sparring. "Come on. Just pretend like you're going to grab me."

His eyes roamed over her. Asher could think of a million ways he'd like to attack her, especially while she was wearing his shirt, the thin material inching up her legs as she bounced in the middle of his living room. Asher shrugged and reached out toward her arm. It was a half-hearted swipe, but before he could blink he found himself twisted around. Lacey had a hold on his wrist and angled his arm up so he was forced to face the ground.

Lacey's victorious laugh tinkled in his ears as she released him. Asher frowned, his ego taking a little hit from how easily she was able to overpower him.

"You think that's funny," Asher said. Lacey nodded, impishly biting her lip and crooking the tips of her fingers to beckon him forward again. "Well, then..."

He flexed the lean muscles in his arms. Asher wasn't a large man, but he spent enough time in the gym to maintain a slightly muscled physique for vanity's sake. His neck popped back and forth on his shoulders and he twisted his torso. Lacey waited for him to make a move. Asher took his time, showing off as he twisted and stretched and then lunged toward her when she least expected it. She screamed as he grabbed her up and threw over his shoulder, tossing her playfully back down onto the couch. She laughed as he landed on top of her and they bounced together.

"That's cheating," she demanded, pressing her palms into his chest, breathless and smiling.

The playful air between them shifted as they both caught their breath and realized the position they'd landed in. Lacey became aware of the way her fingers were splayed over Asher's chest. An urge to press into him tingled in her fingertips and she went still, trying to control the impulse. Asher could feel the fullness of her curves pressed into him as she registered the not uncomfortable weight of his body on hers. He swallowed, hard, as her tongue darted out and wet her tantalizing, pink lips. Before he could talk himself out of it, or remember the restraint he'd been practicing earlier in the night, he let his head dip forward to capture her lips.

The slight worry he'd been feeling that kissing her might have been the wrong move dropped away when Asher felt her hands weave through his short curls, one slender leg hitching around his waist and pulling him closer. His hips answered with a sharp thrust, his erection pressing between the center of her thighs. An encouraging noise rumbled in her throat and he moved his mouth away from hers, going for her neck, trailing a line of wet kisses down her sweet throat.

Lacey arched into him, tilting her head back to give him better access. As he kissed her senseless, Asher's hand slipped down, trailing over her t-shirt—*his* t-shirt—that looked so incredibly sexy on her. He had almost lost it completely when she came into the living room wearing his shirt and nothing else. Asher hadn't missed the cheeky glint in her eye. The minx knew exactly what she was playing at and damn if he didn't fall right into the game. He'd never seen his clothes looks so good on a woman before.

His eager fingers found the hem of the shirt and he slipped his hand underneath the fabric, skimming across her stomach and reaching for her breast before recapturing her mouth.

"Yes," Lacey gasped into his kiss as he tweaked her nipple between his thumb and forefinger. The spoken word was enough to bring him back to his senses for just a moment. He broke through the fog of lust long enough to remember their deal. He remembered the fact that he had agreed that they wouldn't have sex, because she wasn't comfortable sleeping with a man who was a stranger. But she had just said yes when their kissing began to escalate. Did she mean...?

Asher had to know for sure. If she had changed her mind and wanted to take things further, he had to hear it first. He wouldn't make assumptions.

"Lacey?" Her name was a question. Her name was Asher searching for permission. He remained perfectly still over her, the hand under her shirt not moving, and watched her take a deep breath. He felt it against his own chest, the movement shifting her breast against his fingers. Asher swore he would be taking cold showers for the next month if her answer was that their original agreement still stood.

"Well," she said, carefully. Asher dared to hope. Her eyes dropped, before meeting his again, a new resilience within them. "You did say someone would have to pop my cherry sometime."

The words had a been a crass joke when he'd said them in the hotel room, but now repeated as an affirmation sounded like poetry. His anticipation snapped and he crushed his lips back to hers, pressing closer to her. Resuming his earlier path, his hands moved to the edge of her shirt, tugging it off and revealing her naked breasts. He dipped his head down to her chest gently nipping at her perfect, dusky nipples. Lacey's actions mirrored his. She reached for his shirt, pulling at it, silently demanding that he remove it immediately. She let out a frustrated groan when he wouldn't let her have her way. He smiled against her skin, not finished with her breasts just yet. However, he conceded, lifting up and letting her remove his shirt.

Pulling back to undress, he took the opportunity to gaze down at her naked chest. The clingy dress she had worn the night before had left very little to the imagination, but he was enjoying the current, unobstructed view much more.

He raked his hands over her body, starting at her shoulders, moving down her breasts and across her stomach, finally hooking his fingers around her underwear and removing them, sliding the silky fabric down her smooth legs. Now she was completely bare to him. The blood rushed from his brain and directly to his cock at the sight of her and all her naked glory. Shyness wasn't a quality to be attributed to Lacey, she lay still, confident, letting him look.

Asher had been with plenty of women, both hired and not.

He'd observed women in an artistic setting, in studio art classes, practicing how to capture the sweeps and dips of the human body. The female form was beautiful to him, a true work of art, no matter the shape. Lacey was a divine creature sculpted by the gods, with a body created to be worshipped and pleasured. Asher could hardly wait to have her moaning and writhing beneath him, but she had other plans.

Lacey shifted up and reached for him, sliding her hands down his hips and under the waistband of his pants. "Your turn," she said, pulling his sweats down and revealing his erection.

He watched her take in the sight of him. Her cornflower eyes shined with excitement and curiosity. The appreciation in her gaze went straight to his already swollen cock. There wasn't anything innocent or virginal in her look, nothing of the girl who'd been apprehensive about sleeping with a stranger the night before. She looked ready to enjoy the present she had just unwrapped.

"Condom?" she requested.

Asher smirked and reached down into his discarded sweats, fishing out a silver wrapper. He hadn't expected the sex, but he'd thought there was no harm in being prepared when he'd slipped it into his pocket after he'd changed.

Asher leaned forward after rolling on the condom, staring directly into her eyes, and slowly followed her as she lay back on the couch. He pushed her thighs apart and slid a finger deep inside of her. Lacey bit her lip and arched back as he teased the walls of her sex. She was wet and shining; as he pumped his fingers in and out of her, anxious to replace his fingers with his cock.

"Tell me what you want, Lacey." Asher always wanted the women he was with to feel as much pleasure as he did, and he wanted Lacey to feel it even more so.

She opened her eyes, alight with lust. "You. Now." She commanded pulling his head down for a rough kiss. Any lingering doubt about her assurance disappeared as Asher felt her demand for him in the press of her lips and tongue. She spread her legs further apart, draping one off the couch, as he positioned himself in front of her. Lacey squirmed in anticipation, the head of his cock brushing against her center.

Asher didn't make her wait for long; he didn't have it in him to tease or hold out this time. He pushed into her and she gasped out loud as he filled her. Her walls squeezed at him and he removed himself completely, before thrusting in again and settling, letting her body conform to him.

"You feel spectacular," he uttered, beginning a slow rhythm of pumps inside of her. Lacey arched into him and met him thrust for thrust as his pace increased.

He watched her teeth tug at her bottom lip, her hands reaching up to the pillow behind her head, her fists gripping it tight. She was vocal, gasping and moaning. It was something that most escorts did, sounding like porn stars trying to increase the experience. Asher didn't take Lacey for that good of an actress, but either way her sounds spurned him on. He grabbed her hips and changed her angle just a bit, so he reached even deeper, ramping up his speed, getting closer to his peak.

"Asher!"

Soon, he felt her flutter around him and then gasp loudly as her orgasm overtook her. A few more pumps and he followed her over the edge, collapsing on top of her body, sweaty and breathless from their quick tryst on the couch.

"That was...wow." Lacey seemed to be at a loss for words. Asher smirked against her chest as she stroked his curls, silently agreeing. He pushed himself up and took care of the condom, then grabbed Lacey by the hand. She yelped excitedly as he pulled her still naked body into his, her skin still warm, heart still pounding.

"Come, Lacey, I'm not finished with you, yet," he announced, his teeth nipping her ear. "I have an incredibly large and comfortable bed that I think you should become well acquainted with."

Chapter 5

Lacey awoke the next morning momentarily forgetting where she had fallen asleep. Her eyes opened and she was greeted with a crystal clear view of the lake in the early morning sun, fog that would disappear completely before midday rolling gently over the water. Asher hadn't pulled the shades over the glass before they passed out. Lacey hummed contentedly before she sprang up in shock with a gasp.

She was still naked, with nothing but a sheet covering her. She had spent the night with Asher. They'd had sex. They'd had *a lot* of sex. Lacey's skin heated remembering their time on the couch, then him going down on her on the stairs, before they finally made it to the bed and had sex again. As if on cue, the man in her dirty thoughts appeared from the bathroom looking devastatingly sexy with a white towel wrapped around his hips. He flashed her a smile that reminded her of the way he'd looked when she came apart with his head between her thighs; annoyingly proud of his own skill, but drop dead sexy.

"Good morning, sweetheart." The smile on his face fell and he stopped in his path to the wardrobe, noticing the look on her face. "Everything alright?"

"We had sex last night."

"Yes, we did." Asher took a few more cautious steps toward her, trying to gauge her reaction and the meaning behind her words.

Her eyes were turned toward the mattress, focused on nothing, as she realized what their sex meant. A slow smile spread across Lacey's face and she looked back up at him. "Well, that wasn't as I hard as I thought."

Asher breathed a sigh of relief and smirked, walking over and leaning down to kiss her. "Let's hope that's not entirely true," he teased. "I have to be at work in thirty minutes, but feel free to take your time. Shower, eat...there's plenty of food in the kitchen."

Lacey slipped from the bed, dragging his white sheet with her, wrapping it around her body like a toga.

"I need to call Chloe first and check in," Lacey said, making her way out of his room and heading off to find her purse and work phone.

Asher caught her by the elbow and gently pulled her back against his chest. He leaned down and whispered in her ear, his voice low and husky.

"I thought there wasn't anything sexier than you in my shirt last night, but seeing you in this sheet..." He trailed off, placing his lips on her neck and sucking a kiss at her throat.

Lacey closed her eyes and leaned back against him. Even though she was sore from last night—considering it had been the most sex she'd had in a while—she was already aching for him again. Asher's hands came up and unknotted the sheet from her chest, letting it drop to the ground, his thumbs dragging across her nipples. She spun around in his arms and brought his face down to kiss him.

Asher lifted her up and moved them, his towel falling to the ground as he went. Her legs wrapped around him, his cock brushing delightfully against her core as he sat her down on top of his dresser, breaking the kiss. Lacey took his hand and placed it against her, pressing his fingers to her clit. Her leg moved as he worked at the sensitive bundle of nerves and she opened herself to him.

Asher had things to do, places to be, but he wouldn't say no to a quickie. Once he could feel that she was wet and ready, he dashed to his nightstand for a condom and returned to her. Before he could rip open the wrapper, Lacey plucked it from his fingers.

"Allow me," she crooned, ripping it open and taking his cock into her hand to roll on the condom. Asher shivered at the delicate touch of her fingers, gripping the dresser to keep steady.

Once she was done he scooped his hands under her knees and hauled her forward. Lacey reached for him to guide him between her folds.

Asher's thrusts lacked the finesse from the night before, their bodies clashing together, the dresser knocking in rhythm against the wall. It was fast and hard, his molten stare turning up the lust slamming through her. There was nothing sexier than looking at Asher while he fucked her, the way his teeth clenched and his blue-gray eyes went wild.

Asher dug his fingers into her waist, the little bit of roughness sending thrills all across her body.

"Fuck," he uttered, as she tightened her legs around his waist and bucked her hips.

"Yes," she threw her head back, "right there."

Asher buried his face into her neck and complied with her every urge for "harder" and "faster" and a few moments later Lacey felt the sweet rush of an orgasm. Asher was right behind her, gasping against her shoulder.

The rattling of the dresser subsided as they came back to Earth, Asher kissing her lazily as she ran her fingertips over his biceps.

"Thank you," he murmured, a little hazy. "Can't imagine a better way to start my day."

"Likewise," Lacey grinned, brushing her fingers through his hair. Asher separated himself from her and she scooted off the furniture. He picked the fallen sheet off the floor and passed it back to her.

"I suppose I should go shower again," Asher smirked mischievously, "care to join me, sweetheart?"

Lacey thought for a moment before standing on her tiptoes and giving him a quick peck. "I think not. Wouldn't want to distract you again and cause you to be late for work."

His tongue darted out to his lips. "Fair point," Asher conceded. "I am the boss, though."

Lacey giggled and shook her head. "I'll shower when you've finished," she said, "in the meantime…coffee?"

"Fresh pot in the kitchen."

"Perfect," she said, slipping out of the room and leaving him to get ready for his day.

Once they were both showered and dressed, Asher walked her downstairs and hailed a cab. It was the second morning in a row that Lacey was going home in the clothes she had worn the night before. It felt a little scandalous and she couldn't help giggling to herself, even more proud that unlike the previous morning, she actually had a reason for her questionable morning attire. Asher, of course, looked pristine in a suit and tie, messenger bag slung around his chest. He really did look devastatingly good in suits, not stuffy or boring, but effortlessly stylish in the way that only models in magazines could accomplish with good lighting and hours in a makeup chair.

A yellow cab pulled up to the curb and Asher attempted to pass Lacey some cash for the fare. She tried to refuse him but he wasn't having it.

"Call it a work expense," he winked. She rolled her eyes, but laughed and accepted the money, knowing that he probably wasn't going to let it go until she just gave in and took it.

Before Lacey could slip away into the cab, she felt his hand on her arm, drawing her back into his arms. "What are you doing this afternoon?"

She shrugged. "Nothing. No plans. Technically, I'm yours for the week."

"Don't you forget it." Asher gave her a wicked grin and leaned down for a slow kiss. "My firm has tickets to the Cubs game this afternoon, would you like to accompany me?"

"Sure," Lacey smiled, happy to be invited. "I can't lie though. I'm not a big baseball fan."

"I'm not either, truth be told," Asher said, "but in the interest of entertaining clients and our associates, the firm has box seats. There will be free lunch and an open bar."

"Well, I'm not the type of girl who would turn down a free meal."

Asher chuckled. "Good. Meet me at my office around one and we'll all head over together. I'll text you the address."

Lacey nodded and reached up to give him a quick kiss goodbye. To anyone passing by on their morning commute, Lacey and Asher looked like any other normal couple parting ways and going about their morning. Asher watched the cab carry her away and then hailed another so he could get to work.

Since cluing her friends in on her breakup, Lacey had been

camping out at Chloe's until she found somewhere to live. Chloe insisted. Honestly, Lacey was a little jealous and when she envisioned her potential new home, she imagined a place similar to Chloe's. Chloe lived in a one-bedroom apartment on the north side. The apartment was bright, beautiful, and perched over a small café with the most delicious sandwiches in the entire city. Lacey envied her friend's beautiful home, with her cute styled furniture and décor that looked like it came right out of a hip home design blog. It was smaller than the apartment Lacey had shared with Grant, but a single girl didn't need that much space. It was a home that said, "here lives an independent woman, who doesn't need a guy in her life, who can have fresh flowers delivered to her front door every week and doesn't have to share her Saturday morning croissants with anyone."

Chloe was still at home when Lacey walked through her door.

"Hey! Good morning!" Chloe shouted a greeting to her from the kitchen.

"Morning," Lacey returned, dropping her bag on the table by the door. She slipped out of her heels and placed them neatly into the closet. Chloe's neat-freakiness had quelled her habit of kicking her shoes haphazardly by the door.

She walked into the kitchen to find Chloe by the stove.

"I'm making an omelet. Want one?"

"Yes," Lacey said quickly, sliding onto one of the stools by the breakfast bar. "I'm starving."

Chloe laughed. It looked like she had just come home from the gym, still in her black yoga pants and blue sport top, her long hair tied in a high ponytail. "So, how did last night go?"

"It was fun. The gala was really cool. Asher knows a lot about art so he gave me this whole tour of the museum and told me everything about every painting we looked at." Lacey went into detail about the art she saw, a few of the people she met, and her endless love of the champagne fountains.

"Sounds like a nice evening." Chloe cracked a few more eggs

and whisked them around in a bowl before pouring them into the heated pan on the stove.

"It *was* nice," Lacey agreed. "Except…"

"Except?" Chloe prompted.

"We ran into Grant."

Chloe's mouth dropped. "Grant?"

Lacey nodded. "Yeah, turns out he works at Asher's firm."

"Didn't the moniker Knight, Knight, and Sawyer ring a bell when you met Asher?"

"No," Lacey admitted, "I hardly ever paid attention to anything Grant told me about work stuff."

"That speaks of a healthy relationship," Chloe muttered, tapping her wisk against the bowl in her arm.

"Then I guess it's a good thing we're broken up," Lacey snapped, not liking the judgment she heard in her friend's tone.

Chloe set down her wisk and looked up, chastened. "Sorry."

"It's fine." Lacey wasn't really mad at her. She waved it off and let Chloe make up for the remark by making her a latte using the fancy espresso machine she owned.

"So," Chloe said, setting the cup of foamy milk and espresso down in front of Lacey. "Does that kind of put a dent in the whole pretending-to-be-Asher's-girlfriend thing? Won't Grant be around?"

Lacey tested the latte's temperature. "That's what I said, but Asher doesn't seem to think so. It's not like they're friends; Asher is his boss. He said Grant was jealous last night when he was watching us together."

Chloe smirked at her. "I bet that made you happy."

"It really did!" Lacey said, with an enthusiastic nod.

As Chloe finished cooking their breakfast, Lacey filled her in on the rest of the night with Asher, deciding to come clean about one very important detail. She couldn't help herself. When having sex that amazing, a girl needed to commiserate with her friend at how mind-blowingly awesome it had been.

"I have a confession to make," Lacey said, focusing on the curve of the handle on her cup.

"What is it?"

Lacey put on her most not-guilty looking face, hoping Chloe would see the imaginary halo hanging over her head, and not be too upset. "Asher and I slept together for the first time last night."

The confession was sort of mumbled, but it was obvious in the way that Chloe stopped what she was doing that she had caught every word.

"For the 'first time?'" Chloe repeated back slowly. "Meaning, you didn't have sex with him the other night?"

She was giving Lacey a look that hopped between curiosity and exasperation. Lacey could tell that Chloe was trying to decide how to react, or at the very least, control her reaction.

"No," Lacey answered. "I couldn't go through with it."

"What do you mean you 'couldn't go through with it?'"

Lacey really wished Chloe would stop repeating everything she said. Before Chloe could get too irritated and possibly fire her, Lacey explained how she had choked that first night with Asher. She emphasized that he had been completely nice and understanding about the whole thing and took a moment to remind her about Asher's call and glowing review after that first date.

"A 'glowing review' that was a complete lie," Chloe pointed out.

"Not a complete lie," Lacey countered. "He said I was excellent company. Which I was."

Chloe's arms were crossed and she was doing her best to look mad. She sighed. "As your boss, I'm very upset and disappointed with you," Chloe said, "but as your friend, I totally get it."

Lacey relaxed, glad that the little white lie hadn't gotten her into as much trouble as she had been worried about. "Thank you."

Chloe uncrossed her arms and continued finishing up their breakfast preparation. She portioned the omelet out onto two plates. "But again, as your boss, I have to be concerned that this will happen again. Willa and I warned you that this industry isn't for everyone. What if you get cold feet again?"

"I won't!"

"But what if—"

"I *won't*," Lacey said again, with full confidence. "After last night, I realized that sex with a stranger isn't as scary as I thought. In fact, it's kind of nice to be able to let go and not have so much emotion or expectation attached."

"But Asher isn't exactly a stranger now," Chloe remarked, handing her a plate of food.

"I've only known him for two days. Trust me, that still counts him as enough of a stranger, considering I slept with him. Grant and I didn't have sex for the first time until we'd been dating for a month and we grew up together," Lacey poked her fork into the fluffy omelet in front of her. "Plus, it's like you and Willa told me, I showed him a good time and made him happy. That made me feel good and good about what I was doing."

Chloe smiled. "I'm glad to hear it." She put on her boss face once more. "But you can't choke again. We won't always be lucky the way we were with Asher. Some clients would take the rejection personally and that would be bad business for us."

"Yes ma'am!" Lacey promised with a fake salute.

She continued eating her breakfast and drinking her latte, moving along to the juicy bits about her night with Asher that she really wanted to discuss. Chloe switched into girlfriend mode and listened to every salacious detail, laughing along and making faces when Lacey dared to over share a little.

"It's so good seeing you like this." Chloe beamed.

Lacey was grinning back, enjoying the last sips of her latte. "Like what?"

"Like..." Chloe grasped for the right words. "Happy...free...putting yourself out there. I always kind of worried about you a little."

"How so?"

Chloe pressed her lips together in thought. "Grant wanted to make you a trophy wife and put you up on the shelf for everyone to see so they could know what a great and successful guy *he* was. But you're so much more than an accessory for some guy to have on his arm to show off so he can feed his own ego."

"Chlo'," Lacey had to laugh, "I was literally nothing but arm candy for a guy just last night."

"That's different, that's work. I mean when you find yourself in a real relationship again. You deserve a guy who's going to put you on a pedestal, not a shelf." Both of them went silent, Lacey falling back in her seat, taking in Chloe's words. "I'm sorry... I didn't mean—"

"No, don't apologize, you're right." Chloe wasn't saying anything that Lacey hadn't slowly been realizing over the past few days. She reached out and squeezed her friend's arm across the counter. "And I am really happy. Maybe way happier than I should be for a girl who was just cheated on by the love of her life."

"Grant Lucas was *not* the love of your life," Chloe insisted. "You know what I always say, you should be the own love of your life."

Lacey raised her coffee mug in the air. "Cheers to that."

When breakfast was done, Lacey realized it was past time for her to change out of last night's clothes. In the living room, next to Chloe's gray couch, was a rollaway suitcase that contained the belongings Lacey had taken when she'd left Grant. It was mostly clothes. There were things at the apartment she still wanted, but she wasn't ready to face the drama of moving out just yet. Especially when she still didn't have a new place to call home.

Lacey changed into some cozy clothes and flipped on the TV to indulge in some morning talk shows.

"Well, I need to get to the office," Chloe said, when she emerged from her room, showered and dressed. "What are your plans today?"

"Fake girlfriend duty. Asher is taking me to a Cubs game."

"Sounds fun," Chloe replied, not really listening, her attention on her phone. "Oh, that reminds me," she looked up from the device, "Tristen is coming by on Thursday to do a photo shoot with you so we can have pictures for the website."

Tristen was a photographer and also Chloe's younger brother. He'd moved to Chicago a few years after they did. He was also Willa's boyfriend. Lacey felt a little uncomfortable at the thought of posing in lingerie in front of a guy who'd more or less been like a little brother to her growing up, not to mention her best friend's boyfriend.

"Is Willa ok with that?"

"Yeah. He does pictures of all our girls," Chloe reassured her. "Besides, it'll be way less awkward than our typical newbie photo shoots, because you won't actually be trying to hit on him while he takes your picture." She shuddered. "I almost vomit every time I have to watch a half-naked girl try to seduce my brother."

Lacey laughed. "I promise you definitely don't have to worry about that with me."

After Chloe was gone, Lacey went to raid her room for a Cubs t-shirt. Lacey wasn't a sports fan, but Chloe was. Blackhawks, Cubs, Bulls, it didn't matter. Even though Chloe was born a classy, French girl, she loved sports. She could put any body-painted, beer drinking, male fan to shame.

Lacey had no idea who any of the players were, so she chose one at random and went back to her suitcase to dig out a pair of denim shorts and some sneakers.

She still had a couple hours before she had to meet Asher, so she went back to the television flipping through the channels, switching back and forth between reruns of bad reality shows that she guiltily loved. Her work phone dinged inside her bag and she sat up to check it. It was a text from Asher.

224 S Dearborn. 1 pm. Don't be late.

It was the address for Asher's firm. Her phone dinged again with another message from Asher.

I can't get this morning out of my head. Looking forward to a repeat after the game.

A sharp, electric feeling zinged through her body. God, this man was sexy. He could turn her on with just a text message. It helped that she read every word of the text in his delicious accent. She really couldn't ask for a better rebound. Feeling bold, she decided to flirt back.

Me too. I can still feel your hands on me.

She let out a little squeal when she hit send. He replied a couple seconds later.

Keep up the teasing and we might have to skip the game altogether.

Lacey wondered if he was alone in an office, or if maybe he was sneaking a few texts during a meeting. The idea of turning him on while he was working excited her. She was about to take the text flirting another coy step further but was interrupted by another ding, not from the work phone in her hand but from her *real* phone. She scooped it out of her purse and stared at the name on the screen. It was a text from Grant. She slid the button over and typed in her passcode, reading the message.

Can we talk? Please?

Her fingers hovered over the screen, a million responses running through her mind. She tossed the phone back into her purse, deciding to ignore the text and Grant. There was nothing to say to him, nor did she care to hear anything he wanted to tell her. Grant made his slutty little bed and he could lie in it.

It dawned on her that she would probably see him that afternoon. Asher had mentioned it was the firm who had tickets to the game. Whether or not Grant was actually going, there was the chance she could run into him when she met Asher at the office.

Her phone dinged again inside her purse. She gritted her teeth and cursed herself for fishing it back out to read the text,

Ok Lace, I know you're ignoring me. Just call me soon please.

She shut off the phone entirely and slung it down, tears forming in her eyes. That was the trouble about being in a relationship with someone for that long. They knew you too well.

Asher was sitting at his computer answering some final emails when his secretary knocked at his door.

"There's a young woman named Lacey here to see you, sir."

Asher smiled. "Thank you, Mindy, send her in please."

A couple moments later Lacey appeared in his office doorway. She greeted him with a smile, looking absolutely delicious in her t-shirt and shorts. Asher took a moment to admire the view of her legs as he greeted her, recalling the feel of those legs wrapped around him earlier that morning. He looked forward to it happening again.

"So, this is your office," she assessed. "Fancy." Her fingers trailed over the wood of the doorframe.

Asher shrugged, trying not to think about those fingers trailing other places. "It's not much."

He walked around his desk and took her hand, pulling her gently inside and shutting the door.

"Just give me a few minutes to change and we can leave," he said, yanking at his tie.

"I don't mind." Lacey strolled over to his bookshelves and looked over his collection. It was mostly law and political science, but he kept a few historical anthologies on the shelf, just because.

Asher walked over to the armoire in the corner of the office and pulled out the change of clothes he had stashed in there that morning. He switched into a pair of faded jeans and removed his collared shirt, hanging it up and trading it for a blue V-necked tee. As he shook out the t-shirt Lacey appeared behind him, running her hands over his bare shoulder blades and down his arms. Asher half twisted around and glanced at her over his shoulder.

"What are you doing, love?"

"Just trying to be a good fake girlfriend," Lacey said, pressing an open mouth kiss to his shoulder.

Asher turned to face her full on. "From what I've experienced so far, you're the perfect fake girlfriend."

Lacey bit her lip and smiled, running her hands up his chest. Asher slipped his hands around her waist and guided her backwards until her legs hit his desk. He leaned over her, holding her in his arms, and pulled her into a heated kiss. Lacey scooted back onto the desk, knocking over a cup, pens spilling out and onto the floor.

"What about the game?" She asked when he moved his lips from her mouth to her neck.

"We can be late," Asher replied, sucking at her pulse point. He felt her hum delightedly under his lips, those legs he loved coming up and hitching around his side.

He reached down between them to run his fingers along the middle seam of her shorts, letting the rough denim fabric do half his work for him. The gasp she let out went straight to his cock.

A short knock at the door was barely heard by either of them, before the door was cracking open and a head popped through.

"Hey boss, I—"

They both stopped dead at the sound of Grant's voice. There was no use jumping apart. He'd already seen everything there was to see of the moment. Asher was shirtless with Lacey wrapped around him, looking hot and bothered.

"What do you want, Lucas?" Asher barely managed to keep the frustrated growl out of his voice.

Grant sputtered in shock. "N-nothing. I'll just—er, I'll see you at the game."

He made a hasty exit and shut the door behind him. Asher backed away from Lacey and she sat up, adjusting her shirt and shorts and fixing her hair.

"Doesn't he know the purpose of a closed door?" Asher sneered. He looked down at Lacey who was clearly mortified. She folded her hands over her lap, her knees pressed firmly together. Grant had completely killed the mood. "Sorry, sweetheart."

Lacey shook her head. "It's fine," she replied. "His face was pretty priceless."

Asher laughed. "Yes, it was." He took her hands and pulled her off the desk, brushing her hair from her forehead. "Shall we head to the game, then?"

Lacey nodded and stepped away to let Asher finish dressing, going back to her casual perusal of his books. That was the second time Grant had spoiled their moment. Asher hoped, for the younger man's sake, there wouldn't be a third.

Lacey took the train with Asher and Delaney just north of the city to Wrigley Field. It was a beautiful, early summer day in Chicago, when the weather was still mild and it wasn't so uncomfortably hot that being outside meant sweating buckets. Asher escorted her through the private club entrance to the luxury box reserved for the Knight, Knight, and Sawyer employees. The box was like a small, private bar, with a great view of the field. Some of the other associates and paralegals from the firm were already there mingling together at the high top tables around the room, accompanied by other girlfriends and wives. Everyone was indulging in hot dogs and large cups of beer, chatting while they waited for the game to begin.

Her eyes scanned the room and she spotted Grant, standing in a group with two other guys, looking over at her as she walked in with Asher. She quickly looked away from him, still feeling embarrassed from earlier. Seeing Grant's horrified face was an awesome moment of karmic retribution that couldn't have gone down any better if she had planned it. But she was also really glad that he'd only seen kissing and not actual sex.

Before she could think on it too much, a tall, dark haired man approached them.

"Hey, you made it," he greeted.

"The train was packed," Asher replied as an excuse. Their lateness of course had nothing to do with the brief make out session.

"The train on game day is always hell," the man said, turning his attention to Lacey. "I don't believe we've met."

Lacey took his outstretched hand and introduced herself. "Hi, I'm Lacey."

"Good to meet you, Lacey. I'm Gabriel Sawyer." Gabriel struck her with a perfect, white-toothed smile. His eyes were dark, to match his hair, and he possessed a perfectly sculpted jaw that wouldn't quit. Yet for all of his strong features, his eyes and smile made him seem warm and friendly.

"This is my baby brother," Delaney leaned in and hooked his arm around Gabriel's neck. Gabriel scoffed and shoved him off. There was nothing "baby" about Gabriel.

"You both work at the firm?" Lacey asked.

"Yep," Delaney answered with pride. "Trust me, it's no fun having to look out for this guy all the time."

"They pretend like they hate each other, but really they'd cry like babies if you dared to separate them." Asher slid his hand to her back. "Come on, let's go grab a drink."

Asher walked her over to the bar, taking a beer for himself and passing her a bottle of sparkling water. Satisfied with their drinks, he led her through a glass door at the front of the box to the private outdoor seating. Lacey chose a pair of vacant seats at the front of the box. Just below them were the regular stadium seats, fans of all ages with foam fingers cheering and waving their hats as the organ grinder played *Take Me Out to the Ball Game* over the speakers.

The game was about to begin. Delaney took the seat on her other side, giving her a wink, and turning his attention to continue what sounded like the teasing of his brother.

She knew Grant was behind her somewhere, but she tried not to think about it, focusing on the diamond in front of her and the players as they took the field.

"You mentioned you aren't a baseball fan, do you know the rules?" Asher asked her.

"Yes, I know the rules," she replied with a playful roll of her eyes. "I'm surprised *you* know the rules. Don't you guys play cricket over in England?"

"Never was much of a cricket fan," Asher said. "Baseball, I don't mind. It *is* the American past time."

Lacey laughed as he exaggerated his accent and then turned her attention to the game. After the first couple of innings, it was easy to tell who from the firm was there because they were diehard fans and who was there just to drink beer and socialize. Delaney eventually got up and wandered off to chat with some of the junior partners. Meanwhile, Gabriel remained in his seat, eyes glued to the game. His focus was singular. He'd pump his fist or curse depending on how the Cubs were playing. It reminded Lacey of Chloe, who'd yell at her TV at every disappointing play.

A few of his colleagues approached Asher, but Lacey noticed that aside from Delaney and Gabriel, none of the other lawyers interacted with him in any manner that hinted at a personal relationship. It was simple hellos and small talk, as if they were paying homage to a king and flitting away before they might offend him.

Gabriel let out a colorful curse as the Cubs lost their lead and left to get himself another beer.

"He takes this game very seriously," Asher remarked with a grin.

"I can tell," Lacey said, standing up for the first time in an hour. "I'm gonna go find the bathroom."

Asher grinned knowingly. "Bored already, love?"

"Do I lose good girlfriend points if I say yes?"

"Don't worry," he remarked, dropping his voice, "you can make it up to me later."

Lacey pressed her lips together, blushing, thankful that there wasn't anyone close enough to hear their exchange. The luxury boxes included access to a private set of bathrooms just down the hall. Lacey followed the signage on the walls to find them.

Business done, she emerged from the restroom to find Grant waiting for her.

He pushed off the wall and walked toward her, attempting to block her way back to Asher and the private box. "We need to talk."

"No, we don't," she replied, brushing past him.

His hand shot out and caught her arm, spinning her around. It wasn't harsh, but it was a forceful enough action to catch her by surprise. Grant had never manhandled her before, even during their worst arguments.

"Yes, we do," he demanded. "What the hell is going on with you and Asher?"

"We're friends."

Grant snorted. He smelled like beer. "Friends? Don't bullshit me. I saw you two in his office."

"Fine. We're dating. Not that it's any of your business."

"You're not dating him. You just met the guy."

"How do you know that?" Lacey hoped her face didn't give away her unease. She hadn't actually come up with a story to tell Grant for how she and Asher met. Truthfully, she'd meant to avoid him at all costs and never have to come up with a believable lie.

"We only broke up last week! Unless..." Grant narrowed his eyes at her and Lacey glared. She knew him well enough to know where his brain was heading.

"I'm not the one who was cheating in our relationship, Grant."

He dropped his grip on her arm, reaching up to rub the scruff of his neck. Lacey saw the vein in his temple throb, the way it usually did when he was mad or when he was trying not to cry because crying always embarrassed him. "I just don't understand how you ran to another guy so fast."

Lacey smirked. "I'm on the rebound. Asher this week...who knows who next week. You know how it goes."

"No, Lacey, I don't. But I know you and I know you aren't the rebound kind of girl."

Lacey stomped her foot on the concrete. "Stop saying you know me. You don't know me!"

"Yes I do!" His voice was getting louder. "I also know that you have nowhere to live and no money." He paused, figuring something out. "Is this a money thing? Are you with him because he's just a new bank account for you to drain?"

"A bank account for me to drain? How dare you!" She felt like slapping him. "For your information, I have a job now. And Willa is helping me find a place to live. So no, I don't need another person to be my bank account. I'll be fine on my own."

Lacey tried to bypass him again but he stood in front of her and held onto her shoulders, preventing her from escaping once more.

"Let me go," she snarled.

"Not until you listen to me," he said, giving her a shake. "Not until you tell me what is really going on with you."

"Is there a problem here, Lucas?" Delaney appeared behind Grant. Her ex let go of her and turned to face his professional superior.

"We were just talking," Grant replied. The suggestion that Delaney should leave and mind his own business was clear in Grant's posture. His chin was up and he wasn't backing down

97

"Not what it looked like to me," Delaney countered, stepping toward him. He got right in Grant's face, a mean smile curling across his lips. Grant could posture all he wanted, but Delaney held the power. His look dared Grant to say something smartass. "I don't like you, Lucas. Never have. But I'd hate to have to inform Asher that you were manhandling and screaming at his girlfriend."

Lacey watched Grant's jaw tick back and forth, that vein pulsing once more. This time it was definitely from anger. She knew Grant desperately wanted to tell Delaney off. Somehow he found a way to hold his temper and stalked away, heading back to the private box.

"Thanks." Lacey sighed with relief when Grant was gone.

"No problem," Delaney replied. "You okay?"

She smiled and nodded. It wasn't that she thought that Grant would hurt her—he'd always had a temper but he'd never been violent during their relationship—but she also knew that he could be vindictive when he felt that he was wronged. Grant would want answers about her life now that they were broken up, which could prove problematic for Asher if Grant discovered the truth.

"You sure? Look I know you do…what you do… and I don't know what happened with you and Lucas, but no one deserves to be pushed around like that." He dipped his head and made sure she was looking into his eyes. "I'm serious."

Her heart softened toward Delaney. He may have been a silver-tongued lawyer, oozing a particular type of cheesy charm, but his compassion made her think that maybe there was more to the guy than first meets the eye.

"It's not like that, I promise."

Delaney looked skeptical but swept his arm out to allow her to lead them back to the box. He stayed at her back as they walked inside. Grant was standing with his buddies, beer in hand, avoiding her gaze as she passed. She took her seat next to Asher and looked out at the field, letting out a slow breath.

Asher reached over and grabbed her hand, squeezing when she didn't immediately look his way. "Everything okay, love?"

Lacey pushed away her nerves and worry and smiled at him, giving his hand a tiny squeeze right back. "Yep. Everything is good."

Asher couldn't shake the feeling that something was wrong with Lacey. She was no longer reacting in amusement to Gabriel's game related frustration or rolling her eyes at Delaney's annoying attempts at conversation. Between forced laughter and insincere smiles, she stared blankly at the game. He also couldn't help recalling that Grant had slipped out soon after Lacey had earlier. He wondered if something had happened between them while she was gone.

Maybe it wasn't his business to pry, but her sour mood was bothering him. Asher opened his mouth to ask if she was alright, but instead clamped it shut and stood up from his seat.

"Where are you going?" Lacey asked.

"Popping to the toilet before the game ends." His answer put her on edge. Lacey's eyes cut to Gabriel, who was focused completely on the losing game.

"Do you mind asking Delaney to come over here?"

Asher's brow lifted, curious, but he nodded and Lacey looked relieved. Maybe it wasn't Grant he had to worry about.

Delaney was drinking by the bar, frowning at the beer bottle in his hand. Something was up.

He walked over to Delaney. "I'm heading to the restroom," he told him. "Lacey asked for you."

"Oh," he said, straightening. "Sure."

Delaney moved forward, but Asher blocked him. "What did I miss?"

Delaney put a hand on his shoulder. "Calm down, bossman."

The words were nails on a chalkboard to him. Asher hated being told to calm down. "It's not what you think. I caught Lucas more or less giving her a shake down outside the bathroom. I told him to take a hike and brought her back inside. She probably just wants to avoid another awkward situation."

Asher nodded. Of course that was what had happened. He didn't know why he had grown suspicious of his friend all of a sudden. Delaney was a cad, but he wasn't the type of guy to move in on another man's girl, especially a friend's.

He nodded his gratitude, clapping Delaney's shoulder in return as he moved up the stairs and went toward the bathroom. Even though he was lacking in information about the situation, instinct told him it was best if Grant and Lacey stayed far apart, for Asher's sake as well as hers. He turned before leaving the box and made sure Delaney was next to Lacey before he was out of sight. Thankfully, they were almost through the day, and wouldn't have to worry about crossing paths with his associate for the rest of their week together.

An echo of conversation stopped him on his way out of the restroom. He recognized Grant's voice conversing with two others. Asher paused around the corner, listening in on their conversation.

"That girl with Asher is pretty hot." Asher wasn't sure who this man was, most likely another associate who worked with Grant.

"Don't you know who that is?" The other chimed in with a laugh. "Grant's old girlfriend."

"Man, gotta be pretty rough seeing your girl move on to the boss."

Asher heard Grant scoff. "First of all, *I* dumped *her*. Secondly, she's his problem now, not mine. The bitch is a freakin' gold digger. She'll drain a guy dry."

"I don't know man," the first spoke again. "I'd probably let her have a few shopping sprees on me if she paid the right price."

Asher clenched his fists as he heard the boys all laugh and nudge each other in agreement.

"Yeah, she looks like she'd be a freak between the sheets. She's got that blonde, peppy cheerleader thing going on."

"I can't lie there," he heard Grant's suggestive chuckle. "She was always begging for it. And she was creative, too. It was like living in a porn with her."

Asher's eyes narrowed.

"What do you mean?"

"Well, this one time—"

Asher didn't even realize he had stepped around the corner until he burst through the center of the group and his fist connected with Grant's face. His punch sent the younger man spinning around, dropping to his knees. Grant quickly recovered from the pain and surprise and plowed into Asher, throwing him to the ground. A right cross from Grant hit Asher's jaw and Asher felt his teeth bite into his lip. He tasted copper.

It had been a long while since Asher had been in a fight, but he knew what he was doing. Grant had the tale-tell strength of a former jock, someone used to unruly schoolyard brawls, but Asher had lessons from some of the finest boxing teachers on his side.

Their rumble couldn't have had better timing. The game let out and dozens of disappointed Cubs fans from the other luxury boxes began filling the hallway. Men and women stopped to gawk at the two grown men rolling around on the ground, exchanging punches, and cursing.

"Asher!" Lacey's voice broke through the alpha male rage controlling him. He looked up momentarily, registering the shock on her face, giving Grant the chance to land another punch directly to his eye.

Delaney and Gabriel rushed forward, pulling Asher off Grant as Grant's friends made attempts to hold him back as well. Asher spit blood onto the floor, assessing the damage he had done to Grant. The younger man's upper lip was swollen and there was a harsh bruise already forming on his chin. The lawyer in Asher saw an assault suit bound to happen, but it would be Grant's word against his, given that the obvious apprehension rolling off his friends. There was no chance they would cross Asher at the risk of their jobs to aid Grant.

Lacey stepped into his view, reaching for his face. He winced when her fingers grazed his pulsing cheek. "What the hell? Are you alright?"

Asher opened his mouth to respond but Delaney interrupted him.

"How about we discuss this somewhere else? Eh, bossman?"

It was good advice. They certainly didn't need an audience. Nodding, he let his friends pull him from the scene, Lacey following behind them.

Instead of taking the train this time, Delaney, Gabriel, Asher, and Lacey shared a cab back downtown. For once, Delaney had the sense to not make any smart-ass comments and Gabriel wisely followed suit. The driver dropped Asher and Lacey off at Asher's apartment first. Annoyed silence rolled off of her in waves throughout the cab ride, stinging worse than the throbbing wounds on his face. Even in the elevator, she wouldn't look at him.

It wasn't until they were behind closed doors that Lacey spoke.

"Go sit on the couch, I'll deal with you in a second," she ordered.

Asher didn't think twice about following her commands. He ambled to the living room and fell back onto his couch. His back was aching from the fight due to when Grant had tossed him to the ground and his swollen lip felt tender. Lacey came into the room a couple minutes later with some tissues, antiseptic, and a bag of frozen fruit.

"I can't believe you two, rolling around on the ground, fighting like a couple of teenage boys," she muttered, soaking a bit of tissue with alcohol and dabbing it against his lip. Asher hissed at the antiseptic sting. "What even happened anyway?"

Asher bristled. "What happened with you and him earlier? I know he cornered you when you left during the third inning."

Delaney had briefed him, but he wanted more details. He wanted to hear it from her. A stupid part of him was disappointed that he hadn't been the one to step in during her argument with Grant. He could hear his sister in the back of his mind, remarking on what she liked to call his love for playing hero. Gwen always mocked him when he was simply acting in her best interest.

Lacey sighed, dropping her eyes to the bottle again. "I asked you first."

Asher waited until she finished cleaning the cut at his lip to answer. "Grant was running his mouth."

"About what?"

"You."

Lacey laughed humorlessly and shook her head. "Not surprising. He did always have the maturity of a 15-year-old. I expect more of you though."

"You aren't pleased that I hit him?"

Lacey considered it for a moment. "No. I'm not. Violence is never the answer."

"We're men, sweetheart, violence is always the answer." She rolled her eyes at him, not in her usual playful way, and it irritated him.

"Whatever," she muttered, picking up the bag of frozen fruit and pressing it to his eye. He held it in place and she took his other hand to wash the blood from his knuckles.

"You didn't answer *my* question," he pressed. "What did Grant say to you earlier? Delaney said he interrupted something."

"It was nothing. Just basically accused me of going after you for your money."

"If he only knew," Asher mused. Lacey let out a small laugh. He was glad to see a break in her irritation.

"There, you're all better," she said, wiping away the last bit of blood from his knuckles and crumpling up the tissue she had used. "But you're probably going to have a nice purple and yellow eye."

"I'm a quick healer."

"Quick enough to not have a shiner for your brother's wedding?" Asher's face dropped and Lacey nodded. "Exactly. Didn't think of that, did you, when you started throwing punches, hm?"

She stood up and collected her medical supplies, walking to the bathroom to dispose of the used tissue and return everything to the medicine cabinet. Asher got up off the couch and followed her.

"I was defending your honor," he protested, "shouldn't I be getting some kind of reward?" Ignoring his childish, half-serious rant, Lacey walked over and gave him a peck on the lips. Asher hummed delightedly, even though his lip was still sensitive. "I was hoping for something a little less PG, love."

Lacey smirked. "Later. Right now, I'm starving. A girl needs to eat."

Before he could argue, Lacey sashayed away, asking him where he kept his takeout menus.

Lacey ordered some Chinese and they ate dinner at the kitchen island, surrounded by the smell of cheap fried rice and soy sauce. When they opened their fortune cookies, Asher laughed as Lacey warned him that he wasn't supposed to eat the entire cookie before reading his fortune, or else it wouldn't come true.

"I've never heard that rule," he told her.

Lacey gave him a wistful shake of her head. "All those lost fortunes."

"Things have worked out pretty well so far, sweetheart."

Afterward, they settled on the couch for another movie, but they didn't get very far into it before they moved to the bedroom. Coming down from the highs of their sex, they lay together in bed, limbs intertwined, Lacey's head on Asher's chest. His hands traced lazy circles across her back, crafting an intricate pattern of swirls and shapes.

"Do you get along with your family?" Lacey asked.

Asher tensed, his fingers stilling on her back. "Why do you ask?"

The question wasn't quite as out of left field as he imagined. "I was just thinking, some people have weird family drama and we'll be spending a lot time with them this weekend..." she trailed off. "I'm sorry, I don't mean to be nosy."

That wasn't exactly true. Lacey usually took every opportunity she could to nose into someone's personal life. She was a southern girl and she loved her gossip.

"No, it's fine. You're right." Asher disentangled himself from her and rolled over, opening the drawer to his nightstand and pulling out a photograph. He handed it to Lacey. "That's my family. The last time we were all together."

Lacey sat up in bed, keeping the sheet around her chest, and took the photo from him, studying all of the faces in the picture. There were so many, but it was easy to spot Asher. He appeared to be heavier set, not overweight, but with thicker muscle. His hair was the same curly blonde, just longer.

"You look so young! How old were you?"

"Sixteen," he answered and began pointing out his family members, "That's my older brother, Duncan, the one who is getting married. Then my parents, Roderick and Astrid, then my younger siblings, Jaime, Gwen, and Oliver."

Jaime and Gwen looked around junior high age. Oliver

105

couldn't be more than five, seated on his mother's lap. Lacey thought of family portraits taken with her mother and father at the mall when she was little, before they had divorced. Her mom's feathered 80's style haircut and her dad's thick-rimmed glasses, those awful giant bows her dad would make her wear. It was nothing like the Knight family.

Each sibling looked dress for a funeral, in dark navy and black: the two Knight women in dresses and the men in suits and ties. It was a very formal family portrait. Roderick Knight's face was stern and Astrid's smile didn't quite reach her eyes. Each Knight sibling seemed to be hiding something beneath their carefully schooled expressions. Little Oliver's blissful smile stood out in contrast to every other cold expression.

"You really do have a big family," Lacey remarked, not sure what else to say. "If this was the last family photo that was taken, I think the Knights are long overdue for another."

"Well, that would be rather difficult."

"Why's that?" Lacey smirked.

"Because Oliver is dead."

Lacey sucked in a sharp breath, bowled over by Asher's blunt admission. The blissful, post-coital chitchat took a turn.

"What happened?" She was almost afraid to ask. There was a difference between knowing family gossip and knowing family tragedy.

Asher's expression darkened as memories of his childhood returned to him. "Oliver and I got into a car accident about two months after this picture was taken. I flipped my car over a bridge. I made it through with only three broken ribs, but Oliver…there was internal bleeding. He was only five."

Lacey could tell that he barely kept his voice from breaking as he recounted the story. She reached out and cupped his face, running her thumb across his cheek.

"I'm so sorry. That's awful."

He choked out a humorless laugh, but didn't push her away.

"The really awful part came when I was recovering in the hospital. A few medical tests revealed that Roderick wasn't my real father. My mother had been carrying on an affair before I was born and it turned out I was the consequence of her indiscretions. None of us had known, except for my mother. Roderick suspected, I suppose..." He trailed off, resisting the temptation to travel down the road of speculation. He'd walked that path, drunk and alone, many times before. "My father and I had never gotten along before that, but after that revelation and Oliver gone, it became worse. So much worse."

He spoke like he was telling the story about someone else. No emotions, just facts. At sixteen, Lacey's biggest problem had been cheerleading practice and deciding on her outfit for the town beauty pageant. She couldn't imagine shouldering the blame of her own sibling's death. Though, in her eyes, Asher was completely blameless. He'd been a just a kid, too.

Asher continued. "Once I was of age, I moved out and never went back. Then my mother died and my father went *mental*," he sneered, "Roderick was cruel to my mother, but a part of him must have loved her. After she was gone, there was nothing holding him back. Jaime and Gwen suffered the most from it. They were still in high school and there was no way to get them out. In spite of his demons, my father was a respected man and good at hiding his true self." Asher danced around the specifics. Lacey could only assume, but she didn't ask. It was clear that Asher had no desire to go into the details. "As soon as we could, Duncan and I moved everyone to America and far away from our father."

By the end of the tale, Asher's eyes were glassy, his mouth twisted between anger and regret. Lacey didn't know what to say. It wasn't a story she had been expecting. She never imagined Asher to have lived such a tragic life. Sure, he seemed a little pessimistic and guarded sometimes, but she never thought that it was a result of living in such a deep, dark place for so long.

"How's that for family drama?" The smile he gave was self-deprecating. She had to take a deep breath to shove down the swell of emotion.

When he met her eyes, Lacey could see that he was waiting for her to brush him off. He was embarrassed by the secrets he revealed. But there was no reason for him to feel that way.

"Pretty major," she replied. The demons of the past weren't something she or anyone could fix. But Lacey could make him feel less vulnerable in the present by opening a part of herself to him in return. "I know a thing or two about discovering secrets about your parents you'd rather not know." The curious flick of his eyes let her know it was okay to continue. "My parents divorced when my dad realized he was gay and wanted to marry another man. Well, actually he was already dating that man before he and my mom split up but…after they finished yelling and got past being angry at one another, we all still loved each other. My mom and I spent holidays with him and his partner. We were a little dysfunctional, but happy."

For a moment, she thought perhaps her sharing would have the opposite effect she'd wanted. Even though her family had experienced a tough time, their story still ended happily. She wasn't trying to rub that in his face. But the reveal on her part seemed to relax him, and he shifted to hold her again, this time with Asher's head laying on Lacey's chest. She ran her fingers through his hair, trying to soothe him, to bring him out of his dark past and back into the happy present.

It was clear to her now that Asher had set aside his relationships, his goals, and his entire life to protect and provide for his siblings. It was amazing to her that a man would do that.

"Hey," she said after a few silent moments, "maybe this doesn't mean much, but I think it's amazing what you did for your family. You could have kept running after your mom died and it got really bad. But you turned around and you fought for them, to make their lives better. I think that's very brave."

"Well, I don't know how well I did. Jaime has absolutely no

direction nor does he care to find one and Gwen ended up dropping out of university to be a single mother."

Lacey sighed but found his complaints amusing. He sounded like a worried parent instead of an older brother. "Those are *their* choices, not yours, you can only do so much before you have to let people go make their own mistakes."

Asher lifted his head to look at her and awarded her a small smile, leaning forward for a quick, chaste kiss.

She hummed against his lips. "Okay, while we're on the subject, I just have to ask," she said, "what's with all the weird names? Is it like a British thing?"

Asher chuckled. "My mother was an unconventional woman. She was also very intrigued by medieval history and literature."

"Sucks for you guys."

He smirked. "My sister used to call me Ash, but she's the only one who ever did. I stuck with Asher. I don't mind it so much."

"Neither do I," Lacey agreed, stealing another kiss. "Even if it does make you sound a thousand years old."

"A thousand years old?" Dark mischief danced in his eyes. "I'll show you." Asher reached up behind her head and pulled her into a searing kiss that she felt all the way down her toes.

Their bodies melted together once more, heat and passion consuming them, Asher using his lips and tongue to make his point. Lacey was too turned on to care about the small whine that escaped her when he pulled back. She opened her eyes, expecting to see the same heated gaze he'd given her before, or a smug smile because he'd showed her he was much more than his name might imply. Instead, she was struck by the raw gratitude etched into his features.

"Thank you, Lacey," he whispered.

Before she could respond he kissed her again, moving the sheet that covered her away from them, and ending any further conversation.

Chapter 6

Early the next morning, Lacey met up with Chloe and Willa at the Vamp office, ready to do the for her ultra-glamorous photo shoot.

"I went ahead and picked out some outfits for you, since you've been so busy with Asher, Chloe said, handing her a pink striped bag. "Don't worry, you get to keep them," she added before Lacey even had a chance to ask. Lacey accepted the gift with a huge, excited smile and peeked under the pink and red tissue paper.

Her mouth fell open in shock. "These aren't outfits, these are lingerie!"

Chloe winked. "You know you love them."

"I so do!" Her smile was absolutely wicked. Even though the idea of a boudoir shoot that dozens of men would see terrified the

111

daylights out of her, she wasn't going to turn down the free goodies.

"How's it going by the way? With Asher?"

"Good," Lacey replied, pulling out a purple thong and bra set from the bag, giving it hard consideration.

"Willa and I were thinking of maybe adding some more long term arrangements to our service menu. We thought maybe clients and could start booking girls for weekend getaways or—"

"Awkward family events?" Lacey supplied.

Chloe gave her a quelling look, that was mostly affectionate, and moved on. "I've heard of other upscale agencies offering things like that. We're thinking of calling it: Girlfriend for the Weekend."

"Hmm," Lacey said, carefully, "the idea is good. The name might need work."

Chloe shrugged. "So, what's it like being with a client full time? Are you enjoying yourself? Do you feel like it's too much time with a stranger and you need some space? I need to know if this weekend thing is something the girls might be willing to do."

Chloe wasn't always good with constructive criticism, but she was great at gathering input on the fresh idea.

"Definitely enjoying myself," Lacey answered. "I mean, Asher is just so nice and sweet and *god*, the sex is amazing." Chloe smiled at that. "Only, he was being a little weird this morning while we were getting dressed."

Chloe tilted her head, curious. "Weird? How?"

Lacey tried to think how best to describe it. "Quiet. He's pretty low key in the mornings, but this was more so than usual." She pulled out another bra, a white one with feathers across the cups, the edges tipped in silver. "I think it might have something to do with the whole talk we had last night. And the whole Grant thing."

"Wait, time out," Chloe shook her head in confusion. "There was way too much unconnected information in that sentence."

Lacey sighed and started to rehash all the details about the baseball game, Asher and Grant's fight, and everything each guy said to her. She skipped the more personal stuff Asher had revealed to her in bed, simply calling it a very intense conversation about his family and childhood.

"Lacey," Chloe's voice was gentle, "can I ask you something and you promise not to be mad?"

That was a terrible way to start a line of questioning. "Um, okay. I guess so."

"Are you setting any boundaries for yourself with Asher?"

"What do you mean?"

"Well, you seem really involved in each others' personal lives."

Lacey had to laugh. "I *am* pretending to be his girlfriend for a week," she countered. "It's kinda part of the package."

"Not really," Chloe argued. "The girlfriend thing is all a façade. It's supposed to be fun and light. Punching ex-boyfriends and intimate conversations go way beyond that."

Lacey crossed her arms. "It's not *my* fault that Asher punched Grant. And I didn't exactly ask about all the personal stuff. It was his choice to talk."

You did *ask*, a little voice told her. But it wasn't like she'd meant for the conversation to go quite as deep as it had.

"I'm not saying any of it is your fault, but I *am* saying that you need to stay in control. He's a client, you can't allow him, or yourself, to get involved like that." Chloe took her hand and gave it a squeeze. "You have to protect yourself from forming an attachment, just as much as you have to protect him."

Lacey sighed. It was hard to shut the emotional part of her off, she wasn't used to it. "I guess you're right."

Chloe continued. "Sometimes, especially if you start getting regulars, a client might want to open up and vent to you. That's not a problem. The problem is when *you* behave in the same way. Think of yourself as a therapist...you wouldn't go to a therapist who expected you to listen to all of her problems once you were finished talking about yours, right?"

"I also wouldn't expect my therapist to go down on me either," Lacey teased.

"Well, that's why they don't make as much per hour as we do." Lacey snorted at Chloe's uncharacteristic joke and the two of them burst of laughing.

The two girls were heavy into the giggles when a very handsome man pushed the door to the office open.

"Good morning, ladies."

"Morning, Tris," Chloe called to her brother.

Tristen Dane strode into the office, camera bag slung over his shoulder, long brown fringe flopping over his hazel eyes. He tossed it out of his eye line, grinning. The younger Dane sibling was tall and broad; the complete opposite of the way he'd looked when they were still kids. He'd grown up with smooth features and startling hazel eyes, but as soon as he balked up at eighteen, he became a hopeless magnet for anything and everything female.

If Lacey had crossed paths with him as a stranger, she wouldn't have pegged him for the sensitive artist type. She would have assumed he was a college football player or some other kind of athlete. As good looking as Tristen had become, there was still a cloud of shyness that surrounded him.

Willa was right behind him, a tray of drinks in her hands. "Coffee, anyone?"

"Yes please!" Lacey shouted, eagerly accepting the morning dose of caffeine.

Willa passed around the warm beverages and Tristen began to set up his camera and equipment. There was a large sweep that rolled down from the ceiling, installed especially for Vamp photo shoots. Tristen pulled it down and set up flashbulbs and umbrellas, as Chloe advised Lacey on some poses.

"Chloe, *please*, if you remember I was a junior model when we were fourteen."

"Were you modeling underwear back then too?" Tristen joked, flipping his chestnut hair away from his eyes again. Lacey playfully punched him on the arm and went to change.

For her first outfit Lacey decide to bust out the big guns. She put on the sheer, hot pink, flyaway teddy and matching panties. The top tied in the front just at her cleavage and fluttered open to reveal her smooth stomach. She swiped some tinted gloss across her lips and dusted on some extra highlighter, making her entrance just as Tristen finished setting up.

"Damn, Lace," he said, flashing his gorgeous Dane dimples at her.

"Hey!" Willa yelled from her desk in mock indignance.

"Just paying the beautiful lady a compliment." He offered his girlfriend a guilty shrug. "Come on Lacey, let's see what you've got."

Tristen put on some music to relax and inspire her and soon Lacey got into the mood. The more the shutter clicked, the more comfortable she became, and the poses got sexier and sexier. For a few of them she posed standing in front of the sweep, then Tristen had the idea to pull over one of the large automans and have her drape herself across it.

As Tristen continued snapping photos, Willa sat at her desk, editing and preparing Lacey's pictures for their website. Two hours and three outfits later, Lacey had a computer folder full of sexy pictures.

Once she was changed back into her regular clothes, she skipped over to the computer, excited to see Willa's handiwork. The girl in the photos looked like her, but also not like her. Willa knew how to encrypt the photos so no one they didn't want could accidentally find them.

"I gotta say Lace, you look smoking hot," Willa beamed. Lacey studied herself in the pictures. She couldn't help but agree. "I still need to blur these a little more, so you're a little less recognizable, but I already put a few up on the site and wrote a profile for you."

Willa clicked over to Vamp's webpage and revealed Lacey's official listing as a Vamp Escort. It suddenly became real. She was an escort. A real life, paid-for-sex, escort. Strangely, she didn't freak out. Instead, the combination of the barely-there outfits and the sultry look of the photos gave her a new boost of confidence. She didn't see herself in the profile photo, that woman was someone else. The woman in the photo wasn't a girl who was cheated on and left with an uncertain future. The woman in the photo could *do* things. That woman was resilient and resourceful and she could smash the hearts of every cheating bastard with her pointy pink heels.

That was who she could be as an escort. Lacey the girl and Lacey the escort could be two different people, with different lives, working toward the same goals.

"You're sure no one will recognize me?"

"They shouldn't," Willa replied, "unless they know who they're looking for."

"Hey Lace," Tristen called over to her. "Your bag is ringing."

Lacey walked over and picked up her purse off the couch, the sound of her work phone chiming impatiently. She opened it up and saw a text from Asher.

Where are you? Need to have a chat.

Asher sat at his desk, staring at his cellphone as if it were the most offensive object he had ever laid his eyes open. His thumbs had gotten a workout, typing out a handful of different texts to Lacey over the course of the morning, trying to explain why exactly he had turned into an irrational, blubbering sap the night before. The more rational part of him won out in the end and he didn't end up sending any of them. He came to the conclusion that there wasn't any need to explain his behavior. She was his *hired*

girlfriend, not his real one.

The memory of their intimate conversation from the night before still made him uneasy and made concentrating on his work difficult. Lying in bed next to her, feeling the warmth of her skin, and inhaling her rosy scent had lulled him into a sense of safety, and he'd ended up sharing things he rarely discussed with anyone. His jaw clenched as he reread the same line of a contract for the fifth time. He couldn't believe he'd told her about Oliver's death and Roderick's abuse. No one outside of the Knight family knew of their suffering. Not even Delaney's persistent nosiness had been able to drag those secrets out of him.

Asher had always been the only one who could truly see the evil in their father. Duncan had never known the man the way Asher had, or had simply decided to live in denial for far too long. It had all fallen on Asher's shoulders, to protect Jaime, Gwen, and even Duncan at times. When Astrid died, it became impossible to ignore, and Duncan finally came to his aid.

Lacey had reacted as any normal person might. She offered him comfort, physically and verbally, and he appreciated it. But no amount of words and touches could heal that kind of pain. It was the kind of agony born from his father hating him; blaming him everyday for Oliver's death. Though his mother had never become outright hostile toward him, there had been a shift after the funeral. Coldness had descended upon her and he knew he'd lost her as well. He would never deny that it was his fault. He was the chink in their family armor and yet, there was nothing more important to Asher than his siblings. He would make up for the pain he caused his family, whatever it required of him.

It had been a long time since Asher had dared to dig up the past and it had cast its shadow, causing him to think on the things he hadn't consider. He could be facing more than a few demons at his brother's wedding that weekend. Knight family gatherings weren't without their fair amount of drama.

He'd been tense upon waking that morning and the sour

mood continued once he got to the office. Lacey had been more timid around him in response, but he could barely look at her, afraid she might see through him to just how unworthy and pathetic he could be. He didn't even have the willpower to glare at Grant Lucas when the little pissant stepped out of the elevator that morning.

A knock at his office door brought him out of his melancholy musings and back to the present.

"Hey. Nice shiner you've got there." Gabriel shut the door behind him and dropped into a chair.

"Thanks." Asher grimaced. The light purple bruise under his left eye only served to illustrate how wrecked he felt about exposing his soul the night before. Thankfully, the swelling in his lip had gone down. However, his appearance was the least of his worries.

"Lucas looks a bit worse."

Asher smirked at that. "I know. I saw him. Perhaps he'll be smart enough to quit before I fire him."

"I don't think you can fire a guy for being the dick ex-boyfriend of your new girlfriend," Gabriel said. "Delaney filled me in on the story last night." Normally, Asher would have made a comparison about the Sawyer brothers and gossiping hens, but he wasn't feeling up to it. Gabriel seemed to notice. "Something on your mind?"

"How long were you and my sister together before she told you about our family?"

The question caught Gabriel off guard. "Well," he let out an uncomfortable chuckle, scooting around in his seat. "I guess it depends on what you mean as together." Asher shot him a dark look. "It was a few months. And even then it's been in slow pieces. She's even more closed off than you are." Asher nodded to himself. "Why do you ask?"

"I told Lacey..." Asher trailed off.

"Oh," Gabriel said. "Well, you two are dating. Secrets kind of

118

come with the territory."

"We've only been together for a few days. And as you said, I lack the ability to be open with others."

"Maybe things with Lacey are different?"

"Perhaps." They were. Asher knew they were. "I want to be honest with you Gabriel." Gabriel made a hand gesture that invited him to continue. "Lacey and I...we're only going to be together for the weekend."

Gabriel grinned knowingly. "Duncan still bothering you about settling down?"

"Something like that."

"Well that's it then," Gabriel said. "It's that whole 'In-Flight Intimacy' thing. This girl on the plane back from Vegas was telling me about it. It's where you're more likely to tell a stranger your deepest, darkest secrets because you know you'll never see them again."

Asher leaned back in his chair. Gabriel had a point. He could feel safe telling Lacey his secrets, because when the weekend was done, she would be gone from his life. It was certainly a valid explanation for his odd behavior, but it didn't make the knotted feeling in his stomach lessen at all. If anything, something about Gabriel's conclusion just made it worse.

Before he could continue his internal debate, there was another knock, and then the elder Sawyer brother was stepping into his office. The way Delaney was bouncing on his heels reminded Asher of a teenage girl, eager to spread morning gossip.

"Brother," he nodded at Gabriel, "Bossman, I've got something you might—no, *definitely* want to see. It's in my office."

Asher had no desire to play games. "What is it?"

"You just have to see," Delaney insisted.

"Now?"

Delaney nodded, blue eyes wide and impatient. "*Now.*"

Asher blew out an annoyed breath and stood to follow Delaney back to his office. Gabriel tried to follow as well, but

Delaney put a hand to Gabriel's chest.

"Not you little brother."

"What? Why not? What's the big secret?"

Delaney's eyes flicked around. "Surprise. For your birthday. Don't want to ruin it."

Gabriel's droll look said he wasn't buying it. "My birthday isn't for another six months."

Delaney grinned, eyebrows flicking up. "What can I say? We're getting an early start. Come on, Asher."

Before Gabriel could keep up, Delaney quickly ushered Asher away and into his office, letting the door slam shut.

Asher shrugged away from Delaney. "What is so important for me to see that Gabriel can't?"

"It has to with a certain escort friend of yours. I thought you might not want him in on this." Delaney walked around to his computer and Asher settled into the chair in front of his desk. "I was on the Vamp Escort website, trying to find an email for Chloe…"

"Bit of a stalker move there, mate."

"Says the man with morals so high he only dates escorts," Delaney retorted. "Anyway, I was on the website and…take a look at this."

Delaney spun his computer screen to give Asher a peek at what he had found. Asher blinked. There had to be something wrong with his eyes. He leaned closer to the desk, his hand shooting forward to grasp the screen. There was Lacey, spread out, wearing what barely passed as underwear, gazing at him seductively from a photo on the webpage. She was pixelated and calling herself "Layla," but it was definitely Lacey.

Asher's jaw tightened. "What the hell is this?"

"Her escort profile," Delaney answered, much too gleefully. "It says she's a former gymnast, is that true?"

Asher glared at Delaney and rounded the desk, pushing him aside to grab the computer mouse and click through the rest of the available photos. There were half a dozen pictures, featuring Lacey in different variations of sexy lingerie, striking titillating poses, her charms on full display for prospective clients to book.

It took Delaney a little too long to realize that unlike him, Asher was not amused. "Bossman?"

Asher's temper snapped and he threw the mouse in frustration. "Hey! Whoa, easy there," Delaney said, throwing up his hands in placation. "You break it, you bought it. Shit, Asher, I didn't know—I thought—"

"I can't believe she would do this!" Asher fumed, not listening to Delaney.

He pulled his phone out of his pocket and texted Lacey, his thumbs hitting the screen hard enough that it could have cracked.

Where are you? Need to have a chat.

"Did you not know about this?"

Asher read the text twice and smashed the send button. "Does it bloody look like I knew?"

Delaney's brows shot up and he stepped back, no desire to keep poking the lion. That rational part of him that had prevented him from sending any embarrassing texts earlier tried to nudge him, insisting that he was overreacting. However, the side of him prone to jealousy was overwhelming his brain, blotting out the chance of any sane reaction to the situation from fully breaking through.

His phone buzzed with Lacey's reply.

I'm at the office, what's up?

Asher didn't respond. Text message could not possibly convey the things he wanted to express at that very moment.

"I'm taking an early and extended lunch if anyone asks."

Delaney didn't dare question Asher as he tore open the door and stomped down the hallway to the elevator.

121

Once the photo shoot was done and Lacey was back in her normal clothes—jeans and a purple sleeveless top—they all sat down to lunch. Chloe ordered delivery for the four of them and it arrived just as Tristen finished packing up the equipment. He made sure to pay a little bit of extra attention to his girlfriend after he spent the past two hours taking pictures of her half naked best friend. Lacey couldn't help but smile at the two of them, sitting on the couch, looking so in love. Willa had a leg draped over one of Tristen's knees and his fingers were constantly touching the teal stripes in her hair. The way he passed her a napkin and knocked a little kiss on to her cheek was exceedingly cute and cheesy at the same time.

Grant had never been like that with Lacey, even in the early days. Lacey had always thought that maybe it was because he wasn't a very affectionate sort of guy, but they had never had that can't-keep-our-hands-off-each-other passion that burned through two people in love. Sometimes she wondered if she'd ever experience something like that.

"Oh, hey Lace," Willa said, pushing away Tristen's hand from where he'd been teasing her and trying to steal away one of her French fries. "I found a few apartments for you to check out. They're nice and in good neighborhoods. And the rent should fit your budget for what you'll make here."

Lacey opened up the clear container of salad that she'd ordered. "But there aren't really any guarantees I'll pull in money."

"Oh, trust me, you'll be fine," Chloe reassured her. "Plus your profile has already pulled in a couple inquires."

A smile broke out across Lacey's face. "That was fast! Really?"

"Yep!" Willa nodded, knocking Tristen's hand away again and giving him a warning look. He just grinned at her. "I was thinking," she said, turning her attention back to Lacey and passing her boyfriend a fry that he'd wanted so badly, "do you have time on Friday to go look at apartments? I was going to take the day off anyways."

"Sure," Lacey said, excited to see her potential new home. "Asher and I have the wedding this weekend, but we're taking a late flight Friday night because he had some things for work he couldn't miss."

"Perfect," Willa grinned.

"I never thought I'd see the day," Tristen chimed in.

"What day?" Willa asked around a huge bite of chicken sandwich.

"The day that Lacey Hollis got a an actual job."

"Tristen!" Chloe and Willa yelled at the same time.

"What?" Tristen insisted, half laughing at the shocked expressions on both his sister's and his girlfriend's face. "It's true. Lacey and work go together about as well as oil and water."

"Tristen," Chloe hissed. "Would you shut—"

"He's right," Lacey cut in. Now their looks of disbelief were directed at her. "Oh, come on you two, don't look so innocent. Neither of you fully believed that I was actually going to be good at this escort thing."

"Umm..."

"Uhh..."

Lacey laughed and grabbed a fork, starving and ready to dig into her own lunch. Before she could take a single bite, the door to the office swung open. Asher stormed in and the four of them all twisted in the direction of his stomping. Chloe set aside her lunch and stood up, smoothing her down her pencil skirt.

"What can I do for you Mr. Knight?"

Asher ignored Chloe and headed straight for Lacey. He stopped in front of where she sat on the love seat, looming over her.

"I saw the website." His face was colored anger.

Lacey blinked at him. "What?"

"The website, Delaney showed me."

It took her a few blinks to understand what the hell he was talking about. "You mean my Vamp profile?"

"Yes, the profile! What in the bloody hell—"

"Excuse me Mr. Knight." Chloe used her loud voice, taking control of the situation as she stepped in to position herself between Lacey and Asher. She stared up at the lawyer, unintimidated by his anger. "If you would be so kind...I would like to know what the problem is and why you are yelling at my employee?"

Asher's eyes flicked to Chloe and gave her a tight-lipped smile. "Nothing that can't be fixed. If I may speak with Lacey."

"Actually, I think it might be a better idea if you spoke with me instead."

Willa had stood off the couch, ready to put her martial arts knowledge to good use and defend her friends if the need arose. She extended one of her hands out in front of Tristen, blocking him.

Lacey touched Chloe's elbow. "Chlo', it's fine. I can handle this. Asher, we can talk in the hallway."

Chloe seemed unsure and Lacey could hear her earlier warnings ringing in her mind. Lacey gave her a little nod and waited for Chloe to step aside so that she could follow Asher into the hall.

The door between them wasn't much of a sound barrier, but once they were alone, Lacey let him have it. "What the hell is your problem? You can't just come barging in here yelling at me! What are you even mad about anyways?"

"The website, the pictures!" Asher replied, as if it were completely obvious.

"What about them?"

Asher fisted his hair. "Jesus! I had to find out from Delaney of all people. Delaney! Having to fucking listen to him go on about how hot you looked."

Lacey was completely lost. "I don't understand."

124

Asher turned and pinned her with a look so devastating, it almost knocked her back into the closed door. It wasn't anger, it was disappointment. "Have them taken down."

"What?!"

"The pictures, the profile, I want it all gone," he demanded.

Lacey crossed her arms. Now she understood. He was jealous and he was reacting that a total Neanderthal. "Excuse me, but you really don't get to decide that."

"I thought that you were giving up as an escort."

Her brow wrinkled. She had never said that. "What gave you that impression?"

Asher opened his mouth, but closed it again, seeming to reconsider his answer. Lacey tapped her foot, waiting to hear what he could possibly have to say. "How do you think you're going to be manage being an escort, Lacey, if you aren't sleeping with clients?"

His voice had dropped to a calmer octave, but she didn't like it. He sounded like a person who was fully confident he'd just struck the killing blow for their argument.

"I will be," she informed him. "I will be sleeping with clients. It's kind of part of the job. It will be easy now that my escort 'cherry', has been popped."

Asher narrowed his gaze at her, his jaw tightened. "Fine. If you can't be reasonable then I suppose we're done here."

"I'm not the one who is being unreasonable," Lacey retorted. "You're not making any sense."

Asher threw his hands up and walked away from her, retreating toward the elevator. He pushed down hard on the white call button. Lacey followed, stopping next to him with her hands on her hips. She stared at him and waited for him to explain himself but he just stood there, staring angrily up at the elevator numbers and refusing to look at her again.

The elevator was slow, but Asher didn't break. Lacey threw her hands out to her sides. "Fine. We're done here."

She spun, her harsh scoff echoing down the hall, and slammed the door when she entered the office again. Chloe, Willa, and Tristen all jumped and turned away, pretending like they hadn't been listening to the entire argument that had been happening outside.

Lacey heard the elevator bell ding and the doors slide open, knowing Asher was getting in the elevator to ride down and head back to work. As angry as she was with him at the moment, she still had to fight the overwhelming urge to turn around and go after him.

Asher was a sorry excuse for a lawyer for the rest of that day. His irritation was so great, that concentrating on any of his casework was impossible. The words in his files began to blur together and his mind would drift to a place where all he could see was Lacey in her lingerie and that white-hot feeling of jealousy would blaze through him again.

The truth was, he was becoming more irritated at himself than anything else. Why did it matter? Why did he care? What in God's name had he been thinking when he'd jumped in a cab to cross the city to yell at a girl, who was for all intents and purposes, just doing her job?

He pressed the heel of his hand into his eye, trying to rub out the knot of tension behind it and the embarrassment he felt at the overreaction. Not that he was ready to admit he overreacted. Lucky for him, before he did any permanent damage to his eye, his cell phone rang. He grabbed it and checked the caller ID. A number he didn't recognize flashed on screen. For half a second he thought about ignoring the call, but decided to answer.

The last time he'd gotten an unknown call it had been his little brother Jaime, and it had been a good thing he'd answered the phone.

"Asher Knight."

"Mr. Knight, this is Chloe, from Vamp Escorts. I was hoping I might be able to have a few moments of your time."

Asher groaned internally and switched the phone to his other ear. He could hear the forthcoming lecture in her tone and was in no mood. "Chloe, of course. What can I do for you, *Madame*?"

"I'm calling to express some concern for interactions between yourself and our employee, Lacey," the woman began.

Asher wished she could see the eye roll he gave her. "I admire the way you pretend that she's simply an employee and not a friend, Ms. Chloe. It must be difficult to distinguish between the two relationships at times."

"It's interesting that you bring up distinguishing relationships Mr. Knight, because I'm actually calling to let you know I do *not* appreciate the way you berated my employee. I wish to remind you, in the most respectful way, that your relationship with her is strictly a professional one."

"And here I thought the nature of our relationship was sexual, not professional."

Asher was being a dick and he knew it. But truthfully, he had no interest in having Madame Chloe lecture him about his relationships while pretending she wasn't calling to yell at him because he had angered her friend.

"Mr. Knight, if you don't feel that you can uphold the original terms of your contract with our business, we will feel free to terminate it without a refund."

"You—"

"I'll put it in simple terms so that you can understand. Lacey is not your girlfriend. She is a hired escort. You will treat her with respect and you do not have a say in what she can ,or cannot do, when it comes to her personal, or professional life, is that understood?"

Asher's jaw ticked in annoyance. He might admire her tenacity if it didn't irk him so. "Is there anything else I can do for you?"

"Just make sure we don't need to have this conversation again."

Point made, the Madame ended the call.

Lacey was curled up on Chloe's in her PJs with a glass of wine, watching Chloe get ready for a night out. One of their old friends from high school, Tucker, was in town and Chloe, Willa, and Tristen were all going out for drinks with him.

"Are you sure you don't want to come?" Chloe asked for the fifth or sixth time, sliding a black, dangling earring into her ear.

When her friends had made the plan, Lacey had assumed she would be with Asher. Since the fight earlier that day, she'd found herself with some extra free time.

"I want to see Tucker," Lacey told her, "but I'm sure he invited Grant, too."

Tucker had been Grant's best friend since they were kids and all through high school. He usually stayed at their place whenever he managed to make it out of their small town and visit the big city.

"I'm sure Tucker's heard about the drama," Chloe said, "and you know that he's probably already called Grant out on his crap."

Tucker had always been the angel, where Grant had been more of a demon. He was a good guy and he'd never flinched away from letting Grant know when he was being too much of a bully or a jerk.

"Yeah, but it's not like he's is just going to completely shut out Grant because of me. You know how he is," Lacey reminded.

"True. He's too nice for his own good sometimes," Chloe agreed. Lacey smirked, watching Chloe fluff her hair in the mirror by the door. Chloe and Tucker had been a thing once upon a time in high school, but those days were long gone. It didn't stop her from putting on one of her nicer date-night outfit however. "Are you just going to chill here, then?"

"Yeah, I have some delivery coming and a sappy movie. I'll be fine." Lacey did her best to sound casual and not at all mopey. She knew Chloe wouldn't approve.

A little while later Chloe headed out the door, with a promise to glare at Grant the entire time should he show up. Lacey's takeaway arrived and she popped her chosen DVD into the player, settling in to have a nice girly night to relax. The movie failed to hold her attention and her mind began to wander.

We're done here.

She couldn't keep her mind off of the fight with Asher. In typical Lacey fashion, she began to over analyze every word he'd said. Did he mean *over*, over? They still had the wedding this weekend and she was contractually obligated to him until Monday. Was he so mad at her that he was completely done? That he didn't want anything to do with her anymore?

"Damn it," Lacey muttered under her breath, throwing her head against the back of the couch. Her fingers massaged her temples, her brain starting to ache from overthinking.

She was turning out to be a crappy escort. Her very first client and she was already chasing him off. Willa and Chloe had explained how recurring clients could be great assets, and since Asher seemed to be a frequent customer, retaining him would be a good move for her new career path.

On one hand, Lacey felt the need to stand her ground. He had no right to be mad at her. She still didn't even understand why he was mad in the first place—it was a jealousy issue, that much was obvious, but he had no right to be jealous.

Still, she had to be professional about it. She wasn't a girlfriend, so she couldn't react like a girlfriend. She would react like an escort, like a woman paid to please a man. That would mean swallowing her pride.

Lacey grabbed the remote and switched off the TV. She

quickly cleaned up her untouched food and dumped the leftover wine in her glass and rushed into the bathroom to change her clothes, grabbing the pink striped bag from earlier in the day. She decided she'd put her new accessories to good use.

The doorbell ringing was a surprise. Asher wasn't expecting anyone and the doorman downstairs hadn't rung up to announce any guests. He pulled himself off of his couch—where he'd been sulking since he'd gotten home—to see whom it would be darkening his door.

The bell rang again, impatient. "Yes, coming." He groaned at the incessant ringing.

He pulled open the door and was met with a whiff of sweet, rose perfume. Lacey stood before him, glossed lips and a khaki trench coat wrapped around her, tied into a neat bow at the waist. An odd choice for a warm summer night.

A mixture of relief and smugness washed through him. Sitting on the couch, he'd been so close to folding and calling her, especially after ruminating over the conversation with Chloe. That woman had no right to tell him how he could and couldn't interact with Lacey. What happened between him and Lacey was between him and Lacey and not anyone else. But perhaps she'd had a point in suggesting that the lines of their business relationship had become blurred.

Asher was enjoying his time with Lacey. He thought it might be possible to see her regularly. He didn't want to ruin the chance at becoming a regular client for her, especially if her word was true, and she really was giving the escort thing a real shot.

"Can I come in?" The question was tentative. Her hands toyed with the tie of her coat.

"By all means." Asher swept out his hand and moved away, letting her enter.

Her heels clicked across the hard wood of his floor as she strolled through to his foyer. He shut the door, watching her walk toward the living room; blonde curls bouncing around her shoulders.

"I bet you never thought fake girlfriends came with real fighting," Lacey said, spinning to face him.

Asher walked toward her with a shrug. "I would have to admit that it is rather unusual."

"I came to apologize for that" she said, "and, I was hoping to make it up to you."

Her hands went to the ties of her coat and yanked the bow loose. She pulled open the snaps in one smooth motion, letting the fabric fall to the ground. Asher's eyes widened at the sight before him.

Underneath the coat Lacey wore very little. A black lace bra with a tiny pink ruffle, running between her ample cleavage down to her stomach and connecting to a strip of lace between her legs. She sauntered toward him with a sinful look on her face, hips swinging in time with the clack of her shoes. The unsure attitude she had exhibited at the door had all but disappeared. She was putting on a show and Asher couldn't think of looking away.

He smirked and Lacey took him by his hands, walking backwards, leading him to the couch. Her lusty eyes stayed on his as she walked.

"You came all the way here in just an overcoat?" Asher teased. "The driver must have been very excited."

A wicked heat flashed in her blue eyes and she pressed her body against his, putting her mouth just a whisper away from his ear. "I took the train."

The thought of Lacey nearly naked in the middle of the crowded train sent a rush of excitement coursing through him, his cock stiffening. She pressed her hands to his chest and pushed him back. He fell back, barely surprising his grin. He reached up and ran his finger under the ruffled ribbon that fell across her stomach, enjoying the way her muscles tightened at the touch.

"I have to admit, as far as apologies go, I'm starting to enjoy this one."

"Just you wait," she teased, kneeling in front of him and positioning herself between his legs.

She took her time, nimble fingers starting at his tie, unknotting it and sliding it out of his shirt collar. Next, she saw to the buttons on his shirt, flicking each one open and dragging her nails lightly down his chest. Asher shifted, eager, drawing Lacey's attention to the bulge in his pants.

She rubbed his erection through his pants, eliciting a heady groan from his throat. Asher wished she would move faster. He stared at her pert breasts, down to the fabric covering her core. He wanted to reach down and feel her dampness, bury himself inside of her, and remind himself that, for the moment, she was his. But Lacey had an agenda of her own.

She popped the button on his pants and the tugged the zipper, pausing at each notch as it went down, the touch and nearness of her hand to his cock driving him mad. He ached for her hands on him. Finally, the zipper was down, and Asher lifted his hips, letting her pull down everything covering his lower half, embarrassingly relieved to be half naked and damn near ready to come.

The way Lacey ran her hands across his thighs and licked her lips at the sight of him, looking hungry and excited, almost had him coming right there. It was unreal how quickly she could turn him on, frustrating and needy in way that he hadn't felt since he'd been a teenager.

Asher shuddered when her head sunk down and she ran her warm tongue across the length of his shaft. It felt so fucking good; he clenched a fist at his side to keep himself together. She pulled back for a breath and enveloped his length with her mouth. Asher bucked his hips as she began a slow, sucking rhythm, her hand pumping him where her mouth couldn't reach.

His head fell back onto the couch as she sucked and licked, her tiny moans filling him with the sweetest sort of agony. She hummed as she sucked him, the vibrations sending him closer to the edge. He squeezed his eyes shut, trying to think of something else, trying to hold himself at bay but desperately wanting to let go.

"Fuck, Lacey," he cursed through gritted teeth. He wasn't going to be able to hold on much longer.

Taking matters into his own hands, Asher moved her mouth away from him and stood, stepping out of his pants. He wanted to take control. Without warning he hauled her up and pushed her into the sofa. Her giggles turned into gasps as his mouth went to her neck and his hand cupped her wet center.

"You know," he murmured between kisses, his hands making quick work of the scrap of material around her hips. "I'm beginning to really enjoy this couch."

It only took a twist and a single rip before her underwear was gone. Asher pulled a finger through her, enjoying the way she quivered at his touch. She was wet and more than ready. Asher parted from her long enough to fetch a condom and returned. Together they adjusted their positions and Asher thrust inside of her, not bothering to fight for control this time, as he pumped his hips hard and fast.

Lacey's nails dug into his back as she breathlessly called his name. *His* name. Not anyone else's. He knew he had been a barbaric fool, thinking that he had claim over a woman who he was paying to be with him, but damn she had a way of making him forget that. Everything seemed newer and realer with Lacey. Urges he had never experienced came to mind when he was with her. Asher knew he was acting out of his normal character, but with her legs wrapped around him, and lips against his, he couldn't remember why he should care.

A few moments later, Asher felt her walls clench around him and release as she cried out in orgasmic bliss. He thrusted a few times more and followed her, the two of them gasping for breath against one another.

"If this is the apology I get after we have a fight, I must spar with you more often, love." Asher swept his lips across her forehead.

Lacey laughed, her breasts brushing against his chest as she tried to catch her breath. They were still nestled together, Asher still inside of her. She ran her hands along his sides. "To be clear, this is the apology *fake* boyfriends get. Real ones would be spending the night on the couch, without sex."

The smile fell from Asher's face. Luckily, Lacey couldn't see it.

Of course. What had been that possessive vibe he felt moments ago? He had just let himself get caught up in the sex. She wasn't his. Chloe kept had reminded him of that and now Lacey had repeated the sentiment. More to the point, he *really* want to be in that situation? Pissing off his girlfriend and having to spend a sexless night trying to figure out what he did wrong? It was everything he wanted to avoid.

"Hey, I'm only kidding." Lacey nudged him.

Asher shifted away from her, giving her a light kiss, and grabbing his discarded pants from the floor. "I know."

"So, all is forgiven?"

Asher looked over at her. She was a sight to behold, with sex-glowing skin and swollen pink lips. This was what it was supposed to be. Easy apologies. Easy solutions. He was getting what he was paying for, but for some reason he didn't truly feel satisfied.

"Yes," he answered with the most convincing smile he could muster. "All is forgiven."

Chapter 7

Lacey spent the night at Asher's, much to Chloe's judgment. However, when Lacey explained she had only done so for professional reasons, Chloe couldn't really argue. Lacey and Asher never talked about the fight, Asher didn't apologize, and Lacey didn't bring it up again. In terms of their professional relationship together, it didn't matter. The next two days needed to go smoothly, without a cloud of confusing tension hanging over them. While Asher was at work, Lacey spent the day with Willa, searching for a place to live. She was sitting outside a coffee shop, waiting for Willa to return with their drinks, when her work phone rang and she saw Asher calling.

"Hello, love, how's the apartment hunt going?"

"It's the worst," Lacey grumbled. The first two places they had viewed were absolutely horrible. Both of the apartments were in shady neighborhoods and looked nothing like what they saw in the pictures online. Willa told her not to be too discouraged; it wasn't unusual for some places to not live up to expectations.

"I have a realtor friend I could call if you'd like?"

"No, that's okay," Lacey said, pushing at her sunglasses. "We still have a couple places left to check out. Maybe I'll get lucky." She was hoping to sound more optimistic than she felt.

"Let me know if you change you mind," Asher said. "Did you get my message about tonight?"

"Yep, I'll meet you at the airport at seven."

"Good. Good luck with the rest of the hunt, sweetheart."

Lacey smiled and finished up the call as Willa came out of the coffee shop with their drinks.

"Let's go," she said, "We're gonna be late if we don't start walking."

Two hours later, Lacey's luck had definitely changed. The last apartment they visited ended up being perfect. The third one wasn't bad, it was something Lacey could find herself settling for, but the fourth one was an absolute dream. It was a one bedroom, one bath, walkup located in a nice, Northside neighborhood. It was light and airy and Lacey could absolutely picture herself living there.

"This a really good space," Willa had whispered to her, "considering the price."

With Willa's reassurance, Lacey signed the lease and the landlord told her she could start moving in after the weekend, once he had a chance to double check her background report and have the apartment cleaned.

Keys in hand, she looked over at Willa and squealed with delight. Finally! Her first real apartment that would be all her own. On the train back to Chloe's, she dreamed about how she would decorate her new apartment and the furniture she would buy, scrolling through Pinterest and chattering excitedly to Willa about her ideas. No more having to submit to Grant's taste, or lack thereof. It would be her home to do with as she pleased. The single girl life was getting better and better with each passing day.

At seven, she met Asher at the airport. They grabbed their tickets and checked their luggage, making it through the slow line at security and getting to their gate just in time. They slid into their first class seats, the two of them with their own row. Lacey was excited to be flying first class for the very first time.

"How long until we reach New York?" She asked trying to distract herself, as the plane began to back away from the gate and head down the runway for takeoff. Lacey didn't have a lot of flying experience and takeoffs always made her a little queasy.

"About two hours." Asher covered her hand with his own and smiled. Her tension ebbed and she turned her palm up to intertwine their fingers, just until the seatbelt light went off.

The flight attendants came around with complimentary orange juice and snacks. Asher slipped off his jacket and tie, letting open the top button of his shirt. Feeling more relaxed as the plane leveled out, Lacey stared out of the window at 30,000 feet and watched the sun set into the sky, colors splashing across the clouds that rolled below them.

"Tell me about the apartment hunt," Asher inquired. "Did you find a place?"

"Yep," Lacey beamed, "I move in on Monday."

Lacey went off on a excited ramble, describing her new home and all of her plans. Asher smiled in amusement at her enthusiasm, joking that she could possibly have a future as an interior designer, instead of just claiming to be one as a cover for her real job.

"I've just never lived on my own before. I lived with Willa and Chloe for a while in college and then moved in with Grant." Asher frowned at the mention of his associate's name, but Lacey missed it. "It'll be nice having my own space. I can have cute throw pillows and fresh flowers every week and a pink coffee maker if I want."

"Sounds like a perfect life for you." Lacey smiled in agreement, her focus going back to her phone, where she continued compiling a list of things to buy for her imminent move.

A few minutes later, Asher spoke up again. "Can I ask you a personal question?"

"That's depends," Lacey replied, "Can I not answer if I don't want to?"

"Of course," Asher said. Lacey nodded in permission for him to proceed. "In the past week you've been searching for a place to live and you've undertaken a brand new career and from what you've said, it's been no small challenge to you. And from my understanding, the incident with the girl in your apartment was Grant's only indiscretion."

Lacey nodded slowly. "According to him."

"Did it ever occur to you to forgive him? To just go back to him?" Asher asked. "It certainly would have been easier."

"Yeah, you're right, it would have been a hell of a lot easier," she agreed, letting out a breath and staring absently at the flight attendant serve drinks to the passengers.

"I don't mean to offend you, I just know..." Asher stopped himself in the middle of his sentence, recalibrating. "I've known other women who have chosen less challenging paths."

"I thought about it," Lacey admitted. "After I caught him, I spent the weekend in a hotel, crying and crying and listening to apology voicemails and thinking that maybe I *should* forgive him. Maybe he's allowed to have a stupid and selfish mistake every once and a while," Lacey smiled to herself, but the smile lacked any true humor. "It's not like I'm the most unselfish person in the world. I never cheated," she added quickly, "but I was doing a lot more taking than giving for far too long." It was difficult to admit, but it was something Lacey had slowly been realizing over the past week. "And I was sitting in bed crying for stupid, selfish reasons."

"You'd been hurt by someone whom you loved," Asher

reasoned. "It's an appropriate time to grieve the loss of your relationship."

Lacey shook her head. "But that's the thing, I wasn't in love with him," she insisted. It was scary saying it out loud for the first time. "I realized I wasn't crying because I was loosing Grant. I wasn't sad because we'd never go to bed together again or I'd never make coffee for him again or buy him another tie or dance with him or spend another Christmas together. I was crying because I was losing my security and my future and my nice apartment and unlimited spending." She huffed out a laugh. "I'm terrible, but it's the truth."

Asher reached out and brushed his knuckles across her cheek, causing her eyes to flick up to his. "I think you're remarkable," he said. "If you were truly selfish and terrible, you would have ignored everything else to keep your security and your future as you said." He cupped her cheek, running his thumb along her face. "You know your value."

Lacey smiled at him, feeling a little misty-eyed. It was nice to hear. Of course her friends had offered the same support, but there was something different about Asher appreciating her choices. It was different hearing it from someone she hadn't known very long, someone who wasn't necessarily bound by years of friendship to have her back. "So," she sniffed, deciding to change topics, "How was your day?"

"Boring," Asher shrugged, settling back into her seat.

"You always say that," Lacey observed. "Do you even like being a lawyer?"

"I like being smarter than everyone."

Lacey rolled her eyes at his cocky grin. "Are you nervous about seeing your family this weekend? It's been a while right?"

"Up until a few months ago, I saw Duncan all the time. We do run the firm together." Duncan had been spending time between Chicago and New York, networking with new and prospective clients. After his engagement, he'd chosen to reside in

139

Manhattan on a more permanent basis.

"Oh," Lacey said, taking a sip of her neglected juice," that's right. He's the second Knight in Knight, Knight, and Sawyer."

"Indeed. But I haven't seen my younger brother in a while. Or my sister and niece."

"Will your father be there?" Lacey remembered Asher mentioning that things between his father and the rest of his siblings were not so good.

Asher eyes darkened. "Duncan informed him of the wedding, but I don't believe he extended an invitation to the man."

"Then there's nothing to worry about," she said, threading her fingers through his. "All we have to do is make sure no one realizes you brought an escort as your date. It'll be a piece of cake."

Asher smiled and kissed the back of her hand he held. His nerves seemed to run deeper than he was willing to talk about and she let him have his space, letting him keep hold of her hand for as long as he needed.

Two hours later they landed in New York. Asher hired a car from the airport to take them out to the home of Duncan's future in-laws, where the events of the weekend would be taking place. It was nearing midnight when Asher and Lacey arrived at the lavish Hamptons estate.

A large, gated driveway led them through a vast lawn to a large mansion, grand and hulking, complete with white columns and large bay windows. A white washed staircase led up to the porch that wrapped around the entire house. It looked oddly antebellum in design, considering the property was located in New York. Even in the darkness, Lacey could see the well-designed landscape, every shrub trimmed to perfection, every flower arranged in an array of color to match the season.

Asher stepped out of the car and walked around to the other side to open Lacey's door, he watched her wide, blue eyes marvel at the size of the mansion.

"This is amazing," Lacey assessed, her eyes sliding to the swing at the far end of the wrap around porch. "I always wanted a house like this when I was little. There was this huge antebellum house in my hometown—it wasn't actually someone's house; it was renovated into a museum—but I used to walk down the grand staircase pretending I was Scarlett O'Hara."

Asher grinned, having no trouble imaging young Lacey as a hopeful, southern belle.

He agreed the mansion was quite the sight. He was no stranger to wealth, but he also knew that the Nichol family had wealth on an entirely different level from what he and Duncan had grown up knowing.

"Glad you made it, brother." Duncan appeared on the steps, hopping down, and pulling Asher into a hug. "How was your flight?"

"It was a smooth trip," Asher replied. He turned toward Lacey and placed a hand behind her back, urging her forward. "Duncan, I'd like to you to meet Lacey."

Duncan smiled warmly and extended his hand. "Lacey, it's a pleasure to meet you. I've heard so much about you."

Asher caught Lacey's eye as Duncan turned to pay the driver. She smirked at him. His brother was too polite for his own good.

"I take it we're the last to arrive."

"Yes, although Jaime and his...*date* arrived only an hour ago."

Asher heard something in his brother's curdled tone. "What is wrong with Jaime's date?"

"Nothing, she is very beautiful," Duncan answered. Asher shot him a look, knowing that Duncan was hedging around the issue. "Well, one might say she's—"

"She's a complete tramp."

Aleksandra Nichol, Duncan's brash and not-at-all-blushing bride-to-be sauntered down the front stairs and joined them. Asher couldn't help remembering that there was a time he might have said the same of his future sister-in-law. She was the opposite of the refinement that one would expect to find in the mansion before them. She was all tight clothes and red lips with the mouth of a sailor. How this Hell's angel and his mannerly, prim brother had fallen for one another still remained a complete mystery to him. "Hello, Asher."

Aleksa gave him a quick hug and turned to Lacey. "I'm Aleksa," she eyed Lacey from head to toe. "You look much nicer and much smarter than the whore that Jaime brought. And I really do mean whore. Only hookers wear that much polyester and acrylic."

Asher bit back his laughter as Lacey coughed in surprise. Duncan and Aleksa certainly had their tendency for snap judgments in common. Asher picked up the bags and followed the bride and groom into the house.

Aleksa led them through the foyer to the grand staircase. "So, are you going to tell Asher the happy news or shall I?"

Duncan's eyes flashed at his fiancée. Her arched a brow in return, pursing her full, dark colored lips.

"I suppose I will tell him now, my dear Aleksandra, thanks to your suggestion."

"Ooh, he used the full name," she leaned in toward Lacey and spoke in a feigned whisper. "He only does that when he's very annoyed or very turned on. Sometimes it's both."

Asher watched the stare down between his brother and Aleksa, a feeling of dread coming over him. "What is the news?"

"Come on, Lacey," Aleksa broke the silent conversation between herself and Duncan and took Lacey by the elbow. "This won't be pretty. I'll show you to your room."

Lacey glanced at Asher over her shoulder, sending him a worried look, but he nodded, telling her to go ahead. Once the girls were out of sight, Duncan told him the news.

"Roderick is here."

His spine stiffened and white-hot anger overcame him. Roderick Knight, his father, was in the house. It had been more than a decade since they had shared a roof, let alone been in the same room.

"You were never a very funny man, Duncan."

"I'm not joking."

Asher fought the urge to shake his elder brother. "Why would Roderick be here?"

"I extended an invitation to him." Asher cursed, but Duncan ignored his irritation and continued. "I have already spoken to him and he promises to be on his best behavior."

"We already know how much weight his promises carry."

"I wanted our family to be together for this one event. Please, Asher."

Asher glared at his brother, but he already knew there was nothing he could do. It was almost child-like, the way Duncan insisted on still trying to mend their family, when Asher had worked so hard to build a new one. The deed was already done and Asher didn't have any choice in the matter. It was his brother's wedding and there wasn't much he could say to sway Duncan's decision.

"Fine," he growled, stomping down on the betrayal he felt, "but keep the man as far away from me as possible. I don't want to see him and I don't want to speak to him."

Duncan nodded and allowed Asher to head upstairs.

It wasn't the first time he had stayed in the Nichol's home. He didn't need a guide and Duncan was wise to let Asher alone with his temper. Asher clenched his fists around the handle of the luggage so hard that his nails were close to breaking skin. He muttered curses under his breath as he walked down the hall to his guest room.

The house was quiet. He should have asked Duncan which

room Roderick was staying in so he could know to avoid it. Certainly, Duncan was smart enough to house the vile man away from the rest of the family. Then again, he'd invited the bastard to the wedding, so maybe his dear older brother wasn't as smart as he thought. Asher couldn't imagine what Duncan was thinking.

At the end of the hall, he heard Aleksa and Lacey chattering inside a guest room.

"Oh good, you didn't kill my husband before we had the chance to say our vows," Aleksa greeted when Asher when he appeared in the doorway. "I appreciate that."

"Consider it your wedding present," he replied.

"Damn, I was hoping for something prettier. And more expensive." She pushed out her bottom lip. "Lacey, it's been grand chatting with you. I'll see you two tomorrow at breakfast."

Aleksa gave a little wave and made a quick exit, shutting the door behind her and leaving them alone. Asher dropped the bags onto the floor in front of their queen-sized bed and fell back against the comforter next to where Lacey was sitting.

"Not good news?" Lacey asked, stretching out on her stomach beside him.

He dragged a hand across his face, releasing a long-suffering sigh. "Roderick decided to grace us with his presence after all."

"Roderick? As in your father?"

"The one and only," Asher affirmed as he stared at the ceiling.

Lacey whispered. "Are you okay?"

Asher peered over at her, concern etched onto her brow. He rolled over to face her, placing a hand on her back, finding comfort in the touch. "I'll be fine," he assured her, "as long as he doesn't look at me or talk to me, I'll be fine."

"Is there anything I can do?"

Asher gave her a wearied smile. "I don't think family drama is in the contract."

Lacey shrugged, leaning in to press a kiss to his lips. Asher hummed, the taste of her lips giving him an idea.

"You could, however, distract me from the blinding rage I feel right now." He wiggled his eyebrows up and down.

Lacey laughed. "You have to be the most insatiable man I've ever met. Seriously, does nothing turn you off sex?"

The grin he gave her could put the devil to shame. "No."

Lacey pushed him back and lifted herself up, throwing her leg across his hip to straddle him. His hands went to her hips as she rolled them again his growing erection. Lacey removed her shirt and bra, taking his hands and placing them on top of her breasts. Asher felt the weight of her in his hands, running his thumb across her nipples, watching Lacey throw her head back as she continued to rotate her hips.

They'd been exhausted before, from their respective busy days and a long night of travel. But Asher found himself awakening once again at the distraction that Lacey provided. Not only distraction, but comfort, he realized as his lips grazed her jaw and he rolled her over to lose himself in her arms.

Lacey discovered she was alone in bed when she awoke the next morning. There was, however, a note on the pillow next to her.

Couldn't pull you from your coma. Meet me downstairs for breakfast when you wake up.

-A

She smiled and rolled her eyes at his jab about her sleeping habits. Throwing back the covers, she got up to brush her teeth and get dressed. She hurried, unsure how long Asher had been awake. It was only midmorning, but she didn't want to take too long, especially if she was in a house of early risers. It seemed like poor manners to sleep-in when she was a guest. After splashing

145

some water on her face, adding some makeup, and throwing on a sundress, she made her way downstairs.

Because they'd arrived so late the night before, she never received the official tour of the Nichol's mansion. But it turned out to be pretty easy to find everyone. All she had to do was follow the sound of the morning commotion to the dining room.

There she saw Aleksa and Duncan, seated at the head of the large oak table, with the rest of whom she assumed was the Knight family scattered around them. Duncan sipped coffee, already dressed in a suit, reminding her of a modern day Mr. Darcy. Aleksa had swung a chair around to sit beside him, flipping her wild, dark curls before reaching up to ruffle his perfect chestnut coif. The groom-to-be fixed her with an annoyed look but smiled, before settling back to his breakfast, double checking that no one around them had witnessed their display.

At the other end was Asher, a perky, blonde toddler sitting in his lap, with strawberry jam spread around her mouth and cheeks. The little, curly haired girl squealed and squirmed as Asher tickled her sides.

"Ash, please stop encouraging bad manners," the blonde woman across from him chastised in a lilting British accent that matched his.

"Oh no. Mummy's mad," he whispered loudly to the little girl, an impish smile on his lips.

Lacey lingered in the doorway, observing the whole familial scene. It was disarming to see Asher interacting with a little girl. She knew he had an attachment to his family, but his personality didn't scream paternal. Lacey had never been one of those women who were attracted to men that were good with kids, but she couldn't deny that she found the whole scene quite endearing.

Asher's eyes flicked absently, catching Lacey as she was spying on them, and he offered her a welcoming smile. She tossed her hair, ignoring the stutter of her heart and trying to pretend like she hadn't been staring. She joined the breakfast table and took the vacant seat in the middle next to Asher.

"Good morning, love," he murmured to her. "Good to see you alive."

"Love," the girl on his lap mimicked his endearment as she played with a silver spoon on the table. The girl turned and beamed at Lacey as Asher removed the utensil from her grasp. Lacey smiled back.

"Should I be jealous?" She asked Asher.

"Yes, I'm afraid so," Asher admitted. "This is my number one girl, Louise. Louise, can you say hello to Lacey?"

"'Elwo, Wacey,'" Louise greeted her obediently, much more interested in putting more jam on the piece of toast in front of her with her tiny fingers.

"My daughter doesn't usually look like such a monster." The blonde woman across the table pushed back her chair and rounded to their side of the table. Lacey recognized her from the family photo Asher had shown her, even though she looked almost a decade older.

"Lacey, this is my sister, and Louise's mother, Gwen."

"Pleasure," Gwen offered a tight smile to Lacey and reached out a hand for her daughter. "Come on, monkey, let's go clean up."

"Monkey," Louise repeated, taking her mother's hand. Asher kissed her soft, blonde curls before helping her down. The small girl looked up at Gwen. "Dada?"

"You should ask your Uncle Ash. Your father seems to like him better."

Gwen picked up Louise and passed Asher a saccharine smile. He rolled his eyes. "Gabriel will be here after noon."

"Fantastic." It didn't really sound like Gwen thought it was fantastic at all. She disappeared with Louise out of the dining room.

Lacey nudged Asher's side. "Wait a second, back up." She leaned into Asher's space, keeping her voice low. "That's Gabriel's daughter? He has a daughter? With your sister?"

Asher nodded, tidying up the mess Louise had made of her own breakfast, crumbs and jam spread across the tablecloth. "Gabriel and my sister were together a few years ago. Now it's...complicated."

"But you are Gabriel are such good friends," Lacey said, pouring herself a glass of juice and grabbing a banana from the basket of fruit in the middle of the table. "Shouldn't you like, hate him for leaving your sister alone with your niece?"

Asher laughed. "I think you've watched too many soap operas, sweetheart," he said. "They parted on amicable terms. And I understand Gabriel's side of things as well. He may be slightly absent, but he isn't a bad father."

Lacey nodded, chewing her banana. She guessed that compared to what she knew of Asher's father, a little absenteeism wasn't all that bad. The thought reminded her that Roderick would be present that weekend, but he was noticeably absent from the breakfast table. As were Aleksa's parents.

"So, who is everyone?"

"Oh, right," Asher cleared his throat and proceeded with introductions. "You've met my brother, Duncan, and Aleksa, Gwen went off with Louise, and—"

"Saving the best for last?" A young man swept into the room, followed by a busty brunette in a skintight blue skirt.

"This is my youngest brother, Jaime," Asher said, introducing the final Knight sibling. "Jaime, this is my friend, Lacey."

"Lovely to meet you, darling." Jaime swept down into a bow and took Lacey's hand, dropping a light kiss to her knuckles.

Jaime looked like a younger, more devilish version of Duncan. Instead of matching Duncan's refinement, however, Jaime evoked a recklessness that the other Knight siblings seemed to lack. The gleam in his eye was more charming and inviting than even Asher possessed.

The girl on his right was attractive in the plastic sort of way

148

that Aleksa had described. Jaime introduced his date as Krissy—who gave Lacey and Asher a tight-lipped smile—as the pair took their seats at the table. Jaime flashed Lacey a rakish grin from across the table and she couldn't help laughing at the cheesiness as Asher glared in his younger brother's direction. A maid entered and offered the newcomers coffee.

"Is the coffee gluten-free? I can only have gluten-free," Krissy informed the uniformed woman. Lacey caught Aleksa rolling her eyes.

"So, what's on the agenda today?" Lacey asked.

"It's girls' day," Aleksa replied. "The boys are going off to do manly shit, so I'm taking the girls for a spa day. We weren't expecting you, because we had no idea Asher had a secret girlfriend, but you're welcome to come along."

"Thanks! That sounds like fun."

After breakfast—and more overt flirting from Jaime—Lacey and Asher went back upstairs to finish getting ready for the day. Roderick hadn't made an appearance yet and Lacey was burning with curiosity, but she decided not to bring it up. She had no desire to see the darkness from the night before return to Asher's eyes.

Lacey sat on the bed, waiting for Asher to finish up from his shower. "What kind of 'manly shit' will be happening today?" She lifted her fingers into air quotes, repeating Aleksa's phrase from earlier.

"We're staying at the estate. Shooting. Drinking scotch. Nothing nearly as exciting as going to the spa," he teased.

"Hey!" Lacey bristled. "I will enjoy my day of relaxation and girliness, while you get your Downton Abbey on."

The Nichol Estate really did seem like a house out of a different time. Between the maids and the décor and Duncan's chivalrous manners, Lacey wasn't absolutely certain they hadn't time travelled during their flight the night before.

Asher came out of the bathroom, shirtless, and dropped a

light kiss on her nose. He smelled like his usual cologne, classic and fresh, a smell Lacey was starting to love. Lacey caught his hand to pull him into a real kiss, something she had wanted to do since she walked into the dining room that morning.

Asher dipped his tongue into her mouth, carding his fingers through her hair, and climbed over her. Lacey's back hit the mattress, which had been made sometime while they'd been downstairs. The feel of Asher's weight on her body sent a rush through her. "Trust me, I'd much rather spend the day in the room, with you." His mouth descended upon her again, hungry, and Lacey lost herself in his delicious kiss. "But, Aleksa will be disappointed if you miss out. I think she likes you."

Lacey groaned as Asher rolled off of her and stood up. She felt warm and breathless. "I'm willing to risk it, if you are?"

Asher's low chuckle did nothing to settle her desire. "Easy for you to say, she has a terrible temper when she doesn't get her way."

"Coward."

He laughed and tugged on a t-shirt. "Now who's the insatiable one?"

Lacey let out a dramatic huff and headed to the bathroom to fix her hair and lipstick, wiping away the evidence of their much-too-short make out session. She then told Asher goodbye and went downstairs to meet up again with Aleksa.

"Hello, there." A voice behind her made her pause just as she reached the stairs. Lacey turned to see a man, standing alone in one of the bedroom doorways. He was an older man and like Duncan, he wore a suit, but instead of a collared shirt underneath he sported a t-shirt.

"Hello," Lacey replied politely.

The man stepped forward. He was tall and blonde, like Gwen and Asher, a short beard wrapped around his jaw. His face was crinkled by time, yet still attractive.

"I don't believe we met." He extended his hand to her. An

uneasy feeling crept over her as she took it. She became aware of just how big the house was and just how far away her room and Asher were just then.

"I'm Lacey."

"Lacey," the man echoed, as if tasting the sound of her name. "Which of my sons is fortunate enough to be escorting a woman as beautiful as yourself this weekend?"

Lacey's breath hitched as she realized with whom she was speaking. Her hand was still in his and it took everything inside of her not to jerk it back and wipe away his touch. The thought that he might have been Asher's father crossed her mind, but his American accent had thrown her off.

"You must be Roderick?" Lacey let the venom she felt slip into her tone. She didn't know this man, she didn't know the entire story of why Asher hated him so much, but the protectiveness she felt for Asher made her hate Roderick's guts on principle alone.

"I see my reputation precedes me," he replied with a devilish smirk, finally releasing her hand.

"Oh, I've heard all about you."

His chuckle he gave her made her skin crawl. "Judging by your vitriol toward a mere stranger, I'm guessing that you are here with Asher."

"Lacey." She gaze snapped to the bottom of the stairs, thankful to see Aleksa standing there. "Are you coming?"

"My apologies, Aleksandra, for keeping your new friend," Roderick said. He inclined his head to Lacey. "Lovely to meet you, my dear. I look forward to getting to know you."

Lacey didn't hide the look of disgust on her face as she turned from him and half ran down the stairs to join Aleksa. The way Roderick looked at her, like she was a toy to play with, made her want to hide under the covers.

Aleksa threw a look back at Roderick, before taking Lacey by the arm and leading her away. The two girls headed out to the limo that waited for them in the driveway.

"So, now you've met the pathetic patriarch of the Knight clan," Aleksa said.

"Yeah." Lacey was still trying to shake off the uneasy tingle that lingered on her skin.

"He's so fucking creepy." Judging by the sneer, Aleksa had no love for her soon-to-be father-in-law.

As if they could both feel him watching, they each turned to see Roderick peeking out at them from a second story window, a polite yet stomach-twisting smile on his face. He waved his fingers to them. Creepy didn't even begin to cover it.

Chapter 8

Aleksa's family had paid for complete spa packages, including mani/pedi's, massages, facials, and waxes. Lacey was feeling blissfully pampered as she, Aleksa, Gwen, and Krissy — who Aleksa had spent most of the day rolling her eyes at — detoxed in the steam room. At one point, Lacey had given Aleksa a look that said she was maybe taking it a little too far.

Aleksa had only shrugged. "Look, I'm all for feminism but I don't have any patience for a girl without a brain."

The foursome eventually became three around noon when Ruby, Aleksa's best friend from New York, her maid-of-honor.

"Tell me, Lacey, how long have you and Ash been friends?" It was Gwen who finally broke the ice on the subject of her and Asher. Lacey had wondered how long it would be before the family inquisition began. She'd been mentally preparing herself on the plane, making notes about their fake story and coming up with answers to possible questions.

Asher had warned her that Gwen was nothing close to sweet, especially when it came to strangers and certainly when it came to her brother's girlfriends. The look in the blonde's eye said she was out for blood.

"Not long. About a week," Lacey replied. She thought vague truths were the best way to go.

"And here he is already introducing you to the family, he must really like you."

Lacey kept smiling. Gwen couldn't out mean-girl her. In high school, Lacey had written the book on being a Queen Bee and was more than apt at maintaining a bubbly attitude while throwing verbal daggers to anyone who might cross her. She wouldn't be intimidated. "Is that a problem?"

"Not at all," Gwen said, glancing at her nails. "Trust me, we've met plenty of you. Jaime and Ash practically have a competition for who can bring home the biggest feminine disappointment."

"Give it a rest, Gwen," Aleksa interjected, "you're being an even bigger bitch than me, and I've set a pretty high bar."

Lacey appreciated Aleksa's defense, but she could handle herself. She leaned forward and flashed Gwen a sugary smile. "How am I ranking? Is there anything particularly trashy I can do to tip the scales in Asher's favor?"

Gwen narrowed her eyes and Lacey silently called it a victory as Asher's sister strutted away, nose in the air. Excellent Escort- 1, Bitchy Sister- 0.

Krissy, who hadn't even come close to catching the thinly veiled insult that had been thrown in her direction, ignored the entire exchange. Aleksa scooted over the wooden bench closer to Lacey.

"Well done," she commended with a proud smile, "I like you." Lacey beamed at the declaration. "If it makes you feel any better, Gwen gave me the same hard time when Duncan and I started dating. In fact I'm pretty sure she still hates me. She's extremely overprotective of all her brothers."

Lacey waved it off. "I'm not worried about it. It's not like Asher and I are serious at all."

"Just using him for sex?"

Lacey grinned at how closed Aleksa was to the mark. "Something like that," she replied and the two women fell into a fit of giggles worthy of a high school locker room. "What's so funny?" Krissy asked.

"Nothing," Aleksa snapped, "just go back to staring at your nails."

"Pull!"

Asher watched the clay pigeon fly into the air over the barrel of the shotgun tucked into his arms. The orange was easy to spot in the cloudless blue sky. He squeezed the trigger and felt the gun kick back against his shoulder, the clay smashing into pieces in midair a second later.

"Another perfect shot," Duncan said, stepping over to take the gun from him.

One of the game attendants walked over and helped Duncan reload the gun while another congratulated Asher on his excellent aim. Asher took in a breath, gazing at the expanse of land all around. The atmosphere around the Nichol estate was like something out of another time. There were stables and servants and private gardens. Asher and his siblings had grown up wealthy, but the Nichols were in another league. They lived like kings.

"You are certainly marrying well," he quipped.

Duncan gave Asher an unamused look. "I'm not marrying her for her money."

Asher rolled his eyes as Duncan turned and took his position to shoot. His brother could never take a joke.

When they'd first arrived in the back garden, the area had been turned into a driving range. Afterwards, lunch was served and the golf equipment was cleared away to make room for shooting. Gabriel had joined them then, having finally arrived from Chicago. A mini bar had also been set up nearby for their convenience and refreshment. The shooting had become less and less frequent as they continued to pay more attention to the bar.

Jaime had long given up on their sport and instead tried his luck at flirting with the poor girl mixing their drinks.

Duncan called "pull" and made his shot, cursing under his breath when he missed. He handed off the gun and walked back to Asher, as another attendant approached him with a glass of scotch.

"I believe that pulls me ahead by three," Asher declared with a sly smile.

"I think I'm spent," Duncan said, taking a sip of his drink and shaking out his shoulder.

"Giving up so soon?" Asher teased. When they were boys, in had been constant competition between them. Anything and everything could be turned into a game of who was better. Both of them hated to lose and knew just how to egg the other on. "I suppose you aren't as young as you once were."

"I blame the alcohol," Duncan replied, drinking again.

"You'd better be careful then," Asher tutted. " After all, Aleksa forced us to schedule the stag night last weekend so you wouldn't show up with a hangover at her wedding."

"As if that would even happen," Jaime chimed in, joining the two of them. "Has our brother ever been properly smashed in his life? Vegas was wasted on him."

"Oh, I wouldn't say that," Gabriel answered. "In fact Duncan here—"

Duncan quickly cut him off. "I'm surprised you can

remember any of it, Gabriel. Shall I remind you of the finer points of your weekend? Whatever did happen after you found out that dancer was male?"

Asher snickered at the way Gabriel's mouth bobbed open and closed like a goldfish.

"I suppose my invitation to Sin City was lost in the mail." The sound of the voice behind them sucked every bit of merriment from the air.

It was the moment Asher had been dreading all day. Roderick had finally come to join them. He had tried to ignore the sense of foreboding at having to eventually face his father and enjoy his morning with his brothers. Of course as soon as he managed to forget it the terrible moment has come to pass.

"Asher," Roderick said, approaching him. His legs kicked out with each lazy step, his hands tucked into his pockets, as if he didn't have a care in the world. "It's been a long time."

Not long enough.

Asher wanted to snap at him, but he remembered his promise to Duncan to remain civil. "Yes, it has."

Jaime and Gabriel had gone silent behind him. Duncan keeping close watch from his side.

Roderick raised his hands in a show of peace, affecting a slightly more jovial attitude. "Please, carry on. Don't let me stop the fun. Perhaps I'll have a drink."

"Perhaps not." Asher did snap that time.

Roderick chuckled lightly. "I only meant a seltzer."

Asher gave him a hard look, warning him to step out of line, when Duncan stepped forward. "Allow me to get that for you, father."

The lightness of the day was impossible to recover. Even the sky seemed to register the mood, a single cloud moving into their sky and blocking the sun. Duncan kept an eye on both Asher and their father, only making Asher even more agitated. Even Jaime's mood had turned, the younger man scowling into the distance, fist clenched at his side.

Asher tilted his head, really looking at his younger brother. He was happy to know that not all of their siblings felt as ready to cross the line as Duncan seemed to be, and he imagined maybe their eldest brother had given a lecture to Jaime that was similar to the one Asher heard when he'd arrived.

His gaze slipped to the trembling fist at Jaime's side, his knuckles turning white. It was possible that Asher wouldn't be the one that Duncan needed to worry about.

"I think it's time for a drink," Gabriel murmured, breaking the silence, and stepping over to the bar.

"So, Ash, you have to tell us more about Lacey." The darkness that had covered Jaime's features disappeared like lightening, as if it had never existed at all, and he was back to his usual, merry self.

"We met at a work function," Asher replied.

"I don't give a damn about how you met. She's bloody hot!"

"Don't be crass, Jamie," Duncan chided, returning with the seltzer for their father and passing it off.

"Trust me, brother, that was the PG version of what I'm really thinking. If I wanted to be crass, I'd say that I wouldn't mind those pretty lips of hers wrapped around my co—"

"Say another word and I'll tear out your liver," Asher warned.

Jaime pouted. "Don't be like that. You'll dump her eventually, when you get bored or she gets clingy. Perhaps a trip to visit my brothers is overdue. I'd so enjoy being there to pick up those pieces."

Asher glared at Jaime flicking his eyebrows up and down suggestively. He knew his brother was only trying to wind him up, but the thought of him with Lacey made his stomach churn.

"Come now, Jaime, go easy on your brother. You know he has a terrible temper," Roderick interjected. "Even if there is some truth to the matter."

Asher twisted to face him. "What did you say?"

Roderick put on a cool smile. "Forgive me, I've spoken out of turn. I only just met the girl."

Asher sucked in a deep breath, his jaw tightening. Duncan was behind him, placing a hand on his shoulder. "He's baiting you," he said moving between the two. He turned to Roderick, "I warned you that I wouldn't tolerate any disagreements this weekend. You agreed."

Roderick smiled and backed away. "You are right, son. I apologize."

Duncan nodded and glanced back at Asher. He ignored the call for reconciliation and turned his attention toward the gun, preparing to shoot again. After the tiny spar with Roderick, he needed to blow off some steam. Maybe he would picture his father's face as the clay pigeon.

"Pull!"

Duncan went to Jaime as Roderick approached Asher again. "I think I've hit a nerve."

Asher bit his tongue, the vein in his temple throbbing. He said nothing and aimed again.

"You want me to go away," Roderick continued, "but you'll never be rid of me. I'm their father, boy. They'll always feel a connection to me. Duncan and Jaime and even Gwen…they'll always hope for more."

"And you disappoint them at every turn," Asher retorted. "They despise you as much as I do."

"If that is true then why did Duncan invite me here today?"

"I can't imagine. We're far better off without you." His ability to shake off Roderick's barbs was running thin.

"Are you?"

Asher dropped his stance and stalked toward Roderick. "Yes."

Roderick scoffed, unintimidated. "This family is nothing without me. Look at you all. Everything has fallen apart under

159

your watch. Duncan marrying some Bulgarian tart. Gwen impregnated and forced into parenthood without a husband. Jamie dropped out of University and…well, you must be proud. Aren't these things you thought to avoid by stealing them away from me?"

Asher ground his teeth. "We are family. We are happy."

"You barely can be in the same room together. I'll bet Gwen is beginning to resent you as much as she did me. You and Duncan don't even live in the same city because he can't stand to be around you and Jaime…well he can't be bothered about much can he? He hates you and blames you for your mother just as much as he blames me. Even if he won't admit it."

"Don't you dare speak of my mother."

"I have every right to speak of my own wife."

"Your threats mean nothing old man," Asher replied.

Asher's fist clenched, he felt his blood rush, and the urge to throw is fist into his father's jaw. Instead, he threw the gun down and walked over to the bar, lifting the bottle of whiskey from its place.

"What happened?" Duncan asked.

He didn't answer his brother and he didn't dare look back as he walked toward the house, not wanting to see Roderick's satisfaction at chasing him away and hating himself that he allowed the vile man to do it.

The girls arrived back at the house in time to get ready for the rehearsal dinner. Lacey was feeling completely refreshed after her day of pampering. Gwen had even started to be a bit nicer to her after their chat in the steam room. She was now freshly pedicured, massaged and waxed and feeling like a million bucks.

The group walked into the living room and were greeted by Jaime lounging on the white sofa, his legs stretched out and crossed.

"Where is everyone?" Gwen asked him.

"Around," he smirked. "You've all missed out on all of the delicious drama."

Gwen rolled her eyes. "What are you talking about?"

"The usual. Roderick being a bastard and Asher running away to sulk," Jaime explained. "There was a moment where I wasn't sure if Asher would hit him or shoot him."

Aleksa, Lacey, and Gwen exchanged looks.

"Well, at least he didn't shoot him," Aleksa said. "Where's Duncan?"

Jaime shrugged. "Looking for Asher? He kept calling him but he wouldn't answer his phone. No one has seen him in two hours."

"I'll call him. I *told* Duncan not to invite his fucking father," Aleksa grabbed her cellphone and hurried out of the room, muttering about ruined plans. Ruby followed and Gwen went to check on her daughter.

"Welcome to the family drama," Jaime said to Lacey.

Krissy fawned over Jaime which seemed to please him. Lacey listened to Jaime go on for a few moments, milking the attention, and then excused herself to go upstairs to her room.

Asher wasn't inside, not that she was suprised. She reached into her purse and checked her work phone. No new messages, so she messaged him. A chime sounded from the bedside table and she saw Asher's phone light up with her text. Her shoulders sagged.

She didn't see or hear from Asher for the rest of the afternoon or evening. She even attended the rehearsal dinner alone. Duncan had informed them that he had spoken with Roderick and asked him to not come to the ceremony the next day. Aleksa gave her groom an encouraging little hug at this news, but judging by the looks that were passed around, it seemed that they all agreed it was for the best.

Lacey sat with Krissy and Gabriel, the only two attendees not part of the wedding, and watched the rehearsal. The dinner was held at an Italian restaurant a few miles from the house. Lacey sipped wine and twirled pasta around her plate, but didn't speak much. Everyone was too involved in their own little worlds and it was clear that a fair amount of tension still ran after the afternoon's drama. Duncan was attempting to allay his fiancée's worries and Jaime was even looking a little less enthused, enjoying some extra wine and flirting with a little too much smarmy enthusiasm.

Thankfully, she was sitting next to Gabriel, who was nice enough to chat with her every now and again, but Gwen continually pulled his attention away.

That night, as she was getting ready for bed, she still hadn't heard from Asher. Even Duncan admitted that he had no idea where his brother might have gone, but he didn't seem worried.

"He's like Heathcliff on the moors," Duncan told her. "He enjoys his time to brood."

Lacey tried not to worry either as she climbed into bed, shut her eyes, and tried to fall asleep.

It might have been minutes or hours, but her eyes popped open again as soon as she heard the bedroom door click open and shut. A look at the clock on the nightstand told her it was two in the morning. She rolled over to face the door and saw Asher bent over, trying to be silent while removing his shoes.

"Where have you been?" She asked, sounding a little angrier than she had intended.

Asher glanced up at her in the darkness, his shoes hitting the floor with a *thunk-thunk*. "Of course the one time I'm actively trying to not wake you up, I wake you up."

Lacey sat up, scowling at him in the darkness. "Of course I'm awake. I'm pissed. You left me alone with your family all day. I went to the rehearsal dinner by myself, sat in a group of people I barely know, tried to fend off all of Jaime's advances, all after hearing about some argument with your dad and that you just disappeared. Without your phone. Damn it, Asher! I've been worrying non-stop since I got back this afternoon!"

He stopped at the foot of the bed, head hanging between his shoulders, hands in his pockets. "You were worried about me?"

"Yes! It completely ruined all of the relaxation I experienced at the spa."

Asher chuckled and climbed into bed, sliding on top of Lacey and pushing her back. He stretched out on top of her, pressing her into the bed with the weight of his body. She was still angry with him, but her arms welcomed him, glad that he was back and not dead in a ditch somewhere, as her mother might say.

"Are you okay?" She asked, threading her fingers through his hair as he used her chest for a pillow. "You smell like booze."

"The half bottle of Glenlivet might have something to do with that. Did Jaime really hit on you?"

"Is that really a huge surprise?" She asked. "Stop avoiding my question. What happened today?"

Asher sighed, his breath warm against her skin. "I thought you already heard it from everyone else."

"I want to hear it from you."

He sighed again. "Roderick is sadistic, manipulative man who is capable of terrible things. My mother told me she didn't realize until it was too late. She tried to get away, but after two children it became impossible. She wouldn't leave us."

"After Oliver's death and our little discovery about my true parentage, my mother told me some of the details. She told me she did manage to hide for a time and was with my biological father in Paris when Roderick discovered her. She left my father, and went back to Roderick, and soon I was born. When I was eighteen, I abandoned my family and went to France in search of my real father. Hoping…just, hoping. I don't know. I was a stupid boy."

"Did you find him?"

"No. But I did find what was left of him. He'd left me an

163

inheritance and soon Duncan came to France to find me and we left for America together. A few years later, we got a call from Gwen and..." Asher stopped, choking on the words.

"What happened?"

"I realized I had abandoned my family at the worst of times and we knew we had to get Jaime and Gwen away from that bastard. It took almost three years to be completely rid of Roderick. He's been trying to destroy us and everything we've built ever since." Asher let out a mirthless laugh. "He's right. We'll never be rid of him. Why would Duncan even think of inviting him here?"

Lacey knew he wasn't really asking her, he was simply talking through his thoughts, but she answered anyway. "If it makes you feel better, Duncan uninvited him."

"He did?" Asher asked, sounding like a hopeful little boy.

"Yep," she replied. "So no more evil dad. At least not this weekend." Some of the tension in Asher's body seemed to melt away at the news.

They laid together in silence for a while, Lacey running her hands through his hair and Asher holding onto her, listening to her heartbeat, taking comfort from the slow rise and fall of her chest. She didn't even mind his heavy weight on top of her tiny body.

"Sometimes I worry..." he trailed off.

"Worry what?" She asked when he didn't continue.

"He's not a true father but, we share a temper. An impulsiveness. I've tried to erase it all but..." She heard him sniff. "He's right. Jaime and Gwen...Duncan sometimes..."

Lacey didn't know exactly what he was talking, but she grabbed his face and forced his eyes to meet hers. "Asher, you are *nothing* like your father. You take care of your family. They love and respect you. Yes, you ran away when you were younger, but you stepped up to the plate when they needed you, and helped get your brother and sister out of a bad situation. I don't know many men who would do that."

Before he could respond, she pulled him in for a kiss. She wanted to erase all of the bad feelings that his afternoon with Roderick had unearthed.

Asher pulled away and looked down at her. "I'm sorry for leaving you alone with my family today."

Lacey shrugged underneath him. "It's okay, it really wasn't that bad. Gwen gave me a bit of a hard time. But she lightened up."

Asher kissed her again. "Sounds about right."

"Which reminds me, I have something to show you," she gave him a coy smile.

Asher's brows lifted. "Really?"

Lacey bit her lip and nodded, taking his hand and guiding it down, under her pajama bottoms and to feel the smooth skin down below. Asher's finger traced along the seam of her core, her blood heating up from his light caresses.

"That wasn't exactly what I was expecting," he said with a wicked smile.

Lacey giggled, wrapping her arms around him as he captured her lips again.

Chapter 9

Asher stood at the foot of the bed, a steaming cup of coffee in hand, watching Lacey sleep. It amused him to no end how easily she had woken up when he came in early that morning, but now she was dead to the world. He had been up and around for over an hour, making noise in their room. Louise spent some of the morning running and shouting in excitement past their door, but Lacey didn't even stir for any of it.

Perhaps it was a bit creepy, but he couldn't help watching her as she slept. Her beautiful hair splayed out across the pillow, the sheets draped over her delectable body, she looked like a wanton goddess ready for the taking, but at the same time innocent and peaceful.

"Hey, what are you—oh! Sorry." Gwen was standing in the doorway, her voice dropping to a whisper as she noticed Lacey in the bed still asleep.

Asher chuckled softly. "Don't worry. You couldn't wake her

if you tried."

Gwen cocked her head at him, suspicious.

"Why are you looking at me like that?" He asked.

Gwen shook her head. "No reason," she responded. "Tell sleeping beauty that we're doing hair and makeup after lunch. Even though she's not in the bridal party, she is welcome to come."

Asher gave her a surprised look. "How kind of you."

"It was Aleksa's invitation, not mine. This isn't *my* wedding."

Asher heard the bitterness in her tone, but ignored it. "I heard you gave her a bit of a hard time yesterday." He said nodding his head toward Lacey.

"Well, I know your usual taste in women, Ash. I had to make sure she was worthy."

"And did Lacey pass your test?"

Gwen reached up and grabbed his chin, giving it an affectionate shake. "No woman will ever be good enough for my brothers," she replied. "You should keep her around for a while, though."

"I'll consider it."

Gwen left him alone, shutting the door behind her. Finally, Lacey began to stir.

"Mmmm, hello." Sleepy moans bubbled from her throat as she stretched her arms over her head. Asher walked around and set the coffee he'd been holding on the nightstand, taking a seat next to her on the bed. "You've got to stop letting me sleep so long. It makes me a poor house guest."

"Don't worry about it, love. I've brought you coffee."

Lacey smiled and reached for the cup, bringing it to her lips.

"You're perfect," she said in complete earnest. Asher folded his lips together to suppress his grin at the compliment.

"Gwen came by and extended Aleksa's invitation to go down and get ready with the girls after lunch," he told her as she drank her coffee.

"That was nice of her," she replied and looked at the clock. "I guess I better shower."

"Perhaps I'll join you," Asher suggested.

Asher stood and pulled Lacey up with him, catching her lips. She giggled against his kisses as he lead her backward toward the bathroom that was tucked between two guest rooms. His hand was already under her nightshirt, his fingers skimming around her stomach.

They hit the door with a thud and Asher reached behind himself to turn the knob, the two of them falling into the bathroom.

"Pardon me," Jaime cleared his throat. Asher ripped his hands from Lacey's shirt and spun around, glaring at his brother. "All night last night and again this morning? You two are worse than two horny teenagers," the younger Knight said, "and that's saying a lot, coming from me."

Lacey went red, covering her face with her hand.

"Get out," Asher ordered his brother.

"You know, I'm at least respectful enough not to copulate in the common areas of the house," Jaime laughed.

"Out!"

Jaime raised his hands defensively and backed out of the room, winking at Lacey as he went. Asher followed him and locked the door on their side.

"He's been known to 'accidentally' walk in," he explained, stepping back toward Lacey.

"Oh god," she groaned. "I didn't realize we were sharing a bathroom and a wall with Jaime."

Undeterred, Asher wrapped his arm around her waist and pulled her roughly back to him. "Now, where were we?"

Thankfully, she recovered from her embarrassment quickly. Lacey took his hand and put it back under her shirt. "I think somewhere around here."

Asher kissed her again. Clothes were removed and the

shower was turned on, the two of them stepping into the warm spray. Asher pulled back, looking at Lacey, admiring the way she looked wet, hair dripping and matted against her head and shoulders. It never ceased to amaze him how breathtaking this woman could be, in any situation. Whether she was made up from head to toe, like the night they met, or in a simple sundress, or sleeping with tangled hair and pillow marks on her face.

"What is it?" Lacey asked him.

Asher shook his head. "Nothing."

She leaned forward and kissed him again, her hand skimming down his stomach, to his cock. He hummed as Lacey wrapped her long fingers around him and began pumping.

As she worked him with her hand, Lacey set her mouth against his throat, her tiny nips making him even harder than he already was. He had discovered that Lacey was a bit of a biter over the past week. It was interesting to find out that this petite blonde girl was a bit rough in the bedroom, but he adored her all the more for it. She was up for anything all the time and it was a good thing, too. Asher was finding that he could never get his fill of her.

He was close, he could feel it, and he still wanted to be inside of her. Asher removed her hand from his cock, and pushed her gently back against the tile wall. She gazed up at him, her perfect chest heaving in anticipation, drops of water rolling down her naked body.

"Wrap your leg around me," Asher instructed. Lacey did as he said, her knee hooking around his hip.

Asher ran his thumb across her clit and Lacey gasped at the heavy touch. He dragged his thumb down her sex, driving her forward before thrusting up inside of her. They moaned in unison. Lacey threw her arms around his neck to support herself, her leg still wrapped around his hip. Their heads came together, lips brushing over each other again and again with each slow thrust.

"Yes," Lacey urged. "Please."

Her plea was desperate and weak, her body tight around him,

the water pulsing against his back.

Asher increased his pace as she squeezed her leg around him, pulling him closer, letting him in deeper. A few moments later they came together, Lacey's leg falling slowly back to the shower floor, Asher placing quick kisses against her lips. They were breathless and a sated, smiling at one another as the water continued to pour over them.

After the quickie in the shower, they finally managed to clean up properly. Lacey had finished the rest of her coffee and put on pair of shorts and a button up blouse. She parted from Asher with a kiss and went downstairs to join the girls.

The house was alive with energy as the hired help worked to transform the mansion into a wedding venue. The ceremony was taking place outside, just at sundown, on a hill behind the house with a perfect view of the skyline. Through the back doors, Lacey could spot the gorgeous set up that Aleksa had designed herself. There were around 100 white chairs tied up with gossamer ribbons. From one end to the other and there were red roses absolutely everywhere. A long, white runway led to a woven archway in the front, adorned with white lights and more roses. It may have seemed like a lot of red, but the shades of dark cherry, apple, and fiery poppy combined to create a deep, romantic look. Lacey just knew it was going to be absolutely gorgeous come nightfall.

Inside, one of the sitting rooms had been transformed into its own salon. Makeup artists and hair dressers were on hand to make each of the girls look like a princess. She spent the afternoon hanging out with Aleksa, Gwen, and Ruby. Gwen and Ruby were Aleksa's only two bridesmaids.

"My mother tried to make me include my cousins," Aleksa told her, "but I barely talk to those bitches, so what's the point?"

Mrs. Nichol sat in the corner, attending to Louise as well as Ruby's daughter, Emerald, who Lacey guessed was around six or seven. The woman gave Aleksa a chiding look, but didn't say anything, and went back to entertaining the little girls.

"Where's Krissy?" Lacey asked, as one of the hairdressers began combing out her wet hair.

Aleksa shook her head. "Not invited," she said, "you win the favorite new girlfriend award, Lacey."

Lacey smiled triumphantly, but the smile faded as she realized she didn't deserve the praise. She wasn't a girlfriend. New *fake* girlfriend was more like it. Soon to be *ex*-new fake girlfriend. She had to keep reminding herself of that, squirming in her seat a little. The thought stung more than it should have.

"Hey, you okay?" Aleksa asked. "Your face just went from zero to sixty and back again in less than a second."

Lacey gave her a tight smile. "Yeah. I'm fine."

Lacey didn't see Asher for the rest of the afternoon until it was time for the wedding. He was busy with Duncan and the rest of his family. She finished getting dressed on her own, her professionally curled hair going splendidly with her navy colored strapless dress. After double and triple checking herself in the mirror, she ventured downstairs to the ceremony as the guests began to arrive.

In the twilight, the venue looked magical, like straight out of a fairy tale. The light from the lanterns blended perfectly with the oranges, blues, and purples of the night sky. If she looked to the left, a large tent area had been set up where the reception would take place after the wedding. Lacey walked down the aisle, not sure if she should be sitting on the bride's side or the groom's side until she saw Gabriel seated on the groom's. Since he was the only person around that she knew, she decided to join him.

"Is this seat taken?"

"It is now," he said, flashing her his winning smile.

A few minutes later, the music from the string quartet

172

changed and the wedding procession began. Duncan, Asher, and Jaime entered from the side, along with the priest. Asher looked amazing in his black tux, a red flower pinned to his jacket. His eyes searched the crowd until he found Lacey. He gave her a little wink and she smiled back at him.

The guests turned as Gwen entered first. She looked stunning in her scarlet bridesmaid gown. Ruby came next, holding the same small bouquet of cream color flowers that Gwen had.

Emerald serving as the ringer bearer came next, holding dutifully onto the pillow with the rings, she was outfitted a feminine styled mini-tux. Louise shyly rounded out the procession, looking completely adorable in her flower girl dress. The gentle "aww" from the guests gave her confidence a boost, and she gleefully trotted down the aisle, tossing out rose petals from her little wicker basket as she went.

"She looks adorable," Lacey whispered to Gabriel.

"That's my girl," he replied.

Louise dumped out the rest of her petals at the alter and spotted her father. Everyone quietly laughed as she ran over to climb in his lap. Gabriel gave her hair a kiss and took the basket from her, setting it on the floor.

"Good job, kiddo."

Everyone stood as the music changed again. The big moment arrived.

Aleksa appeared on her father's arm, looking every bit the fairytale bride. Her dress had round taffeta skirts flowing out into a train that would put Princess Diana to shame. The bodice was strapless with tiny diamonds tracing around the top. The veil she wore was pinned neatly to her curled hair, sweeping down Aleksa's back and along the length of her train.

Lacey barely recognize her as the feisty woman she had gotten to know over the past couple of days, in skin tight clothes with a wicked look in her eye. Aleksa slowly marched down the aisle, her eyes focused solely on Duncan, who stood in awe of the beauty walking toward him.

Everyone was seated and the ceremony proceeded. Lacey couldn't help feeling a little emotional and romantic while watching. The way that the bride and groom were looking at each other made her feel jealous and hopeful all at once. There was a love story there. A really good one.

"Need a tissue?" Gabriel teased her.

She gave him a playful poke in the ribs with her elbow. "Shut up."

"The couple would now like to recite their own vows," the priest announced. Duncan pulled a piece of paper from his breast pocket and read from it.

"I never believed in love. I always thought that love was a fantasy confined to the pages of a book. That was until I met my darling Aleksandra. She is my opposite in everyway. Loud, obnoxious, blunt," Aleksa made a face and the guests laughed. Duncan gave her an endearing smirk and continued. "But she is also beautiful and fierce and loyal. I found that every moment I spent with her, I felt like a better version of myself. She made me feel...fuller. And I realized, that I wanted her in my life, every day, for the rest of my existence. Perhaps love is just a story, but I'm glad that it has become a part of ours. I will love you, my darling Aleksandra, all the days of our lives."

Duncan finished and Ruby handed Aleksa a paper with her vows. "Unlike Duncan, I *always* believed in love. When my mom read me fairytales like Cinderella every night, I knew that that was the exact kind of love I wanted, and I would wait an eternity to find it. Lucky for me, I didn't have to wait quite that long. Duncan wasn't the prince I dreamed of...he was so much better." Her voice caught and Duncan lifted his palm to her cheek. "I will love him," Aleksa finished, "all the days of our lives."

Rings were exchanged and Duncan stepped forward to kiss his bride. The guests clapped for the newlyweds as they made their way down the aisle, hand in hand, as man and wife.

Chapter 10

After the ceremony, everyone made their way toward the reception tent. A string quartet played near the corner of the area as cocktail hour began. Champagne ran in abundance from fountains and little candles flickered on every table surround centerpieces filled with Roses of every color. Roses seemed to be the running theme at this fairytale wedding.

Lacey meandered through the tables and chairs until she found Asher's name and "guest" on a card. She was seated with Gabriel, Gwen, Jaime, Krissy, and—

"Delaney?" Lacey asked, picking up his name card. "Where is he this weekend?"

She hadn't even thought about the older Sawyer until just that moment.

"He had to stay behind," Gabriel said, setting Louise down in her mother's seat. "Some last minute stuff came up at work."

Lacey nodded and set her purse down, walking over to one

of the champagne fountains to for a drink. When she returned to the table Gabriel had disappeared again, but Jaime had seated himself, Krissy beside him, fully immersed in the reflection in her compact mirror.

Satisfied with the line of her lipstick, she excused herself to grab a drink and Jaime turned his attention toward Lacey.

"Did you enjoy the ceremony?"

"It was great," Lacey replied.

"Wasn't it? Didn't I look handsome?" he asked, wiggling his eyebrows.

"Jaime, go bother your own date," Asher said coming up behind them. Lacey turned and wrapped her arms around his neck.

He pulled away and looked down at her, leaving his arms around her waist. "You look ravishing."

"So do you," she smiled.

Asher leaned down for a quick kiss before pulling out her chair. She was happy to finally have him back. Even though he'd been nearby all day, she found she'd missed being around him and being able to talk to him.

The reception was just as amazing and extravagant as the ceremony. After a delicious dinner came the dancing and dessert. The string quartet had moved on and a DJ had taken over. There seemed to be an endless supply of cake and champagne and Lacey could feel herself getting a little buzzed.

She watched Gabriel dance with Louise, twirling her around the floor, until her Uncle Jaime came in and scooped her away, letting Gwen cut in. The pair swayed slowly to the music, completely wrapped up in one another. Maybe it was the fizzy champagne getting to her or the abundance of love in the air, but Lacey couldn't help but think that the two of them would eventually find a happily ever after. They just looked too happy in one another's arms for things to end up otherwise.

"Come on," Asher said, interrupting her romantic musings,

"Let's dance."

Lacey happily accepted and let Asher lead her onto the dance floor. He pulled her close, her chin resting near his shoulder. As they swayed and spun, she gazed at the couples; Gabriel and Gwen, Aleksa and Duncan, everyone looked so happy and in love.

"What is it, love?" Asher whispered in her ear as they twirled.

"Hmm?"

"You just sighed. Very heavily I might add. Everything alright?"

Lacey pulled back to look at him. She met his warm, blue-grey eyes, crinkled slightly by his dimpled smile. It was infectious. Every time he smiled, she couldn't help smiling too, even when it was his usual cocky, self-assured grin. She recalled the very first night she met him; his smile had put her completely at ease.

"Yeah, everything is perfect," she said.

"Excuse me, some people are trying to dance," Aleksa said, interrupting their moment. Lacey hadn't even realized that they had just been standing still in the middle of the floor. "Mind if I dance with my new brother-in-law?"

Lacey gave her an exaggerated bow and stepped back to let the bride cut in.

"Lacey," Duncan offered his hand, "May I?" Lacey nodded, taking his hand, and letting him guide her along the floor. "I saw Jaime making his way over and I thought I might spare you my brother's inability to concede to rejection."

Lacey laughed. "Thank you. He does seem pretty persistent."

"He enjoys irritating those he cares for, a misplaced means of affection, " Duncan explained. "Have you been enjoying yourself this weekend?"

"Yes, thank you."

Duncan smiled, giving her a spin and bringing her back in. "Glad to hear it. I know it must be difficult to meet all of the family at once, especially so early in a relationship."

"It's fine, really," Lacey insisted, "I was happy to be included."

"I hope I'm not too bold in saying that I hope things work out between you and my brother. You seem very well matched and you appear to make my brother very happy." Duncan paused, glancing off toward Asher and Aleksa dancing. "I haven't seen him smile the way he has this weekend since…" Lacey waited, watching him shake off whatever memory swept through him just then. He returned to himself and to the moment, smiling at her once again. "Well I just hope that you and I meet again Lacey. Many times."

The song ended and Duncan thanked Lacey for the dance, making his way toward Aleksa once more. Asher stepped back toward Lacey, flashing her that smile that she enjoyed so much. The one Duncan said he hadn't seen in…how long?

"How about a break from dancing?" Asher asked, taking her hand. Lacey shrugged and he pulled her away from the dance floor, leading her out of the tent and away from the reception.

They walked down the grassy hill, toward the giant lake that sat at the very back of the Nichol's estate. The moon glowed high in the sky, casting a blue reflection on the water. The night was warm, but not too hot. A light breeze swept the air. They strolled hand in hand, in companionable silence, until they reached the boathouse at the bank of the lake. A long dock stretched out in front of them with a tiny boat tied up at the end. Lacey could hear the sounds of the rippling water and the creak of the small boat mixed with the soft echoes of music from the reception.

"Are you having a good time, love?" Asher asked stopping and turning to face her.

Lacey nodded, reaching up to straighten his bowtie. "I suppose the question is, are *you* having a good time?"

Asher wrapped his arms around her back. "Of course. Seeing my brother get married, I suppose it puts things into perspective, a little."

"Yeah?" Lacey wondered where he was going with that line of thought.

"Yes," Asher affirmed without further explanation. "So, are you going to tell me what that sigh was about while we were dancing?" Lacey repeated the sigh, this time disappointed at his evasion. "Ah yes, that's the one I was talking about."

"I don't know," Lacey replied, brushing the toe of her heel through the grass, "I guess just getting caught up in all this wedding, romance stuff. Seeing Duncan and Aleksa together. Even Gabriel and Gwen—everyone in love. It just makes me think…it makes me think about Grant."

"Lucas?" Lacey's head popped up at the harsh change in his voice. She noticed some dark look in his eye and how his grip on her tensed. She tried to ignore the theories that reaction posed for her.

"Yeah, just that, I thought I was going to marry him. I really did. When I imagined my future, I imagined Grant and two point five kids, and a big house in the burbs with a dog and tennis court that we never use. I just completely shut myself off to anything else, including college and dating and other people. I never considered anything else. If he hadn't cheated on me—if I hadn't caught him—then that's what my life would have become within the next couple of years. Not exactly barefoot and pregnant but not far off."

"But that's not what you want now? The children, the home, the dog?"

Lacey's gaze flicked off, over his shoulder, to the ripples in the lake. "I don't know. Listening to Duncan and Aleksa talk about their love—Grant and I didn't have that. Not ever. I couldn't have said those things about him. I mean look at me, I haven't cried over him. Not once. I didn't even when we first broke up." Asher gave her a look of disbelief. "Okay, I did cry a little, but not because I missed him. It was because I was scared for myself. For the first time in my life, I was alone. I didn't have anyone making

179

choices for me, and I didn't know what I was going to do." She dropped her head against her arm hanging over around his shoulder and released a small laugh. Asher rubbed lazy patterns across the small of her back, listening intently as she spoke. "I'm a bit intoxicated. I'm rambling."

"Don't worry about it, love."

"I guess what I'm just saying is that in the end, I'm really glad Grant and I broke up and—" Her long lashes fanned out over cheeks, glowing in the starlight above. She lifted her eyes and peered up at him, taking a deep breath, and confessing the thought that had been filling her with giddy warmness that couldn't be blamed on the champagne. "I'm very glad I met you."

She stood up on her toes and sealed the admission with a kiss. Asher gripped her tighter and slipped his tongue past her lips, deepening the kiss. Lacey just couldn't help herself, she knew that she was breaking every boundary rule in Chloe and Willa's book of escort self-preservation, but she needed to tell him. For once she needed to stop pretending and let herself feel—even for one brief evening—what she knew had been developing since their first night together.

Asher pulled away and pressed his forehead against hers. She closed her eyes, listening to the music play in the distance. She almost didn't hear him when he whispered, "I'm very glad I met you as well, Lacey."

She crushed her lips to his once again, letting her kisses speak what she couldn't put into words. Asher broke from her, taking her hand and leading her into the boathouse.

Inside was a large white cruiser. Asher led her onboard, to small the cabin below, where there was small bed. He turned toward her, leading her backwards by both hands, that ever-present cocky grin on his face. A giggle escaped her throat as he folded her in his arms again and they collided onto the tiny bed. The boat and bed seemed like such a happy convenience that she wondered if this was his intention all along when he led her from the reception. Not that she minded either way.

His hands slid down her zipper, while she unfastened his tie and buttons, sliding off his jacket and shirt simultaneously. They undressed each other, bit by bit, laughing and kissing the entire time. It was dark inside the boat, not even moonlight was visible within the cabin. Asher reached over to a control panel above the bed and flicked on a cool, greenish light that illuminated the space just enough to see shapes in the darkness. Water lapped at the sides as the boat rocked gently.

He paused, laying over her, brushing the hair from her face. Reverence and surprise shone in his eyes under the nightlight. "You are so beautiful, Lacey. You have a beautiful future ahead of you." His tone was very serious. "You don't ever have to be scared of anything at all. You can have and be anything you want. Anyone who would keep you from that is a fool."

Before she could take a breath to respond, he kissed her again, his words wrapping around her heart. Each kiss drove deeper meaning into his belief in her. He didn't just tell her that she was beautiful and capable, he made her feel those things, too. His hands glided over her skin, his mouth exploring every curve of her neck and dip of her chest. The energy within her grew into something new and her body hummed with desire and the feeling of his devotion.

Asher took his time in the boat cabin, exploring every inch of her, savoring every single gasp and whimper and moan. He knew the place under her ear, that if kissed, made her sigh. He knew that a thumb swept under her breast made her moan and arch her back, begging for more. Her skin tasted of vanilla and honey. No woman Asher had ever been with compared to Lacey. Every little thing about her, from the top of her brow, to the curl of her toe was exceptional. She squirmed under him, impatient, and he smirked against the skin of her breast. He wanted this to be slow. He wanted to take in every bit of her he could, committing each second to memory, enjoying their final night together.

The bed they were on was small, but they didn't need much room when they were completely wrapped up in one another. Asher crawled down her body, leaving a path of reverent kisses across her skin. He reached the apex of her thighs and she opened for him. He sunk two fingers into her core. Lacey moaned, arching her back at the touch, the sound making his cock twitch.

Asher dipped his head down, feathering kisses along the inside of her thighs before his tongue met her center. He took one, long lick of her, tasting her sweetness in his mouth. Lacey's fingers twisted into the striped sheets. He continued his passes, sweeping along her walls with his tongue, rubbing her clit with his thumb. He stole a glance at her face, seared by the fire and ecstasy in her eyes. One of her hands squeezed her breast, massaging it as he licked her. The sight of her touching herself made a rumble from his chest. His will to take things slow crumbled as the need to be inside of her surged.

He continued his ministrations, flicking his tongue across her heat as she moaned his name, beginning for him to brig her to the brink.

"Please," she strained.

Asher nipped at her clit and sent her over the edge, drinking her in as she pulsed around his tongue. He kept hold of her thighs as she cried out, not worried about any wandering wedding guests that might hear them. They were in their own little world, inside the small rocking boat.

Asher made his way back up to her, bringing his face was level with hers. Her bright eyes hooded, shadows of her long lashes stretching over her cheeks in the lamp's glow. A satisfied smile played around the corners of her mouth as she looked up at him, but he wasn't finished with her yet.

He kissed her again and flipped her onto her stomach. Asher hadn't taken her in this way yet and he wanted to experience every part of her. Lacey followed his lead, maneuvering back so that she was on her knees, her back pressed into his chest. Without any words, they understood one another, her body responding to his.

Asher slowly entered her from behind, filling her up, feeling her walls tighten around him. Lacey's head lolled back against his shoulder as their bodies connected. His lips went to her throat and began sucking as he set a rhythm of his hips. Lacey took his hands and placed them over her breasts, curling her fingers through his. He smirked into her neck; there was that demanding girl he had grown to love.

He stilled for a moment as he realized the thought that just sliced through his brain without warning. *Love.* He had thought of loving her.

Did he love her? He loved things about her, certainly. Her smile and laughter and warmth; the way she made him feel, whether he was happy or sad. They had only been together a week, but it felt like more than that to him. It was as if she had always been with him, he needed only to turn around and see that she was there.

But a week was all he had with her. She deserved so much more than he could give. He had seen her wistful expression during the wedding, and the way she watched the couples with a hint of envy in her eyes. He knew from her reflections about her previous relationship that Lacey wanted the white picket fence and fairytale ending. Asher wasn't the man to give that to her. He liked his life the way it was. He was happy living his life as he did. He didn't want anything to change.

But for the moment, he couldn't ever remember not wanting her.

Lacey's walls squeezed around him and he increased his thrusts, blocking out all other thoughts, and only concentrating on the pleasure he gave and she returned. The way Lacey's fingers intertwined with his as he kneaded her breasts, the delicious curve of her back and ass, they fit together perfectly, and there was no denying it.

Lacey reached back and turned her face to his, brushing her lips across his as he continued to pump inside of her. She could feel the tension mounting in her stomach as she climbed higher and higher toward her climax. Even though her body screamed for release, part of her didn't want it to be over. A door was being shut on something, before she got the chance to see where it led. The way Asher was touching her told her that he was committing the experience to memory, to store it away, but never to live it again.

"Lacey." It was a whisper against her cheek. He was getting there, too.

He moved one hand from her breast and pressed down on her clit with his finger. She squeezed her eyes shut as another intense feeling of pleasure overcame her. She couldn't hold on for much longer, soon she would have to let go.

"Asher," she whined, her voice shaky.

The orgasm hit her like a hurricane, sweeping through her, leaving her breathless. The intense feeling pulsed through her and she felt Asher reach his release, groaning into her neck, and gasping at their shared climax.

Lacey tilted forward, rolling over and Asher followed, lying down on his side to face her. She reached her hand up and cupped his cheek. His face was smoother than usual. He had shaved it for the wedding. She rubbed her thumb back and forth across his cheek as they lay together in the afterglow. Asher turned his face and kissed her palm, smiling at her. She smiled back and let her eyes flutter close, his arm slipping under her body and pulling her closer as they both settled and drifting off to sleep.

Chapter 11

Someone shaking both her shoulders awakened Lacey.

"Ow," she grumbled, attempting to escape by turning over. No luck.

"Sorry, sweetheart, time to wake up," Asher said, as she opened her eyes and focused on his face hovering above her, "We have a plane to catch."

Lacey nodded with a yawn and stretched out her arms, her eyes adjusting to the light from the small table lamp in the room. The windows in the boat's cabin were still dark.

"What time is it?" she asked, voice thick with sleep. Asher was sitting across from the bed, in just his trousers, grabbing socks from the pile of clothes he'd discarded last night.

"Five in the morning," he answered. "Our flight is at 7:15."

They had fallen asleep in the boathouse and missed the rest of the reception.

They dressed quickly in silence with secret smiles on their face as the previous night came back to them. Asher laced his hand through Lacey's as they headed back toward the house through the dewy fog, laughing to one another about their rustic walk of shame.

They only had about twenty minutes to pack up and head out to the airport. Lacey sleepily changed out of her dress and gathered her things, dumping them all into the suitcase without any time to worry about organization. Before she knew it, they were in a cab and heading away from the fairytale mansion.

Lacey felt sad at missing a chance to say goodbye to Aleksa and wish her well. There had been a small spark of friendship that had formed between the two of them. Unfortunately, it wouldn't have the chance to develop beyond that weekend. Peeking back at the house from the rear window, Lacey silently wished Aleksa a happy honeymoon and a joyful life with Duncan.

Her hand rested on the seat near Asher's. His face was turned toward his phone as he checked their flight schedule and the traffic to the airport. Her finger twitched toward his hand before she brought her hand away from the seat and folded it into her lap, turning her face toward the window.

It made her even sadder to think that she wouldn't see any of the people she'd met that weekend ever again. Not Aleksa, or Duncan, or Gwen, or even Jaime.

The plane touched down at O'hare just two hours later. Exhausted, Lacey slept through most of the flight. It was full morning in Chicago when they arrived, humid and bright.

"Where're you headed?" the driver asked when they stepped into their hired car. She recited Chloe's address as Asher climbed in beside her.

Lacey fell asleep once again and magically woke up the exact moment the cab stopped in front of Chloe's building.

"Lacey," Asher murmured into her ear. "You're making me nervous. Every time you fall asleep I worry that I won't be able to wake you again."

She poked her tongue out at him and he laughed as she got

out of the car. Asher stepped out too, helping her with her bag. They lingered on the stoop of Chloe's building, Asher gazing up at her from a few steps below.

"I suppose we've broken a rule," he mused. "I now know where you live."

She chuckled. "I technically don't live here anymore. I start moving out today." She yawned again and smiled. "I guess I'm officially off the clock."

Asher's mouth twisted into a wry grin. "I guess you are." He took another step up toward her and took her hand. "Thank you for a wonderful week, Lacey. Truly."

"Thank you, Asher. I had an amazing time," she smiled. She was trying her best to make it polite and professional, but deep down, she was sad to see him go. She didn't want to think about not seeing one another later that evening. There would be no more texts or take out dinners. She wouldn't be next to him when she went to bed. It was so strange how one week with this man had affected her so much.

"I was thinking," Lacey ventured, "I mean, I don't know if this would be weird but, maybe we could keep in touch? Stay friends?"

Asher blinked at Lacey. Oh no! She had read the situation completely wrong. He'd seemed sad too, and she thought —

"I would like that, Lacey." But for some reason, his response didn't convince her.

"That was weird, wasn't it? You don't have to be nice to me — "

Asher chuckled and shook his head. "It's not weird. It's fine," he reached up and cupped her cheek. "You're an extraordinary woman and I would enjoy being your friend."

Lacey smiled, relieved to hear him say so. "Maybe I should give you my phone number. My *real* phone number. Not the business one."

Asher handed her his phone and she typed her number. "Don't be a stranger."

"Of course not," he replied, "I'll call you soon."

He stepped up, giving her a quick kiss on the cheek, and then went back to the cab. Lacey watched the cab disappear down the street and around the corner, wondering if he really would call and if they really would be friends. She hoped so.

Once his cab was out of sight, she shouldered her duffle bag and turned to go upstairs, letting out another gigantic yawn. She didn't even want to think about moving that day. She was excited for it, but she wasn't looking forward to lugging all of her boxes up and down the stairs. Or going over to Grant's to retrieve the rest of her things.

She stuck her key into Chloe's lock and turned the doorknob.

"Good morning! Anyone hom—Oh my god!"

Lacey's mouth dropped open in shock as she spotted a very naked Delaney Sawyer sneaking out of the bathroom. She immediately slapped a hand over her eyes, hoping the image wouldn't be permanently seared into her brain. Her bag dropped to the floor as she fumbled around the door, trying to get into the apartment without looking.

"Lacey, I didn't know you were coming back this morning," she heard Chloe's voice enter the front room.

"Apparently not," Lacey replied, shutting the door, hand still over her eyes. "I came straight from the airport."

"Have a good weekend with Asher?" Delaney asked. She could practically hear him waggling his eyebrows.

Lacey extended one hand in front of her, trying not to run into anything.

"Delaney, go put pants on," Chloe ordered. "It's ok now, you can uncover your eyes."

Lacey slowly withdrew her hand and peeking around her fingers first to make sure Delaney was gone. Chloe stood there in her purple bathrobe.

"Oh my god!" Lacey exclaimed in a whisper. "You and Delaney?"

Chloe gave her the we'll-talk-about-it-later look. Lacey shook her head, noticing the take-out containers and clothing strewn around the living room floor. Something told her that it had been a little bit more than a one night stand.

Delaney came out again in pants and a fresh shirt, scooping up a discarded tie and threading it around his neck.

"The boss man is back, which means it's time for me to get to work."

Chloe walked him downstairs and then came back, starting a pot of coffee while not making eye contact with Lacey.

"Sooooo," Lacey teased.

"Sooooo, nothing," Chloe replied. Lacey gave her a look and her friend sighed. No way was she getting out of spilling the beans. "He kept emailing me at work and I finally agreed to go out with him Friday to get him to shut up. He's not as annoying as he seems."

"Okay," Lacey said, pursing her lips to hide her smile. If there was any chance that Chloe might actually like Delaney, she didn't want to push it.

"Enough about me. What about your weekend? How was the wedding?"

"Good. Asher's family was nice, for the most part," she said, thinking about the Roderick debacle. She told Chloe about the gorgeous wedding and how much she liked Aleksa.

"Good. I'm glad you had fun," Chloe smiled. "Speaking of work, I have a surprise for you."

Lacey perked up behind her coffee cup. "What is it?"

"It's good news and bad news. Bad news: Willa and I have decided not to keep you on as an escort."

The perkiness disappeared as quickly as it came. "What? Why not? Is this because I was too personal with Asher?"

"That's part of the reason," Chloe admitted. "But also because we're your friends, Lace. We know you and love you and you are just not cut out for this sort of job."

"Chloe! I am cut out for this job! Asher had an *amazing* week. No complaints! And I'm over the whole sex with a stranger thing, I promise."

Chloe held up her hand to stop her. "I did say I have good news." Lacey pressed her lips together and waited for her to continue. "Willa and I have decided to instead, hire you as a personal assistant."

Lacey opened and closed her mouth. "A what?"

"Well, like you always say, you're good at shopping. And the girls always need things like lingerie, toys, supplies. And they need styling for new photoshoots every six months. All of those things will be your job. Plus, doing some stuff around the office. Willa has plans for a host club as well, so we'll for sure need help with the planning."

"That sounds amazing!" Lacey beamed. "But wait, can you guys afford that?"

Chloe nodded. "Willa's been looking over the budget for the past couple of days and we definitely have room to hire another employee," she explained. "Regardless, we would have figured it out. We wouldn't leave you hanging."

"Chloe!" Excited, Lacey stood up and shuffled around the breakfast bar to hug her friend.

Lacey couldn't have been happier. In a week she went from no boyfriend, no apartment, no job to fantastic new job, her very own place, and a new sense of self that she wouldn't have traded for anything else in the world.

"Oof, last one." Lacey heaved one last cardboard box onto her new living room floor. She brushed the bit of hair that had fallen out of her messy bun and wiped at the sweat on her brow.

"Damn, you have a lot of stuff," Tucker said, taking a look around at all of the boxes he'd just helped move.

It had taken all afternoon, but she was completely moved in. The best part was she didn't even have to go to Grant's to get her things. As it turned out, Tucker was still in town, staying at the apartment she'd shared with her ex and agreed to bring over all of her things in his truck.

Lacey was super grateful, even though she felt kind of bad about putting Tucker in the middle of their fight. He'd said that Grant had tried to convince Tucker not to go so Lacey would be forced to come over and talk to him.

"Well Tucker Donovan, I think I owe you dinner," Lacey announced.

He chuckled. "I will definitely take you up on that," he said, his mouth turning into the same boyish grin that had made all the girls giggle during their high school days. "But first, I need a shower."

"Help yourself," Lacey said. "Wait, I don't have a shower curtain. Or towels. It's all packed."

He laughed again, shaking his head. Tucker had a blonde haired, blue eyed, all-American boy easiness that could roll with just about anything. "Okay, how about this? I head back to Grant's and change and we'll meet up later."

Tucker left and Lacey quickly found the box labeled "Bathroom". She unpacked her shower things. Baths it would be, until she had a chance to pick up a shower curtain.

A couple hours later, she texted Tucker and they made plans to meet up for dinner downtown. They'd decided to go out for Tex-Mex and margaritas. Lacey opted to wear her new favorite dress. It was red with an empire waist and an A-line skirt that fluttered out when she spun around.

She'd purchased it when she had been out shopping for the Art Institute Gala she went to with Asher. It had only been a week ago that they'd had their second date. Her eyes went to her phone. Asher hadn't called or texted, which felt unusual. Then again, he wasn't her fake boyfriend anymore and they had just seen each other that morning. They were just friends from here on out. Maybe. If he ever called.

The restaurant was full when she and Tucker arrived, but they didn't have to wait long to get a table. The hostess sat them in a booth by the window, where they could watch the people walking down the city sidewalk, the sounds of evening traffic accompanying the nightlife. Tucker ordered Lacey a margarita and a beer for himself, claiming margaritas were "too girly".

Tucker marveled at the people on the street and mused about how different the big city was from their little hometown. Lacey thought it was good for him to get away and experience something different. He was the one person in their friend group from high school who hadn't branched out yet and flown on to new and exciting things.

"So, who's this new guy you've been seeing?" Tucker asked after they had given their orders.

Lacey rolled her eyes. "I take it Grant told you?"

Tucker ducked his head, realizing he was caught. "He said that you were dating his boss?"

"I didn't know he was Grant's boss at the time."

"How did you even meet him? I mean, it all seems pretty fast after you and Grant just broke up."

"He cheated on me, Tucker. That made it all really easy to get over." She took a big gulp of her margarita and looked pointedly out of the window.

Tucker reached across the table and took her hand. "I know Lace, and I'm sorry. Grant's a dick. We've all known it since high school. You didn't deserve any of that."

Lacey looked back at him and offered a smile, appreciating the sentiment, even though she knew Tucker and Grant were still good friends and always would be, no matter what Grant did.

"So, is it serious with this new guy?"

Lacey sighed, thinking about her phone inside her purse and fighting the urge to check it. "No, it wasn't."

"Wasn't?"

"We decided we just worked better as friends."

Tucker took a sip of his beer. "Well, don't worry. If you and Grant can't work things out, I'm sure there's a guy out there who will be perfect for you."

Lacey smiled at Tucker's attempt at encouragement.

"Thanks Tuck, I hope you're right," she said, reaching across the table to take his hand again and giving it a squeeze.

Asher walked down the street with Delaney, his eyes fighting the desire to shut after such a long day. He had gone straight to work after dropping Lacey off earlier in the morning. After traveling and working all day, he wanted nothing more than to go home and crash. But Delaney had set up a dinner with some clients that they were trying to woo over to their firm, and Asher decided that he had better attend.

His fingers fidgeted against his phone in his pocket. He had thought about ringing Lacey, or texting her, to see how her day had gone. He remembered that she had mentioned she was moving into her new apartment and he considered checking in with her.

That afternoon, he'd mentally chastised himself for not offering to hire movers for her, but then realized it could have been a misunderstood attempt at controlling her. Developing her independence was important to her and he didn't want to once again present himself as patronizing ass.

Still, he wished for some excuse to open the lines of communication and continued to argue with himself back and forth for most of the day.

In the end, the conclusion to not contact her won out. At least, for the moment. She probably wanted some space and he didn't want to become clingy. Asher Knight was not a clinger.

Christ, she had practically friend-zoned him outside of Chloe's building that morning. He'd been hoping...well, he didn't know what he had been hoping. She was a girl who had just gotten out of a long relationship. She was in the middle of getting her life together. Of course she wouldn't want to jump into anything right away.

And there was also the lingering fact that he wasn't the relationship kind of guy. It was strange to have to remind himself. Being friends was probably the best way to go in the end. He didn't want to let her out of his life just yet, but at the same time, he wasn't sure in what way he wanted to keep her around, or if she was ready for anything more. He'd sit back and let everything just take its course. Inaction in this case, seemed like the best action.

Delaney and Asher walked into the restaurant. It was a hip Tex-Mex place, the kind that specialized in fancy tapas and fishbowl sized margaritas.

"This is where you choose to take out potential clients?" Asher asked, incredulous.

Delaney shrugged. "We want to show them a good time. Trust me, when you meet them, you'll get it. Alcohol will help."

Asher rolled his eyes, thinking about how many times the phrase "trust me" had gotten him in trouble. Delaney turned to speak to the hostess and Asher surveyed the restaurant. It was a trendy, younger crowd. There were couples on dates, a few groups of friends sharing large drinks, other professionals mixed in with the bunch enjoying a nightcap. His eyes stopped when he saw a familiar blonde across the restaurant in a cozy booth next to the window.

She was with another man, a handsome looking blonde. He looked like the All-American, former high school star, athlete kind of guy. She was smiling and laughing with him.

"Hey, who are you looking at?" Delaney asked, following the direction of his gaze. "Is that Lacey?"

"Yes," Asher replied.

"Who's that guy? Is he—He's not another client, is he?"

Asher watched Lacey reach over and take the man's hand, holding it in hers just long enough for a bolt of jealousy to hit Asher so hard it almost knocked him off his feet.

"Right this way, Mr. Sawyer," he heard the hostess say. Delaney nudged him into motion.

Asher turned away from watching Lacey and followed Delaney as the hostess led them to a more private section on the opposite side of the restaurant.

He fumed through each cocktail and the entire meal, completely useless and anti-social. Delaney passed him a few odd looks, but gave up trying to include him, and played it off as Asher being a surly work-a-holic who didn't get out much.

Asher kept staring in the direction of Lacey's table, wondering about her evening. Was that man a client? Or was it a date? He wasn't sure which was worse. The thought of her still working as an escort unnerved him. It hadn't even occurred to him before now that she would still be doing the job. Even more to the point, that she'd be with a new man the very same day her contract had ended with him. The thought of that blonde man putting his hands all over Lacey made Asher want to punch something.

From where he was sitting, he could see Lacey leaving the restaurant with her date. The man's hand was at her back as they walked out the door and down the street, out of sight. It took everything in him not to get up and follow them and demand who the man was and what the fuck Lacey was doing with him.

"You okay, boss man?" Delaney asked him under his breath.

"Fine," Asher muttered through his teeth.

"Does this have to do with a certain blonde distraction?"

Asher frowned at Delaney and motioned to the server for another scotch.

Tuesday morning. Not their usual coffee date day, but that morning Lacey was sitting at the coffee shop with not only her best friends, but her co-workers. Chloe, Willa, and Lacey had decided to treat themselves to breakfast before heading to the office for Lacey's first day as not an escort, but a receptionist/personal assistant. Not the most glamorous job in the world, but it was a start. She held her head higher and felt prouder of herself than she had in a long time. Going to work with her two best friends was like a dream come true. Willa asked her about her weekend at the wedding and Lacey regaled them with all of the details.

"Aleksa sounds...interesting," Chloe remarked, sipping at her latte.

Lacey knew what "interesting" was code for, but she let it slide, sharing a smile with Willa. "She was nice and fun. I'm sad I won't see her again. I thought about asking Asher for her number, maybe."

"What do you mean?" Willa asked. "You're still seeing him?"

"Um, yeah," she replied carefully. "We decided to keep in touch. Be friends."

"Oh please, you are completely crushing on this man!"

Lacey's eyes widened. "What!"

"Come on Lace, we know you have a thing for him," Chloe said. "We knew it the whole time. How do you think we realized you were not born to be a paid escort?"

Lacey's mouth twisted in offense before she let out a groan and finally came clean. "Okay, okay! Yes, I like him. He's just so amazing and warm and caring and sometimes funny and god the sex! It's just like, wow! And I love being with him. It's been like, twenty-four hours and I already can't stand that I haven't talked to him once."

Willa answered her crush ramble with a haughty smile. "See.

196

Told you."

"Well, it doesn't matter," Lacey said, coming back down to Earth, "he doesn't do relationships."

"How do you know?" Chloe asked.

"He told me. The first night we met. He said that's the reason he dates escorts, because he doesn't want to deal with relationship drama."

"We've heard that one dozens of times in this business." Chloe's statement did not make Lacey feel better.

"I don't know," Willa reasoned. "I mean, come on, you spent an entire weekend with this guy. Went on dates, slept at his house, met his family. He punched your ex-boyfriend and had a hissy fit over your pictures on the Internet. He treated you like an *actual* girlfriend the entire time. Men don't do that with escorts. He likes you, too."

"You think so?"

"Oh my god! Yes!" Willa exclaimed. "I know you've been out of the dating game since the twelfth grade, but it's so obvious."

A smile spread across Lacey's face. She definitely didn't hate having her friend convince her that Asher maybe also had feelings for her.

"Well, what should I do?"

"Tell him you like him," Willa advised. "That you want to date him and maybe try a relationship."

Lacey snorted. "Easier said than done."

"It *is* easy when the guy in question is into you." Which describes Asher is," Chloe told her. "Delaney said he thought so."

Lacey's eyebrows shot up. "Delaney?"

"Wait," Willa held out her hands to stop them both. "When did you talk to Delaney about Lacey and Asher?"

"Yeah Chlo', was it before or after you two played naked tonsil hockey," Lacey teased. Willa gaped back and forth at the two of them and Chloe was forced to spill yet again about her tryst with Delaney.

The conversation shifted from Lacey's love life to Chloe's as they finished up their breakfast. Lacey listened to her friends while she tried to plan what and when and how she was going to talk to Asher.

Chapter 12

Lacey sat at her new desk at Vamp Escorts. As a surprise, Chloe and Willa had gone shopping over the weekend and set up a workspace for her full of cute accessories. She took a few moments to enjoy her new surroundings—breathing in a new chapter—before getting straight to work.

First thing, she called each of the girls to introduce herself (professionally that is, she knew some of them already anyways) and asked them for supply lists, which they had been more than happy to give her. The things they needed made her giggle and blush, but she would get used to it. Honestly, she was relieved that Willa and Chloe had given her a job other than being an escort. After thinking on it, she decided they were right. She wasn't cut out for the call-girl life. She had gotten lucky with Asher.

The thought of Asher made her heart stop for a half second. She still hadn't heard anything from him. To be fair, she also hadn't contacted him, either. It took some time to plan what would become the big feeling reveal, the next step was to call him and find out when it would all be taking place. After running out for a mid-morning latte, she took out her phone on her walk back to the office and dialed Asher. He picked up after the second ring.

"Hello?"

"Hey! It's Lacey."

"I know," he replied.

Duh. Of course he knew. Caller ID. She felt nervous and couldn't read his tone. "Oh yeah, um, how's your day going?"

"Fine. Busy."

Lacey frowned at his shortness, her inner confidence balloon deflating. She didn't want to over-analyze. He did say he was busy and probably didn't have much time to chat.

"I was thinking...if you aren't too busy tonight maybe you would want to come by my new place and check it out. I'll make dinner."

"Uh sure, what time?"

"Seven-ish? I can text you my address."

"Fine. Seven. I'll see you then."

Asher disconnected before Lacey could even say goodbye. She watched her screen go black and got into the elevator of the building, feeling an overwhelming sense of dejection as she shoulder opened the door to the Vamp office and walked inside.

"Oh, hi."

"Hi," Lacey said, tilting her head in confusion at the woman standing in the middle of the office.

The woman was gorgeous, short, with dark hair, and full, dusky lips. She walked toward Lacey, extending her hand. "You must be, Lacey. I'm Jolie...or 'Scarlett' as I'm known on the website."

Lacey laughed in recognition. "Oh right, Scarlett! I filled in for you!"

"Oh, you can call me Jolie," she smiled.

She took Jolie's outstretched hand and shook it, admiring the woman's big smile. She remembered Willa telling her that Jolie was pre-med at Northwestern, working as an escort to pay her school tuition.

"I can never thank you enough for that, all the nights of working and studying and not sleeping finally caught up with me, I guess," she grinned. "I am jealous, though. I heard you got a pretty great gig out of that week."

"Yeah," Lacey said, walking over to her desk and setting down her coffee. "Asher was pretty great."

"No doubt," Jolie agreed, snapping her fingers in disappointment. "I'm so bummed, that could have been me. Maybe I'll get a second chance next time he books."

Lacey shot her a confused look. "What do you mean?"

"Willa said he was a regular client. Since you are off booking, he call back and I can give it a go. And who knows, maybe he'll want another girlfriend experience, that's a pretty cool idea you girls had."

"I don't know about that." Lacey became interested in shuffling the pens and papers on her desk, feeling a little less friendly.

"Oh," Jolie whispered in gentle understanding. "Oh no. You fell for him."

Lacey didn't answer or look up at Jolie, not feeling as chatty as before. She took a seat and turned to her laptop, hoping she would see how busy she was and leave. Instead, the escort grabbed the chair at Willa's desk and slid it over to sit next to her.

"Look, we've all been there. Every single one of us. We get all wrapped up in the moment, especially with regular clients, thinking that things are more than they are," Jolie placed a hand on top of the desk. "Occupational hazard, ya know? We have to be Oscar-worthy actresses and sometimes we're so good, we even fool ourselves."

"No offense," Lacey said. "But you don't know me or Asher and you don't know what you're talking about. We're friends. It's different."

"Okay," she backed off a little, "don't know you or this guy, but I can promise it's not different. You'll see. Once things start getting real, he'll realize that he was just in the sex haze and so were you, and the fun stops when the money gets cut off. He'll start to distant himself and go back to escorts. Trust me, save yourself the hurt. It's a hard truth."

Lacey didn't want to believe it. This woman had no idea what she was talking about. She didn't know Asher. He was different. He didn't just want Lacey because she was easy fun. Very little about their week together had been simple. There'd been ex-boyfriends and belligerent fathers and fights...though most of those things ended in sex.

She'd even admitted to herself after their argument over his possessive over-reaction to her website photos that if they had been in an actual relationship, things would have been handled differently. It would have been an apology from him, not a make-up blowjob from her.

Lacey shook her head. No, that didn't matter; it was just them figuring things out. It was different. They were different.

"Look, I'm really busy," she said to Jolie, who was still hovering near her desk.

"Right, okay," Jolie took the hint. "Well, I came by to see Willa and Chloe and let them know I'm ready for booking again so...if you could tell them."

"Sure," Lacey said, giving her a smile that didn't reach her eyes, and turning her attention back to her work at her laptop.

Lacey dashed to the front of her apartment when her doorbell rang at 7:15. Asher was standing in the doorway clearly having come straight from the office, his messenger bag slung over his shoulder. Lacey smiled at him moving to let him inside.

"Hey," she said, trying to keep her voice level and casual. She was still worried about his short tone from the call earlier, but also excited about showing off her new home.

"Evening, love," he smirked as he walked past her, dropping the bag near the door.

He seemed like he was in a better mood, but there was still something that bothered Lacey. Maybe it was just because she felt so keyed up that she couldn't fathom why he would be so calm.

"So, this is it," she swept out her hand, proud of her new home. "I know it's not much compared to your fancy bachelor pad."

Asher walked around, examining the space. There wasn't much to see, really. Large brown boxes were still piled everywhere and she didn't have any furniture yet. Her TV was sitting on the floor in front of some large pillows that were currently serving as her couch.

"I'm going out furniture shopping this weekend with Chloe," she explained. "And Grant let me have some stuff from our apartment."

The bonus furniture had all been thanks to Tucker pressuring him.

Asher's eyebrows flicked up. "How generous of him."

"It was the least he could do," Lacey quipped. "So, I know I said I would cook, but I realized that I don't have any pots and pans. Or silverware. I ordered some take away instead. Hope you're in the mood for Thai."

"I suppose I don't have a choice," he replied.

"Guess not." She bit her lip, trying to stay light-hearted, and hoping he was just teasing and she wasn't being dramatic in thinking that he was for some reason mad at her.

She led him over to the little carpet picnic table she'd set up in her living room, with the coffee table Grant had given her. Peanut-y smells of Pad Thai filled the tiny living room. Lacey handed him a box and a pair of chopsticks.

"Sorry we have to sit on the floor," she said, opening up her white box of noodles. "I really can't wait until I have real, actual furniture."

"I'm guessing that moving out on your own is proving to be more difficult than you thought?"

Lacey shrugged. "I guess I just forgot that I have get all this stuff now for myself. It doesn't just appear. Do you want some wine?"

Asher ignored her question. "It must be quite an adjustment not having everything handed to you all the time."

Lacey frowned, defensive. "I never had anything handed to me. I was just taken care of so I didn't have to do things by myself. I never had to learn how to do all this adult stuff."

"How is that different than having things handed to you? Like your current job? Oh, and didn't your friend Willa find this place for you?"

Lacey slammed down box and chopsticks. "Okay, what the hell is your problem?"

"I don't have a problem," he replied, with a fake smile.

"Then why are you being such a dick? Did something happen at work today?"

"Am I being a dick? Or am I just telling you things you don't want to hear?"

Lacey stood up abruptly. "If you don't want to be here, then maybe you should go."

Asher chuckled. "What's the matter? Are we not having a nice time?"

"No, we are not having a nice time. You've been nothing but rude since you walked through the door. I don't know what your problem is, but I'm not here for you to take it out on."

Asher stood up in front of her. "Would you be happier if I paid for your time?"

His words felt like a slap. In fact she felt like cracking him a good one herself for that statement.

"You know what, fine. If that's how you're going to be, then screw you. You know, the only reason I even invited you over tonight was to tell you that I like you, that I want to keep seeing you. But I don't want any of that if this is how you are going to be now."

She didn't know why she told him her feelings, especially now, but the words came out of her mouth before she could stop them.

Asher trailed his fingers along her bicep. "Well love, I told you before. I'm not the relationship kind of guy. But I've enjoyed your company. Perhaps we can work something out. At a discounted rate of course, since this arrangement would be to your benefit as well."

Lacey snatched her arm away from him, hot tears stinging her eyes. She refused to let herself cry in front of him. She couldn't believe he was standing in front of her, saying these things, acting this way. But then again, did she really know him at all? Maybe these were his true colors.

"You know, you really are fucked up aren't you? With all your family issues and dating escorts. I mean, what kind of man only has relationships with women that he can pay for?"

"That's a pretty rich judgment coming from the mouth of a whore."

Lacey's hand flew up and there was a loud crack as her palm connected with his cheek. Asher's head snapped to the side. He stared at the wall, cheek reddening, and his jaw clenched. Her palm throbbed from the force of the slap.

"Get out," she sneered.

Asher looked at her out of the corner of his eye, his mouth pressing into a tight, lifeless smile. With a casual grace he walked over and picked his messenger bag up off the floor. He paused before pulling the door shut and gave her a small nod.

"Have a nice life, love."

☎
One Month Later

Asher walked into his office, slinging his messenger bag down without a care as to where it landed. He just had an absolutely lousy day in court. With a frustrated groan he fell back into his leather desk chair, dragging his hand over his face and considering the bottle of scotch hidden in the secret cabinet within his bookshelf. His cell phone vibrated on his desk and he grabbed it , inspecting the number flashing on the screen.

It was the new escort agency he'd called last week. Most likely they were calling him back about booking an appointment. He hadn't been out with any escorts in a long while, not since...He swallowed down the uncomfortable feeling in his throat and pushed ignore, not wanting to deal with anything escort related at the moment.

"Bad day?" Delaney was there, darkening his door.

"Not the greatest," Asher admitted. "I'm hoping for better tomorrow."

Delaney nodded, shoving his hand into his pockets and walking toward his usual chair in front of Asher's desk. "I'm sure it'll turn around."

"I hope so," Asher said. "I have some emails to run though, do you fancy grabbing a drink once we head out?"

Delaney smirked. "Are you asking me out on a date?" Asher glowered at him. It was rather awkward for Asher to be the one asking Delaney to hang out. Usually it was the other way around.

"Anyways, no can do," he replied, "I'm on boyfriend duty tonight with Chloe. Engagement party."

"Still seeing her?"

"One whole month now," Delaney replied, ducking his head to hide his smile. "It's great. *She's* great."

"Wonderful," Asher muttered, turning his attention to his computer. He wasn't particularly interested in hearing how happy Delaney was with Chloe Dane. He had never particularly liked the woman that much.

"Lacey's pretty great too," Delaney added.

"Thriving in her new escort career, I'm sure."

"She's not an escort anymore. She quit after the wedding weekend and they hired her as this stylist-slash-personal assistant or whatever."

"If she is no longer an escort, then why are her pictures still up on the website?" Asher countered.

"So, you've looked her up."

Asher's eyes flicked over to Delaney, noticing a smug look on his face. Damn it, he'd slipped up. As a lawyer, he shouldn't have fell into this trap. He was disappointed in himself.

Yes, he had looked her up on the website. At first he was checking to see if she was still working as an escort. He always reckoned that she would have quit or maybe it was just that he wished she would. When her pictures never went away, he started to feel angry, and decided that holding onto his anger was the only way to ignore the niggling idea that maybe he'd been kind of a prick to her. It was useless, though. He couldn't be angry with her for finding a way to support herself.

When the anger faded, he started looking her up because he missed her. He missed seeing her; it was as simple as that, even if he wouldn't admit it out loud. He had been a complete ass that evening in her apartment. As always, his impulsiveness got the better of him and he sabotaged the one relationship it turned out he actually wanted.

"They leave them up because she pulls in clientele. But Chloe can usually convince them to book someone else," Delaney explained. "It's a little misleading but not a completely bad business move."

Asher continued to stare at the emails on his computer, hoping that Delaney would take the hint and leave him alone. He didn't care to discuss Chloe or her business or anything else that even remotely related to Lacey.

"Okay, well I'm out," Delaney said, finally realizing that his company was no longer wanted. "Have a good night."

As soon as Delaney was out of his office, Asher picked up his phone. His thumb hovered over the button, trying to decide whether or not to dial the number on the screen. Taking the plunge, he pushed the button and squeezed his eyes shut, lifting it to his ear. It was time he stopped torturing himself and just got on with it.

"Yes, hello, this is Asher Knight calling," he said, when the woman on the line answered. "I know it's short notice but I'd like to make an appointment for tonight, if you're free."

Lacey ran from one end of her apartment to the other, trying to find the heel that would match the red one that was already in her hand. She was already running late for Willa and Tristen's engagement party. They were doing drinks at a bar over in Wicker Park and it would take her around twenty minutes to get there by train. Chloe had already texted her twice asking where she was. Lacey smothered a yawn with her wrist, exhausted from being out all day, running errands around town.

Her life had done a complete one-eighty in the past month. Being a stylist and assistant at Vamp and working with Chloe and Willa was greater than she'd ever imagined. She never expected to fall into the working world as seamlessly as she had. Willa was even helping her figure out how to freelance her skills as a personal shopper and stylist in addition to what she was already doing at Vamp. She was so busy all the time establishing a brand and a fresh business for herself; she barely even had the chance to breathe.

Being busy was fine though, because the opposite meant being bored, and boredom meant thinking, and thinking meant thinking about…no, she did *not* want to go there. Any time her mind even tiptoed around the subject, she would slam the door shut, lock it, and bury the key. She had rehashed the entire heartbreaking scene long enough to give Chloe and Willa all the gruesome details, and then immediately banned the subject or his name from ever being brought up again.

Well, that wasn't entirely true. She had brought it up herself, last week, when she couldn't stand it anymore. It was last Tuesday morning. Willa was out for the day and Chloe and Lacey had been in the office by themselves. It had been one of those rare moments when Lacey had had a moment to breathe and think and her mind waded into dangerous waters.

"So," Lacey started, "I was wondering…has he who will not be named, you know, made any…appointments?"

"Voldemort?" Chloe teased, but gave her a sympathetic look. "Nope, I haven't heard from him at all."

Lacey had only felt half relieved. She was glad that he wasn't going out with other women that she worked with, but at the same time, she knew better than to assume that meant he hadn't hired any other escorts. She'd considered asking if Delaney had mentioned anything, but her pride won out that time, and she dropped the line of questioning.

Lacey's phone buzzed angrily on her coffee table, bringing her back to the present. She lifted her head out from under her couch and answered it.

"Where are you?" Willa asked on the other end.

"I'm leaving right this second. Walking out the door," she said as she got up and continued searching around for her shoe. Ah! She spotted the little devil in the corner of the room. Scooping it up, she smiled victoriously. "Be there in 20 minutes."

Willa and Tristen had reserved a cute garden area behind a

trendy hipster bar for their party; a buddy of Tristen's giving them the hookup. The warm summer air and electric glow of fairy lights over the terrace were soft and romantic. It was hard for any Chicagoan to resist an outdoor bar in the summertime and Lacey group of friends were no different.

Lacey spotted Willa and Tristen hanging out in the corner, surrounded by some of Tristen's old art school friends. She went over to say hi. Willa looked relieved to be pulled from the group as Lacey hugged her.

"I know I've said this, like, eight hundred times this week, but congratulations!"

"I'll never get tired of hearing it," Willa beamed from every angle, glowing from the top of her now completely aqua colored head to the bottom of her spiky her heeled toes. Lacey grasped her hand, demanding once again to see her ring. It was a simple blue sapphire Tristen had selected himself with a silver band. It was perfect for Willa, unlike the traditional diamond. Blue *was* Willa's favorite color after all.

Chloe joined them and the three girls chatted away, sipping cocktails, and teasing Willa about her lost single life. Lacey couldn't help but feel a little envious. This could have been her, engaged and happy, celebrating with friends and enjoying her time basking in the attention. It would have been with Grant, though. And she would have ended up in marriage that she would have eventually realized was a terrible mistake.

She didn't need to have regrets or reminisce about what could have been; she was happy now, being single, working on a career of sorts, hanging out with her friends...even though they were both in relationships now. Of course, Delaney chose that moment to walk in and slip his arm around Chloe, stealing her away.

Lacey swallowed the twinge of pain that Delaney's presence brought and continued to mingle with all of their other friends at the party, trying to flirt back with one of Tristen's cute photographer friends.

A few girls from Vamp showed up and pulled her away for some shots together. Tucker was visiting again and he bought her a couple drinks. Before she knew it, she was feeling rather light and tipsy, and having a great time in spite of the fact that she was single. Instead of letting what she didn't have weight her down, she let the possibility of what each night out could now become lift her up.

"I'm gonna find a bathroom," Lacey said to Tucker as he ordered them fresh drinks from the bar. He nodded and she turned to search for the sign to the restroom.

She hadn't taken two steps when all the good feelings she'd been floating on moments ago flew away and dropped her on her ass.

"Grant."

It had been a while since she had seen him. The last time had been when Asher had punched him at the baseball game. He had continued to text her and call her intermittently, still trying to get her to forgive him, but she stubbornly ignored him.

"Lacey, I—"she held up a hand to cut him off. She was drunk and she had no desire to bring up anything about their past relationship. Frankly, she just didn't give a damn about any of it anymore. Not when someone else had stomped on her heart so much more thoroughly than Grant Lucas ever had.

She shouldered past him and continued to the bathroom. By the time she was finished, she decided it might be best to leave the engagement party and avoid any potential drama. Peeking out the door to make sure the coast was clear, she rushed out and over toward Willa.

"Hey, what's up?" Willa asked, noticing the way her eyes darted around the party. "You okay?"

"Yeah. I'm sorry, I'm going to cut this short. Grant's here to stalk and bother."

Willa peered around her to see Grant standing in the middle of the room, his eyes on Lacey's back. "I understand," Willa said, giving her a pat on the shoulder. "Thanks for being here."

Lacey smiled, and pulled her into another hug. "Wouldn't miss it for the world."

She waved goodbye to Chloe and Tucker as she walked out, sure they would eventually cross paths with Grant and know why she ducked out early. The sidewalk outside was mostly clear of foot traffic, everyone already settled into their chosen bars and activities for the time being. Not wanting to waste the pleasant night air, she decided to walk a little ways before calling an Uber.

"Lacey!" Grant called after her running out of the bar. "Lace! Wait!"

Lacey stopped in her tracks and turned around, groaning loudly at him. "What, Grant? What do you want?"

Grant pulled a piece of paper out of his jacket pocket. He unfolded it and held it in front of her face. She groaned again when she recognized what he had. It was a printed screen shot of her profile from the Vamp website. She knew she shouldn't have let them keep it up.

"I knew it," Grant accused, "I knew when you said you got a job that Chloe and Willa had hired you. I didn't want to believe it. I thought 'no, not Lacey'. But then dating Asher Knight out of nowhere? I thought, 'well how did she meet him'? And when Tucker told me you two broke up, I couldn't help but wonder why it all happened so fast. I mean you went to his brother's wedding right? Met his family? It's all pretty serious for someone you've only known for a week."

Lacey crossed her arms. "I don't want to talk about Asher, Grant. It's none of your business."

"I don't give a fuck about Asher, Lacey. I care about *you*! What the hell are you doing? Working as a fucking prostitute?"

"I'm not a prostitute," She protested. "And if I were, what exactly would be the problem with that, huh? You've never judged Chlole and Willa. Why me?"

"So, what was Asher? He wasn't actually your boyfriend."

"I thought you didn't give a fuck about him?"

"Just tell me."

"It was a one time thing!" Lacey shouted, the alcohol in her system making her louder, angrier. "I agreed to fill in for one of the girls for Chloe and Willa because I needed money. We were supposed to go on one date and then he ended up paying me to spend the week with him and attended Duncan's wedding."

Grant gaped, his hazel eyes reflecting hurt and betrayal he had no right to feel. "You *are* a whore then?"

Lacey held back the urge to slap him. She wanted to scream at him that it was his fault. That he didn't leave her with a lot of choices and he only seemed to care about her when he thought he couldn't have her anymore. But it was pointless and she had had enough of his temper and judgment and bullshit. Instead of wasting another stupid word on him, she spun on her heels, needing to get away as fast as she could. Grant reached out and grabbed her.

"I didn't mean it," he pleaded.

"Fuck you," she cried, shoving him away. She spun again and darted away to cross the street.

"Please, Lace—"

The moment she stepped into the crosswalk the world tilted and everything got slow.

A car horn blasted in her ear, drowning out the fearful cry of her name from Grant. Her blonde hair whirled in front of her face as she twisted her head toward the sharp screech of tires. Two bright headlights barreled toward her before she even had a chance to move.

Her body was no longer her own. She was crumpled by a sudden force, rolling up and back down again, then dropped onto the ground. Numbness flooded her system, wind rushing from her lungs, leaving her gasping. The next thing she saw was Grant's face over her, blurry, but recognizable. His lips were moving but she couldn't understand what he was saying. The view of the night sky above her became fuzzy, stars behind Grant's head blinking out of existence as she tried to understand him. She couldn't move or breathe. Her head lolled to the side and then the sky and Grant disappeared.

Asher rolled over, dragging a hand across his face. It had been a few days since he'd shaved, his beard a bit longer than he usually kept it. It took him a few moments to realize it was his mad, vibrating phone that had pulled him from repose. His tired eyes looked at the alarm clock. It was just before midnight. Grumbling, he picked up the noisy device and inspected the caller ID. It was Delaney.

"Aren't you a bit old for the drunk dial, mate?"

"Asher." Delaney's voice was sober, bordering on somber. A sour feeling crawled down Asher's neck.

"What is it?" Delaney remained silent on the line for a few moments. Asher thought he heard a paging system in the background say something about a doctor. "Where are you?"

"I'm at the hospital."

"Why? What's happened?"

Delaney sighed. "I was at the engagement party with Chloe. It was her brother's and her friend Willa's engagement party…"

"Yes, and…"

"Lacey was there," Delaney told him. "There was an accident."

Asher's heart skipped a beat at the words "Lacey" and "accident" in the same sentence. He swung his legs over the edge of the bed and stood up, needing to move.

"Delaney, what happened? Is she alright?"

"She stumbled out into traffic, got hit by a car and it…it's pretty bad, boss man."

Pretty bad. Was she alive? Was she dead? What the fuck did

pretty bad mean? His jaw ticked back and forth.

"I just thought you would want to know."

Asher tried to remember to breathe. "Where are you?"

"Althaea Memorial."

Asher ended the call and placed the phone back on the nightstand. His head dropped into his hands and he fought against the quickening of his breath. It had been years since he'd experienced a panic attack. Not since his mother had died.

"Everything okay?" A female voice said behind him. A manicured hand slid across his shoulder and around his chest. Asher glanced over his shoulder at the naked brunette behind him in his bed. He had never felt more disgusted with himself that he did at that moment.

"No, it isn't," Asher murmured. "You need to leave."

Chapter 13

Asher had pulled on the first t-shirt and pair of jeans that he'd grasped and ran out of his apartment, jumping into a cab. The driver drifted through the empty streets at a leisurely speed despite Asher's offer of more money if he sped the hell up. His eyes stayed on his phone in case Delaney called him again. With little information to go on, he feared the worst. Time could be in short supply. Surely Delaney would call him if she...no, he couldn't think that.

At last the cab pulled up at the front of the ER and Asher tossed a wad of cash into the front seat, bursting out and heading through the sliding doors. He all but ran straight up to the reception desk to find out where Lacey was located.

"What's the name of the patient, sir?" The nurse in purple scrubs asked. She was young, possibly just out of school.

"Lacey," Asher replied.

"Lacey. . .what? Last name?"

217

Asher opened his mouth and then shut it again. He didn't know her last name. The small but important detail had never even occurred to him before. She hadn't given it to him the first night they met for security purposes, and he had never thought to ask.

"Hollis." A male voice answered from behind him. Asher turned and saw Grant Lucas's glare fixed in his direction. "Lacey Hollis."

He wanted to be angry at the younger man, but the shame he felt at not knowing Lacey's last name kept him silent. Asher stepped away from the reception desk and toward Grant. He was dressed nicely. Asher quickly presumed that he'd also been a guest at the party, his brain filing that assumption away for later examination. His eyes drifted down and noticed the blood stains on Grant's blue button up shirt. Asher wondered how it got there. What part had he taken in this accident?

"What are you doing here?" Grant questioned.

"I think that's obvious," Asher answered.

Grant scoffed. "Look, I know about the escort thing. I know that you paid Lacey to pretend to be your girlfriend." He stepped forward, getting right in Asher's face, his chin raised to challenge. "I'll ask one more time. What the hell are you doing here?"

Gone was the boy who had been nothing but a suck-up and an irritant since the moment he'd stepped into Asher's law office. In front of him stood a man, with an actual backbone. Asher might have admired it if he didn't hate him so much. Grant had become irritating in a whole new way ever since Asher had met Lacey.

"I called him." Delaney appeared in the hallway.

Grant transferred the angry glare in Delaney's direction. Delaney stood there, relaxed and completely unbothered by the younger man's attempt at authority. Grant finally gave up and left, heading back around the corner and away from Asher and Delaney.

"What happened?" Asher asked once they were alone.

"Grant showed up and Lacey decided to leave the party. He followed her outside and according to him they got into a fight. She was trying to run away from him and ran right out into the street...she didn't even see the car. He claims it hit her and she rolled right up onto the roof and back down the hood. At some point we heard sirens inside, ran out, and saw him freaking out as paramedics loaded her up."

Asher listened dejectedly as Delaney recounted the story for him, dark imagery of Lacey smeared on the side of a busy Chicago street filling his mind. The bloody mental image turned his stomach. "Where is she now? Is she...?"

"She's in the OR. They're still working on her. The doctors aren't saying much until they get her stabilized or whatever. But I heard the words internal bleeding a couple of times."

Asher nodded silently and followed Delaney over to the waiting room. Chloe was there, along with Willa and another guy Asher didn't know. Perhaps Chloe's younger brother, since they possessed the same sparrow like features. Chloe glared at him as he walked in and sat down, but she didn't say anything. He didn't care. Every single one of them could scowl at him as much as they wanted to. There was no way he was leaving until he knew Lacey's fate.

The wait was unbearable. The television hummed in the background, some crappy, low-budget movie no one paid attention to. Asher overheard Willa on the phone with Lacey's mother, letting her know the condition of their daughter. Delaney brought him a cup of stale hospital coffee, but it remained untouched on a small table surround by old copies of National Geographic. Asher slumped in his chair, staring at the wall, counting tiles just so he wouldn't go insane with waiting.

"Hey, sorry it took so long. I was halfway to the lake house when Tristen called," a blonde man came up to the group and joined them. "How is she?"

"It's okay," Chloe said, hugging him, "there hasn't been any news yet."

Asher recognized him. Tall, blonde, all-American, he was the guy he had seen Lacey out with that night at the Mexican restaurant. Lacey's new boyfriend, perhaps? Because of the gossip he'd heard from Delaney, he now knew that the man hadn't been a client after all.

Asher stood up and left the waiting room, feeling crowded. What had been going through his mind when he decided to come to the hospital? Lacey wasn't a part of his life anymore, and he wasn't a part of hers. He'd never given himself the chance to be.

"Hey," Chloe called after him, running to catch up. "Where are you going?"

Asher stopped and faced her. "I thought it might be getting a bit crowded. I don't know if Lacey's boyfriend would appreciate my presence."

"Tucker?" Chloe asked. "Tucker's a friend from high school. Not Lacey's boyfriend. Look—I don't even understand why you're here in the first place or why Delaney insisted on calling you. I thought you didn't give a damn about Lacey after the way you treated her."

Asher narrowed his eyes at her. Once again, Chloe Dane was making assumptions about things that were none of her damn business. He opened his mouth to respond, but Delaney interrupted, poking his head around the doorway.

"Doctors are out of surgery. They have news."

Asher and Chloe shared a nervous look and followed Delaney back into the waiting room. Everyone circled around a woman in blue scrubs. Delaney, Chloe, Willa, Tristen, Tucker, and Grant. Asher stood behind them, holding his breath in anticipation.

"My name is Dr. Weatherford," the petite woman began. "I've been with your friend, Miss Hollis."

"How is she?" Chloe asked.

"We've stopped her internal bleeding. Her vitals are fair for the moment. From what we can tell, she has four broken ribs and several contusions. We'll know more about any possible bone damage once we are able to get her in for a CT."

"Can we see her?" Willa chimed in.

"She's currently comatose I'm afraid. We've moved her into the ICU for further observation. I suggest you all go home and get some rest. One of you can leave your information with reception and they'll contact you if there is any update to her condition."

Chloe thanked the doctor and let her return to the OR. She volunteered to leave her number at the front desk and told everyone she would keep them informed. Asher watched Lacey's friends hug each other goodbye and head out one by one. It was almost three in the morning and everyone was exhausted. Chloe lingered in the waiting room, not noticing Asher lingering, too.

Once she turned and saw him, she seemed unsure by his continued presence. "I don't have your number, but I know Delaney does. He can call you if we hear anything."

It was as polite as a dismissal as she would probably give him. He ignored it.

"I'm staying."

Chloe let out a breath that indicated she had no energy to argue. Delaney gave Asher a nod and tugged Chloe away, leaving Asher alone in the waiting room. Once they were gone, he strolled over to reception again.

"Can I help you, sir?

"Where is Lacey Hollis located?"

The nurse typed something into the computer in front of her. "She's in room 6A." Asher turned to head through the doors to the ICU. "Excuse me sir, are you family?"

"No, I'm—I'm her boyfriend." The lie slipped out half-heartedly.

The nurse narrowed her eyes at him, but conceded. "We only allow 20-minute visits per hour."

With that she turned back to her work and let Asher pass

through.

He ventured down the too bright, sterile hall until he reached the room marked 6A. There was a stillness in the ICU, punctuated only by the beep and hiss of machines or the murmur of night-shift nurses. Asher hovered outside the door to Lacey's room, his hand motionless against the silver knob. Memories of his own car accident flashed before his eyes. Oliver still on a bed, tubes surrounding him, his mother's silent sobs and his father's fiery rage: Gwen, Duncan, and Jaime all begging Oliver to open his eyes once more. But he never did, and Asher would never forgive himself.

Before he could lose any more nerve, he turned the knob and pressed onward. Lacey was still as stone in the bed, engulfed by tubes and machines. A small desk lamp was the only thing breaking the darkness in her room. A low beep counted the slow and steady rhythm of her heart. Asher walked to her and stood over her bed. He hadn't seen her in more than a month. The last time he had looked at her face it had been red with anger, eyes hot with tears, and now...

She was pale and cold and too quiet. Tubes pulled her mouth down at an odd angle. Asher catalogued the injuries on her face: A nasty purple and yellow bruise covered her right cheek, her lip was spilt open, a cut sliced over her right eye, just above her brow. Pain sliced through him, pain at seeing this girl that he cared for in a state of near lifelessness. If she looked this bad on the outside, how bad was it on the inside? Her arms hung out over the sheet that tucked her in and he could see slashes and bruises there, too.

Asher pulled the chair up against the wall closer to the bed, and sat down, keeping his locked eyes on her face. The monitors next to him beat in a continuous rhythm, reminding him that no matter how bad it looked, she was still alive.

He stretched his fingers toward her hands but pulled back as the tips brushed her cool skin. He couldn't do it. He broke everything he cared about. Everything about the way she looked

222

reminded him of the past. He couldn't do this again. He couldn't lose someone else. It was his fault, in a way. He couldn't help but think that if he hadn't been such a self-destructive ass, he would have been with Lacey at that engagement party and she never would have fought with Grant or ran out into the street or gotten hit by the car.

For possibly only the second time in his life, he felt completely helpless. Not even when he was going through all the shit with Roderick did he feel this powerless. There was always an answer to those problems. After Oliver died, he knew that has been the worst thing he could ever experience. Every other problem or trial he would encounter in life would have a solution. Enough money or will power could fix anything.

Death and pain had no answer. He didn't know how to deal with either of those things. There was nothing he could do but sit and wait and hope that she would come out of this alive. He promised to whatever god was listening that he would make things right again with her. Or if she hated him and never wanted to see him again, he would honor that, too. Just as long as she would wake up and be alive and happy.

"Sir, your twenty minutes are up." The reception nurse was standing in the doorway. Asher hadn't even heard it open. Any energy he might have had to argue was completely drained. He looked over at Lacey's sleeping form one last time before following the nurse out to the waiting area. His head hanging between his shoulders, he walked over to the same chair he had been occupying before and sunk into it.

"Sir, as I said before, we only allow one twenty minute visit every hour."

"So, I'll wait an hour."

The nurse blinked in confusion. "It's 2:30 in the morning."

Asher's head rolled up to fix her with a bored look. She was slow on the uptake and it was irritating. "Then I'll be seeing you again at 3:30."

223

She sighed, finally seeming to get it. "There's coffee and tea around the corner if you need it."

Asher sat with Lacey for twenty-minutes, every hour. He never said anything or touched her, just sat and watched over her, listening to the draw of her breaths and the beeps of the monitors.

Eventually, the sun announced a new day. Light bled through the blinds, strips of orange appearing over Lacey's bruised face. The nurse came in to remind him it was time to leave once again. Her attitude had adjusted and she had become a little bit nicer over the past two hours, letting him stay for twenty-five minutes instead of just twenty. Asher sat in the main waiting area and pulled his phone out of his pocket to dial Delaney as the TV above him reported the traffic for the coming day.

"Everything okay?" Delaney answered.

"As okay as it can be," Asher replied. "Just wanted to let you know I won't be in the office today."

"Are you still at the hospital?"

"Yes."

There was a pause before Delaney spoke again. "Do you need anything?"

For her to wake up, to open her eyes, to survive.

"No."

"Whatever you say." Delaney didn't sound convinced, but Asher didn't care as he hung up and dropped his tired head into his hands. He rubbed at his eyes with the heel of his palms.

The nurses changed shifts just after nine. The next nurse—an older woman this time— wasn't as kind about visitors. She claimed that no one but family was allowed in. Asher narrowly avoided getting in a screaming match with the woman before Dr. Weatherford showed up and solved the problem. Asher overheard the doctor informing the nurse that he had been there through the night and was allowed to visit under the established visiting guidelines. His mouth twisted into a slight smirk. Small victories. He continued his silent twenty-minute visits throughout

224

the morning.

Delaney stopped by just after noon. Asher saw him sitting in the waiting area as the nurse escorted him back from another visit. Chloe was there with him.

"They won't let you in right now," he said to her, "they only allow one visit per hour."

"I'll go talk to them." Chloe stood and headed out of the waiting room. When she didn't come back, Asher assumed they must have let her pass.

"You look like hell," Delaney remarked, as Asher fell into the chair next to him.

Asher had caught his reflection earlier in the restroom mirror. His eyes were a raw red, purple shadows swooped underneath. His entire face was heavy with sleep and exhaustion, but he refused to rest, plying himself with the complimentary brown tar they called coffee in the hospital cafeteria.

"I went by your apartment and brought you a change of clothes, your phone charger, and a sandwich from the deli around the corner. I'm guessing you haven't eaten. Anything else you might want?"

Asher took the duffle full supplies and the brown bag with the sandwich and tossed them onto the vinyl chair next to him. "I could use a bourbon."

Delaney let out a soft chuckle. "I bet."

Asher sighed, pinching the bridge between his eyes. "I was with someone last night, when you called me. There was another woman in my bed."

"You're a free man." Delaney's reply struck him as too automatic, too flippant.

"You don't understand. It was the first time since her. The first time, and I—"

"Hey, you didn't know."

"That's not the point!" Asher raised his voice, drawing a few eyes of others in the waiting area. "Remember that night we saw her? At that restaurant? I thought she was with another client. I couldn't stop thinking about her and him—together—and I lost it. I completely lost it. I never felt so furious in my whole life. I—I had this thought that she was going to quit escorting and want to be with me or...something. And then, when I saw her the following evening, I just threw all my anger at her even after she told me exactly what I was wanting to hear: that she *did* want to be with me, but I just bloody sabotaged myself. And the truly ridiculous part of it all is, I don't even know why I did it. I could have had what I wanted, but..."

Asher poured out his frustration, knowing he wasn't making any sense, voicing thoughts that had only been echoes in his mind. Delaney reached over and put a hand on his shoulder.

"Do you love her?"

Asher's eyes snapped up, his brow furrowed. Of all the things Delaney could have said, that was the very last one he would have ever guessed to hear. Neither man was well acquainted with the notion of being in love. Delaney had been just as much of a bachelor as himself. It was one of the first things they found in common. But the introspective look on Delaney's face made him consider the thought. The way Delaney had been there with Chloe had escaped his attention before, but now that he thought about it, perhaps his friend was gravitating in the direction of something like love.

Asher let the question roll over in his mind. Did he love her? Did he even know what love was? He had only known Lacey for a week. He had only learned her last name the night before. Was that even long enough to be in love with someone?

"Hey." Chloe returned to the waiting area, interrupting his musings.

Delaney looked over at her and Asher found himself paying attention to the way Delaney acted toward her. There was a tense concern in the space between his eyes as he stood to hear her report, like he shared the pain that Chloe felt in someway. The way Asher felt Lacey's pain also belonged to him, in a way. But that was absurd.

"Hey, how does she look?"

"Awful," Chloe folded her arms across her stomach. "They said her vitals are pretty much the same. They only let me have 10 minutes because her boyfriend has been in and out all night."

Chloe's gaze slid to Asher. Her mouth was twisted slightly, but not in anger, more in amusement. Acceptance even. Asher had proven something to Chloe, but he also didn't care about her opinion.

Delaney and Chloe said their goodbyes soon after—Delaney needing to go back to work and Chloe still having a business to run—leaving Asher once again alone with his thoughts and worries. A check of the clock said he still had another forty minutes or so before the nurse would let him back into Lacey's room, so he decided to change into the clothes Delaney had brought.

He walked into the restroom and opened the bag. There was another pair of jeans and a t-shirt inside. After he changed, he pulled out the sandwich and tried to eat, but it turned out he didn't have much of an appetite. Asher put the sandwich back in the bag and noticed his phone charger. He pulled his phone out of his pocket. The battery was nearly flat. He took the charger out of the bag and plugged it in to the wall to charge his phone while he finished waiting.

At the turn of the hour, Asher walked back into Lacey's room. It was short of an entire day of seeing Lacey in bed, but it felt like weeks to Asher. She still looked the same. Her vitals hadn't changed, as Chloe had reported. Dr. Weatherford had come by to speak to him when she finished her midday rounds.

When she had gone, he pulled the chair that had been moved back against the wall over to the bed and sat down. His throat felt tight. With careful fingers, he traced the seams of her fingers, at last finding the courage to intertwine his hand with hers.

A single tear slipped down his face as he grasped her small hand with both of his and kissed the top of her fingers. "Remember when we were at the wedding and Duncan told me Roderick was going to be there? I came upstairs and got into bed and you held me in your arms. I felt so safe. No one ever made me feel like you did then. *No one.* Only you." He brushed her hair back with his palm, gaining some sort of odd strength as he touched her again. "I wish I had that now. I need you. I'm sorry it took something like this to make me realize that."

He chuckled a little at the realization that he had no idea whether she could hear him or not, and another memory coming to mind.

"You know, every time you slept, you were always completely comatose," his voice crackled against the emotions seizing his chest. "I never told you this, but every night, after our first night together, I played this game. I would try to do things to get you to wake up. I'd talk to you, play music, touch you, I could be as loud as I wanted and you wouldn't even blink an eye."

A shaky, panicked breath left him, something close to a sob, more tears following the one that had come before. "I love you.. I love everything about you. You are the best woman I've ever met, Lacey Hollis. And if you open your eyes I'll spend every day showing you just how bloody amazing I think you are. If you want me to, I will. If you can forgive me for being the world's biggest fucking idiot, I'll give you the world, because you deserve it all."

A frantic beeping sound ripped through the steady beat of the room, causing him to jerk away. Some type of alarm was going off. Two nurses burst into the room pushing past and rushing to check the monitors.

"She's in V Fib. Page Dr. Weatherford."

The other nurse rushed out while the first continued to work on Lacey. Asher backed into the corner. Two more nurses rushed in along with Dr. Weatherford. He heard them calling out instructions to one another, but the noise was muffled. His head was spinning.

He felt like he couldn't breathe. His own chest constricted as he watched them lay paddles on Lacey's chest to shock her body. She lifted slightly, but the monitor continued with its erratic, fast paced beeping. Another shock. No change. Asher held his breath, his fists clenching, knuckles going white. Another call from the doctor and another shock. They waited.

Chapter 14

Lacey blinked against the harsh light cutting in through her eyelids, blinding her. Not a great way to wake up. Her mouth tasted like cotton, her tongue like sand paper. She reached up to try and block some of the light, but couldn't move her hand. Taking a moment, she recognized someone's palm pressed into her own. Curious, she peeled back her eyelids slowly, to see who was holding her hand. She focused in on the top of the head lying against her bed, next to her hip, and a tuft of blonde curls.

"Asher?" Her voice sounded scratchy against her throat.

Asher's head snapped up, his blue eyes instantly alert. "You're awake."

He sounded relieved and terrified all at once. Lacey's vision began to settle and more of the scene came into view: cool blue walls, vinyl chairs, a door the restroom in the corner. She was in a hospital room, machines hooked up to her limbs, beeping behind her head.

"What happened? What are you doing here?"

"You were in an accident, love. A bad one. You've had two surgeries and have been in a coma for over 72 hours."

Lacey shook her head, trying to clear her thoughts. Two surgeries and three days missed. The last things she remembered being angry. Memories flickered into her consciousness and she recalled the last moments before she blacked out: Willa's engagement party, the argument in the street with Grant, the flashing lights of the car slamming into her.

Asher's hand was still in hers and she looked down at their joined palms, confused.

"But, why are *you* here?"

His face dropped and he pulled back his hand, only adding to her confusion. Even though she remembered the moments of the accident, her brain still felt fuzzy. She hadn't seen or heard from the man in over a month and only to wake up from coma and find him sitting by her bed, holding her hand. She didn't understand. Before she could ask him any more questions, Chloe and Delaney entered the room.

"Lacey, you're awake!" Chloe rushed toward the bed

"I'll grab the nurse," Delaney said, disappearing from the doorway.

Chloe gave her a timid hug, trying not to hurt anything. Lacey's arms felt like jelly, moving was difficult, and her right side hurt like hell. A nurse walked into the room, followed by Delaney.

"Hello Lacey. I'm Amanda, it's good to see you awake."

Lacey gave her a half smile and a weak hello. "I'm just going to take your blood pressure, sweetie."

Asher had stepped back, closer to the wall, watching over them. The nurse slipped the blood pressure cuff around her arm, her glance cutting back to where he stood. "Your boyfriend has been keeping quite the vigil since you came here."

The cuff tightened and Lacey let out a small gasp. Boyfriend? Asher? The cuff released again and Nurse Amanda stepped back.

"I've paged Dr. Weatherford. She should be along shortly to talk to you."

Satisfied with her checks, she left. Chloe approached her side again. "How are you feeling?"

"Tired, if that's even possible," Lacey said. " And thirsty."

"I'll find out if you can have some water," Chloe offered. "And I should probably call your mom."

Chloe left the room, Delaney following her out, and Lacey was alone with Asher again. She noticed her friend also didn't seem that surprised by his presence. He stood by the window, watching her carefully, his mouth turned down into a serious pout. But she was interrupted before she could ask him any of the questions running through her mind.

"Hello Lacey, I'm Dr. Weatherford, your surgeon." The doctor approached her, medical chart in hand, and read her monitors. After checking her vitals again, Dr. Weatherford began explaining to her the complicated collection of injuries she had acquired.

"Lacey, you were struck on the right side of your body. When you first arrived, we assessed internal bleeding which we were able to stop. From there we found two broken ribs and one bruised. You were in surgery and then moved to our ICU. Less than 24 hours later you suffered from cardiac arrest."

"A heart attack?"

The doctor nodded. "A puncture from one of your ribs caused air to build up and collapsed your lung. We inserted a tube into your chest and relieved the pressure. During your CT scan we found a break in your tibia. We preformed surgery again, but we're keeping an eye on the swelling, and once you're discharged you'll be on crutches for a while."

Lacey swallowed hard. Cardiac arrest, broken ribs, broken leg. She had gone through hell and slept through most of it.

"I feel like I can't move. Am I paralyzed?" She asked, dreading the doctor's answer.

"You're most likely suffering from slight muscle entropy due to the coma. And we've got you wrapped up pretty tight."

"What about my leg?"

"You'll be on crutches for a while, and you'll have to do some physical therapy once you get up and around again, but you'll be good as new."

"Did I have any head injuries?"

The doctor shook her head. "Not any we ascertained. Are you feeling any pain in your head?"

"No," Lacey answered, "I just—no."

The doctor eyed her cautiously, but nodded, accepting her answer. "Well, make sure you get plenty of rest. Your body is still healing."

"Thanks, Dr. Weatherford," Lacey replied.

The woman smiled and left the room, letting Lacey know to have her paged if she needed to discuss anything else.

"So, I don't have amnesia or anything?"

Asher pushed himself off the wall he had been leaning against while the doctor spoke, coming closer to her bed again. "Wouldn't you know?"

She shrugged and winced at the movement, it kind of hurt. "The last thing I remember is you being a complete dick to me and not seeing you for a month. Then I wake up in a hospital and you're here and the nurses are calling you my boyfriend."

The frown on his face deepened and he shoved his hands into his pockets. He looked so very tired, dark circles under his eyes and a few days worth of stubble across his jaw. "Is it terrible that I wish you did have amnesia? At least about certain things."

"So, getting hit by a car is what it takes to get your attention and get an apology from you?"

"I was an idiot."

"You were a dick," Lacey repeated. She was tired and it was difficult to pull off indignant while lying down, but she held her ground as best she could.

"If you hate me, if you want me to go. I'll leave. I just needed to know that you were going to be alright."

The look on his face crushed her. It reminded her of a kicked puppy. Part of her wanted to be frustrated that he was the one looking hurt when it was he who did the hurting. But the fact that he'd been at the hospital with her—for a long time from what she could guess based on everyone's reactions to his presence—made her swallow the irritation down.

"Asher, I don't hate you. I don't think I'd ever be able to hate you. Even though I did try, I still missed you."

Sadness still crinkled his eyes as he reach for her hand again, threading their fingers together. It felt like a first step back into good graces. His lips touched the back of her knuckles and Lacey's couldn't feel much because of whatever pain medication she was on, but her heart skipped at the contact.

"I was so scared. More scared than I've been in my whole life," he admitted, "I thought I'd lost you for good."

She grinned, squeezing his hand back, knowing that they had a lot to talk about. "You can't get rid of me that easily."

The day seemed long for Lacey even though she was only awake for the afternoon. Tiredness got the better of her in spite of being asleep for three whole days. Her body was recovering. She'd talked to her mom on the phone—who apologized repeatedly for not being there. Lacey reassured her that she was okay, and that there was no reason for her to spend money on a plane ticket to Chicago just to watch her lay in bed. It was a little disconcerting hearing her tough, deputy mother cry over the phone.

Chloe and Asher had hovered nearby all day. Chloe made calls to their friends and let everyone know that she was awake, but she was too tired to see anyone currently. Delaney hung around too, mostly divided between supporting Chloe and Asher. Something was still bothering her about Asher being there, but she couldn't put her finger on what it was. It wasn't that she didn't want him to be there, something was just off about it.

Delaney came to pick Chloe up and tugged her out of the room to go out to dinner. The doctors informed Lacey that she would be extending her stay at least a few more days. Chloe, the dutiful friend that she was, offered to run by Lacey's apartment and bring her anything she needed.

"Shampoo, I guess? Toothbrush. I don't know how I'm supposed to take a bath," Lacey frowned. "Make up?"

Chloe noted her list and then headed out to grab dinner, promising to be back soon. Lacey was alone with Asher once again.

"Make up? How shallow am I?" Lacey laughed, hissing when a sharp pain shot through her ribs. She grabbed her side where is hurt the most, feeling the bandages underneath her hospital gown. Asher rushed to her side.

"Are you alright?"

"Fine. It just hurts to laugh." She shifted a bit as the pain subsided, trying to get comfortable.

"Do you need pain mediation?"

"No . . ."

Asher narrowed his gaze. "Lacey..."

"I don't want any right now. It will make me fall asleep."

"You need sleep. You need to rest."

"But I'm scared that I won't wake up again. What if I fall into another coma?"

Asher sat down beside her, his tone gentle. "I don't think that will happen."

Lacey's teeth worried her bottom lip. She could feel a bump there, where there was a cut she hadn't noticed before. How horrible must she look right now, she wondered. She hadn't seen herself, but judging by the way she felt it was probably pretty bad.

"You should go home," Lacey suggested, noticing Asher's eyes look even more downcast, if that were possible, and she quickly clarified. "You need a shower, and some food. Have you even left the hospital at all?"

"No."

"Seriously. Go. I'll be fine, like you said." Lacey tried to give him a reassuring smile.

"I'm fine, I—"

"Asher, I don't want you to take this the wrong way, but…I need some time. Alone. For just a while. Please?"

His shoulders fell, but he nodded. "I'll be back in an hour?"

"Perfect," she answered, giving him a small smile that she hoped he read as encouraging. He leaned forward, as if he was going to kiss her, but then changed his mind. Lacey watched him grab his small duffle bag from the corner, letting her eyes slide close as he left the room.

She wasn't kicking him out; she just really needed alone time to sort through her thoughts and trauma of the accident. It had been impossible with everyone hovering over her since she had woken up.

"Hey—oh, sorry. You're sleeping."

Chloe walked through the door, waking Lacey up. She hadn't even realized she dozed off.

"It's okay. I don't really want to sleep anyway," Lacey said, rubbing her eyes.

"Where's Asher?"

"He left to go home for a little while. He's coming back."

Chloe's eyebrows flicked up in surprise "Wow. I can't believe it."

"What do you mean?"

"Lacey, the man hasn't left the hospital in four days. He stayed with you in ICU. They would only let him in to see you in intervals and he would come in, sit with you, and then go back and wait until the next turn."

"He stayed?" Lacey asked.

Chloe nodded. "Yeah. And when they moved you to a room, he sat in that chair. He wouldn't leave for anything. Not for me or Willa or Tucker. Delaney brought him food and clean clothes. I don't think he's slept the entire time."

Lacey couldn't believe it. She thought of seeing his sleeping head when she first woke up, and she wondered if that had been the first time he had fallen asleep since he'd been with her.

"I just don't understand it..."

"Lacey," Chloe said, taking the chair next to the bed. Asher's chair. The one he had apparently been camping out in. "I know I haven't really had the best opinion of Asher since he came into your life, but I have to say, he definitely cares about you. I see that now. And I think he regrets what happened between you two."

Lacey sighed. "I know he does. We talked. Kind of."

"And?"

"And, I just—"

"Hey," a new voice interrupted. The two girls looked over to see Grant hovering in the doorway, his hands shoved into the pockets of his jeans.

"Hey," Lacey returned. Grant ducked his head toward his chest and Lacey could guess that he wanted to talk. She recalled echoes of their fight seconds before the car had struck her. His tentative gaze passed to Chloe.

"Chloe, could you give us a few minutes?" Lacey requested.

Chloe looked back at her and Lacey gave a nod to let her know everything would be fine. Maybe in the past she would have been hesitant to be alone in the room with her ex, but it seemed the near-death experience was giving her a little perspective.

"I'll head home, unless you need anything else?"

Lacey shook her head. "I'm good."

Chloe left and Grant stepped into the room.

Chapter 15

It had been nearing two hours when Asher walked back through the sliding doors of the hospital. He hadn't meant to be gone for so long, but he'd accidentally fallen asleep the moment he sat down on his bed to remove his shoes. After a quick shower, shave, and a stop to grab a decent cup of coffee, he returned to the hospital. He hoped to find Lacey resting. Someone would have called him if something happened, wouldn't they? He'd left his number with almost every nurse he could find, in case of emergency. He tried to shake away the paranoid thoughts as he stepped off the elevator and continued down the hall. She was fine now, awake and stable. She would be fine.

Asher approached the door pausing, when he saw Grant slipping out. The younger man turned and saw him, too. His hand remained on the silver knob and he stood, their gazes locked and sizing up the situation. Grant was the first to speak.

"So, you're still hanging around?"

"That's right," Asher replied.

"I'm surprised you haven't fired me yet," he said.

Asher shrugged. "It's not exactly legal to fire someone because they've hurt the woman you love."

Asher didn't miss the way Grant's face twisted at the mention of "love."

"You love her?"

Asher wasn't even sure why it slipped out. Maybe he felt a need to stake claim, but it didn't make it any less true.

"Yes."

"You barely know her. You didn't even know her last name until I told you, four days ago."

Asher couldn't argue that there was a lot he didn't know about Lacey. He didn't know her birthday or her favorite food or color. He didn't know her mother's first name or where she grew up. But he knew she was a strong woman, smarter than anyone gave her credit for, shallow sometimes, but kind to almost everyone she met. He knew the essence of her soul.

"You're wrong about that, mate. I know her better from a week in her company than you did in all your years together."

Grant's jaw ticked, but he had no response, brushing past Asher and disappearing around the corner. Asher smirked to himself, heading into the room. Lacey was still in the bed of course, her eyes opened as he walked into the room. He didn't realize how tense he'd been until a smile from her allowed him to relax.

"You're back."

"Of course," he replied, resuming his usual seat.

"Coffee for me?"

Asher chuckled. "I believe you are restricted from heavy food and drink at the moment, love."

Lacey's pout made him chuckle. The playfulness faded though, as she turned serious once again. "Grant was just here."

"I saw him."

"We talked," she explained. "He felt like the accident was his fault, but I told him it wasn't. I'm pretty sure it's the first civil conversation we've had since we broke up."

Asher tried to keep his expression indifferent. He didn't know if he agreed with the part about who was at fault. "Well, good for you."

"I think he finally gets that we're over."

Asher nodded and took a sip of his coffee, letting the silence hang, filling the sterile air between them.

"Ugh! Would you stop, please?"

Asher tilted his head to the side. "Stop what?"

Lacey's voice raised an octave, her hands waving wildly in front of her. "Sulking. Being dramatic. I'm the one in the hospital! I should be sad and moody! Not you! You should be telling me to cheer up. You're stealing my thunder. Ow!"

Her face twisted and she held her side to ease the shooting pains caused by her outburst. Asher's mouth twisted into a smile, a slight chuckle making his shoulders to bob up and down.

"There, that's it," Lacey pointed at him. "That's what was off."

"What are you talking about?"

"You've been so serious, I haven't seen you smile once since I've been awake. I miss it. I like your smile. I'm a sucker for dimples."

Asher smiled again, it was a small one, but if it made her happy…"My apologies for not smiling enough. It's been a taxing few days."

Lacey shrugged. "I wouldn't know. I was asleep for most of it."

Asher reached over and squeezed her hand, entwining their fingers, letting the warmth of her skin chase away the coldness he felt. She failed to hide the tiny yawn that bubbled from her lips.

"You should sleep, love."

"Not tired," she murmured.

"That's a lie if I ever heard one."

Lacey poked out her tongue and he laughed. This was good, he thought, *this* felt like them, her lightness dispelling his tendency toward darkness.

"On one condition," she said. Asher raised a brow, eager to hear her negotiation. "Stay with me."

"Of course," he replied without hesitating. There was no question that he would sit right next to her all through the night.

"No, I mean in the bed." The purple bruise on her cheek mixed with the warm blush that crept up at her timid request.

"I don't know if I can. I might hurt you."

Lacey shook her head. "You won't," she said, her voice shrinking again. "Please? I know it's a lot to ask but—"

Asher silenced her, leaning forward and placing a gentle kiss on her lips. He could feel her twitch in surprise, but her lips melded into his. It was the first kiss they'd shared in a long time. "Alright, love."

Lacey tried to shift over, but moving proved to be difficult, so Asher helped her as best he could. He stretched out next to her on his side, looking at her with his head propped in his hand. They couldn't cuddle properly, because of her wraps and casts and tubes. He settled for placing a hand on her cheek, brushing his thumb back and forth over her soft skin, mindful of the scraps and bruises.

"Close your eyes," he whispered. She gave him a small smile and did as he said. Almost immediately he heard her breathing even out as she fell asleep.

A week later, Lacey was heading home. She had never been so happy in her entire life. Asher had stayed with her the entire week, hardly letting her out of his sight. A couple days after she had woken, Dr. Weatherford had her up and out of bed, trying to walk. It hurt, but it also felt good to move her limbs after being still for so long.

"Now, it will be painful and cumbersome for a while to do daily activities like showering and dressing. But as long as you take it slow and stick to your physical therapy, you should make a full recovery," the doctor had told her.

The nurses wheeled Lacey out to the exit and Asher was waiting there, in the driver's seat of a blue Ford Escape. He climbed out and walked around the car to help her get in as the nurses loaded her one small bag into the back seat. She put her weight on Asher's arms as she stood, carefully stepping toward the car.

"Whose car?"

"Gwen's," he replied. "She traded with me for the time being. An R8 is much too low for you to sit in."

Lacey raised an eyebrow. "R8? Aren't you impressive?"

He leaned forward and gave her lips a quick peck. "Don't you forget it."

She giggled as he shut the door and walked around to the driver's side. He was in a good mood, which made her glad. Over the past week he had a few mood swings, but was gradually getting better the more she improved.

Asher drove her to her apartment, landing a lucky parking spot right in front of her building. He ignored her when she fought against him carrying her up the stairs and sat her down on the couch, mumbling about how it was too low for her to be sitting in and ran down to grab her bag.

She was still pouting when he reappeared inside her living room. "I think stairs are a bit of a fantasy yet, love."

The doctor had given her crutches, but using them was beyond difficult with her broken ribs.

"Oh my god." Lacey's hand covered her mouth as some realization hit her.

"What's wrong?" Asher was in front of her in an instant, his face turning a shade whiter.

"I can't use stairs."

"No," he affirmed. "Probably not until your ribs heal and you can use the crutches."

"But how am I supposed to leave the house? Go to the grocery store? Go to work? Live?"

Her eyes widened and her voice got louder with each item she listed. Asher took her hand, holding it in both of his and placed a gentle kiss over her knuckles. "You don't have to do any of that. Well, except the living part," he told her. "Your job, for now, is to rest and get better."

"But what am I supposed to do for money?"

Asher shrugged. "Don't worry about it."

She narrowed her eyes at him, understanding the insinuation. "Asher, no."

"It's not a discussion."

"No!" She aruged. Damn it! She wished she could stand up. "I can't take money from you."

"Why not? It's done. I've already paid your land lord for the next six months and opened a line of credit for any other expenses."

"Because I—I can't have things handed to me, Asher. You said that yourself."

He frowned. "I wish you would forget that. I didn't mean anything I said that night."

"Yes, you were an ass about it, but it was true. You were right about that. I did have things handed to me. But you know what? In the past month I finally started learning how to live as my own person and to take care of myself."

A sob nestled itself into her throat, the tears welling. She finally realized what had truly been bugging her the past week since she had woken up. It wasn't Asher, or Grant, or anyone else. It wasn't even the physical pain she constantly felt. It was the loss of her new found and treasured independence. No one thought

244

she would make it on her own after Grant had left her and she'd wanted to prove them all wrong.

Life was unfair. Just as she was finding her footing, the stupid accident had to happen to ruin it all.

Asher walked over and took a seat on the coffee table in front of her "You're owed a break, love. You've been in a terrible accident," he cupped her fae and she leaned into his touch, trying to feel reassured. "It's okay to accept help from friends."

"I guess you're right," she muttered, not entirely convinced.

"I am right," he smirked. "Now, we have to see about getting you another couch."

"Asher!"

He ignored her shout, grabbing her laptop from the kitchen counter and setting it in her lap. "Pick whichever you'd like and make an order. Consider it another apology present."

Lacey rolled her eyes. He wasn't giving up. She opened the computer and began her quest for a new, more accident-recovery-friendly couch.

Two weeks later Chloe and Willa stopped by for a visit. It had been forever since they'd spent time together. Lacey spent most of the time on the couch, watching bad daytime TV and hanging out with Asher. He indulged her and watched all of her girly shows and movies, brought her magazines and food and kept her entertained, but it didn't make up for the girl time she missed. As soon as her friends got there, she immediately sent Asher away. He reluctantly left, promising to be back before her friends were gone.

Chloe and Willa brought over food and set up at the small dining table in Lacey's kitchen, another Asher-approved furniture present.

"He complains about all the furniture being too low, forcing me to sit at odd angles, and against doctor's orders. I swear he would just redecorate the entire apartment if I let him."

"Why don't you?" Willa winked. She'd gotten her nose

pierced since Lacey saw her last, a little blue jewel on the side of her nostril that matched her hair.

"I can't do that!"

"Does he ever leave?" Chloe asked, handing Lacey the takeout salad she'd brought her.

"No! He's taken a leave of absence from work to stay here all the time. He takes me to physical therapy, runs my errands, cleans, cooks, he does everything!"

"Aw, that's sweet. Do you think you could teach me how to get Tristen to do all that?"

"It's kind of annoying is what it is," Lacey muttered, shoving a forkful of lettuce and dressing into her mouth.

"Annoying?" Chloe asked. "He just wants to take care of you while you're recovering. I'm sure he'll ease up in a week or two when you start to move around a bit more on your own."

"Maybe," Lacey sighed. She felt bad for complaining that he was being so wonderful. "I love him and I appreciate it, but damn, I need some space sometimes."

"Wait," Chloe halted the conversation. "Did you just say you love him?"

Lacey blinked. Did she say that? The word had just sort of popped out. She considered it for a moment, letting the idea actually take shape in her head.

Yes, Asher was irritating the daylights out of her lately, but truth be told, she had started missing him about thirty seconds after he walked out the door. He'd been nothing but considerate and kind to her since she had woken up from the coma. It would have been difficult for anyone else in her life to devote that much time to her needs.

Over the past couple weeks, she'd kept thinking about their time apart. That month had been agony. She'd felt all the things over their ending than she had over her break up with Grant. Now that he was back in her life, she didn't want him to leave again.

"I think so," she said finally. "Maybe I do."

"You should tell him," Willa encouraged.

"Oh yeah, cause it went so well the last time I tried to tell him I had feelings for him."

"It's different though," said Chloe. "Because he *definitely* loves you."

"I don't know," Lacey said.

"What makes you say that?"

"Things are different than they were before. We don't have sex. Sometimes he'll kiss me, but it's like a friend type kiss. Not a passionate, romantic kiss. And he barely touches me. I mean, we sleep in the same bed together, but he doesn't even touch me then. Most nights I wake up and he's moved to the couch."

"Well, can you even be having sex yet?" Willa asked.

"I actually don't know. But I'm sure Nurse Asher does." The three of them laughed, joking about how he would look in a cheesy, nurse Halloween costume.

Before long, Willa and Chloe had to get back to the office, there were a couple new girls coming in to interview about being escorts. Lacey wished them luck and they left. She was alone for the first time in weeks.

She glanced at her phone and thought about texting Asher to find out when he would be back, but thought better of it. She wanted to enjoy some alone time and didn't want to give him any indication that he should rush home.

Slowly, she stood up from the table and limped out of the kitchen. The combination of her tender ribs and the cast on her leg made movement more than a little difficult. She was slow as she hobbled through the living room and toward the bathroom. It had been ages since she'd had an actual shower. Standing for long periods of time still hurt, so she usually opted for baths instead when Chloe could come over and help out, or just washing up in the sink. But today she would try a shower.

Lacey walked into the bathroom and began to undress, which was also difficult, since it hurt to lift her arms. She gingerly removed her t-shirt and pajama shorts and wrapped a towel around herself, carefully bending to reach for the faucet knob. There were plastic wrappings that Willa had found for her on the Internet to protect her leg cast whenever she bathed. Once her cast was secured, she took out her toothbrush and waited for the steam to fill the bathroom. She examined herself in the mirror while she brushed her teeth. The bruises and cuts on her face had healed quite nicely, although she still had a scar above her eyebrow. She wondered if she would always have that scar.

Lacey heard her front door open and close and Asher call out to her.

"I'm in here," she yelled back.

Asher opened the door to the bathroom, finding Lacey in her white fluffy towel. She tried not to roll her eyes at him just barging in without knocking.

"What are you doing?" he demanded.

"I was going to take a shower," she replied, ignoring his irritation.

"Have you lost your mind? A shower?"

Lacey glared. "Yes, a shower. I haven't showered in weeks. I'm tired of baths and feeling completely gross all the time."

"What if you slipped or fell?"

"I think I can manage standing still in a shower for ten minutes, thank you."

"Out of the question," Asher said. "Call Chloe back over later and have her help you if you want a bath."

Lacey wanted to explode from frustration, but as Asher reached across her to shut off the water, another idea popped into her head. She reached out and stilled his arm.

"Wait, I have a better idea."

Asher glanced over at her again skeptically, irritation still creasing the corners of his eyes. He could be so stubborn. "What is it?"

"Why don't *you* help me take a shower?" Lacey bit her lip,

gauging his face for a reaction. What she hadn't said to Chloe and Willa before was that she was worried that he wasn't sexually attracted to her anymore. Maybe they were really just friends now. Maybe after seeing her look awful and beat up and at her very worst he didn't think of her as sexy anymore.

Asher straightened up and stared at her as if she had made the worst suggestion he had ever heard. She pulled her towel closer around her.

"I don't know if that would be a good idea," he said, his voice very low.

"Why not?" She let out a half-nervous laugh. "It's not like we haven't seen each other naked before. Or showered together."

"The doctor said no strenuous activity—including sex—for six weeks, love. We've still got another three to go."

Lacey's eyes snapped back up to him. "So, you *do* want to have sex with me?"

"Of course I do," Asher replied, dumbstruck by the question. "Why would you—"

"You always leave me in the middle of the night. I wake up sometimes and find you on the couch."

"I don't want to accidentally hurt you while I sleep," Asher explained.

"I just thought that after everything...seeing me this way—"

Asher cut her off with a crushing kiss. He fixed his hands on each side of her face as his tongue cut through the seam of her lips and invaded her mouth. Lacey could feel the arousal hit her fast. Asher pulled away, but touched his forehead to hers, keeping them close.

"Lacey, trust me, once you are fully healed I plan on throwing you down on the bed and ravishing you until you beg for mercy."

A sharp thrill coursed through Lacey's body at the rakish smirk that spread across his face. She reached her hand around the back of his head and pulled him in for another kiss.

"Well, showering is innocent enough," she remarked.

"Not the way I remember it, sweetheart."

Lacey could hear the husky quality of his voice and sensed that he was very close to giving in to her suggestion. Feeling bold, she stood and reached up to unknot her towel, letting it fall to the floor.

"Lacey…" Asher warned, but she lifted a finger to his mouth to quiet him.

She reached down to the hem of his t-shirt and lifted it up. She tried to hide her grimace as her ribs protested the movement of her arms. Asher noticed and stilled her hands. Lacey frowned, preparing to argue that they keep going, until she realized that Asher was helping her remove his clothes. He got rid of his shirt and she reached down to unzip his pants.

Once he was completely naked, Asher turned to check the water's temperature.

"Come on," he said, holding out his hands to help her into the shower. Lacey carefully stepped up and over the tub, while Asher held on to her waist and joined her.

"Tell me if you start to feel too much pain," he said, the worried look still on his face.

Lacey nodded and gave him a delicate kiss, determined to make him stop treating her like his patient.

Asher held on to her as she stood under the spray and let the water soak through her hair and skin. It felt so nice to tip her head back, close her eyes, and let the warmth wash over her. She couldn't help the dulcet moans that rumbled from her throat. When she tipped her head forward again to look at Asher, his eyes were on her breasts. Lacey grinned, removing one of his hands from her wait and placing it on her chest.

"There are things we can still do, other than sex," Lacey suggested.

This time Asher didn't need much convincing. He dipped his head down to kiss her as his hand began to massage her breast.

Lacey sighed at the feel of his fingers kneading her flesh. She wrapped her arms around his neck to support herself as he drew her in closer.

"Take a step back," Asher instructed. She did and he pressed her up against the wall. The cool tile shocked her warm skin and she flinched. "Are you alright?"

"Yes," Lacey answered, forcing herself not to groan at his concern.

Asher nodded and went back to kissing her, trailing his lips along jaw and throat. His hand skimmed down her stomach, blazing a trail down to her core. He traced his fingers over her entrance, teasing her. Lacey could feel the throbbing ache. She gave her hips a little thrust, which hurt like hell, but thankfully Asher was too distracted to notice the painful reaction in her face. She didn't care about that anyway. She wanted him inside of her now; she didn't care which part of him she had to settle for at the moment.

He slid one finger through her slit and then added another, moving in and out in a slow rhythm, circling his thumb across her clit as he worked her with his fingers. The pace and roughness of his hands felt amazing inside of her. It had been so long since he had touched her and she couldn't wait to be able to experience him fully. But for now, she was just glad he was touching her.

Asher nipped lightly at her throat and before long she came undone under his ministrations. She gasped as the bubble of pleasure inside of her burst and grasped onto his shoulders for support as her orgasm overtook her. Her breaths came quick, causing her ribs to ache, but she focused on the feeling of bliss and relief his fingers pulled from her. When she met his gaze, she smiled.

"Thank you," she said, for lack of anything else to say.

"Thank you," he smirked, giving her lips a small peck.

"Your turn." She could feel his hardness twitching against her belly.

Asher chuckled and pushed away the hand that was reaching for him. "Let's get you washed up first."

Lacey frowned, but didn't protest. He held onto her while she washed her hair and body. When she was done he shut off the water and grabbed another fluffy white towel to dry her off. He was slow as he ran the material over her body. It was like he was studying every corner and curve of her, getting himself reacquainted. It wasn't lost on Lacey that Asher had ended their shower before she had a chance to return the favor.

She brushed her hand over his cock as he stood, eliciting a slight hiss from his lips.

"Lacey, you don't have to..."

"I want to," she replied. "If this is all we can do now, let me have this."

"You're not in too much pain right now?"

The standing and walking hurt her leg and the heavy breathing from her orgasm had made her ribs feel extra tender, but she chose to shrug it off. "Asher, trust me. This whole caring thing is really great, but I could use a little less chivalry right now and a little more action."

Asher smirked and lifted her out of the shower. He carried her toward the bedroom and gently laid her on top of the bed, making her more comfortable. Careful not to let any of his weight fall on her, he hovered over her and kissed her, taking her hand and guiding it to his cock. She began to stroke him slowly, running the tips of her fingers over his velvet shaft. As she pumped him with her hand, she nipped at his neck, tracing random patterns on his skin with her tongue.

Before long he found his release. He went to the bathroom to clean up and then came back into the bedroom, pulling Lacey onto his chest. A little glow settled over Lacey.

"So, how long do we have until actual sex?" She mused.

"Three   weeks."

Lacey smirked into his chest, tracing the lines of his muscles with her finger. "Three of the longest weeks of my life. To add to the seven on top of that."

Asher chuckled, running his fingers through her damp hair. She couldn't help but notice that he hadn't agreed with her on the lack of sex in his life and her mind began to wonder. It could be nothing, but the thought was nagging her and she couldn't help but pursue it.

"Did you see anyone else while we were apart?"

Asher unconsciously tensed and that told her all she needed to know. It hurt, but honestly he had every right to date other women, escort or otherwise. Although, the romantic in her hated that he hadn't just curled up in a depressive ball after their fight.

"There was one," he finally admitted.

"Oh."

She kept quiet, not knowing what else to say. One wrong word and Asher would think she was hurt or angry. She didn't feel either emotion, not exactly.

"It was the night of your accident," he explained. She could hear the regret in Asher's voice and it helped to alleviate some of the negativity she felt over his admission.

"It's fine," she told him. "I mean, we weren't together."

"It doesn't matter, I still regret it."

"There's no need for regret."

"Yes, there is." Asher let out a heavy sigh and moved her so that he could get up from the bed. He walked over to Lacey's dresser and opened the drawer where he kept his things, pulling out a pair of briefs and putting them on.

"What do you mean? Because of our fight?"

"Yes and no," he answered over his shoulder. "I don't want to talk about this."

Lacey sat up and wrapped her purple sheet around herself. "But we never talked about any of it. We just sort of pushed everything under the rug. I'm not mad or anything, I forgive you like I said, but I still don't understand why you went off on me the

253

way you did. At first I thought you realized you didn't want anything serious, and you were just having a typical guy freak out. But with everything that's happened the past few weeks, I don't think that was right. What happened?"

Her voice sounded so small and vulnerable on the last question. Asher turned around and went back over to the bed, sitting down next to her. "I know most people don't mean this when they say it, but it wasn't you, it was me," he explained, brushing a curl behind her ear. "I saw you out one night with your friend, Tucker, and I thought he was a client or another boyfriend."

"So, you were jealous?" Lacey asked. Asher nodded and she couldn't help the slight chuckle that gave way. "Why didn't you just ask me?"

"I'm an impulsive man, darling; more action, less talk. And perhaps, I was a bit scared of where we were heading."

"Well, you're doing a pretty good job of talking now," she said, cupping his face, brushing her thumb along his cheek.

"Thank you," he said. "Any other questions then?"

"Just one."

Asher sighed, almost afraid of what she would ask. He felt like he was just barely staying out of trouble with her, even though there were no more secrets being kept between them. "Go ahead."

Her grin turned mischievous. "What was it you were saying about more action, less talk?"

Asher returned her smile with one of his own. He leaned her back on the bed once again and kissed her lips, pulling the sheet away from her body. "Allow me to show you, love."

By the end of her fourth week home, Asher had practically moved into Lacey's apartment. He only ever went home to grab more clothes and other miscellaneous items. Thankfully, he was allowing her to be home alone during those trips, no longer bothering her friends to babysit. He continued to take care of her and help out while she was still recovering. Of course, they often had different views of what constituted as "care" which caused one or two minor spats between them.

In spite of everything, they had settled into a nice routine. They had even figured out a few more creative work-arounds in the bedroom. Although, Asher had to admit, he was looking forward for the next two weeks flying by, keeping a careful eye to make sure she was healing at a steady pace.

"Are you ever going to go back to work?" Lacey asked over dinner one night. They were eating take-out on the couch he had given her that first week home.

"I reckoned I'd give it another week. Duncan and Delaney are fine with me taking some time."

"Don't you miss it?" Asher shrugged noncommittally. "Oh, come on, when we met you totally gave up on all relationships because you were such a self-proclaimed workaholic."

"That wasn't the only reason."

"Still…"

"Still what?"

"Nothing," she said, chewing her food. "Did I tell you I really liked the care package that Aleksa sent me? It was really nice. Especially the tiny soaps."

"Twice," Asher narrowed his eyes at her. "What did you mean by 'still'?"

Lacey sighed, wishing she hadn't brought it up.. "It's just…I don't want you to feel obligated to stay here and take care of me."

Asher regarded her with weary eyes. Was she growing tired of him? He thought things had been going well since their talk the week before. They had cleared the air and he had even started to feel less guilty about his indiscretion. He had thought they were past it, but maybe he had been wrong. "Do you want me to leave?"

"No!" She said quickly. " It's just—I mean, the thing is, I can't do this."

"Do what?"

"The friends-with-benefits thing. I'm not that kind of girl."

Asher blinked at her. "Friends with benefits?"

"You know, the sex and the non-commitment. I'm just not cut out for that. We figured that out when I completely bombed as an escort," she grinned.

Asher sat down his bowl and turned toward her. He removed the dish from her hands and cupped her face, looking into her eyes and reading her insecurity. He couldn't believe that she still didn't get it. After all these weeks she still didn't understand what he was trying to show her. They had talked about the accident and about their time apart and he'd remained by her side. He'd made promises to her while she slept in the ICU. Asher knew how he felt and he had said as much to Grant that day in the hospital corridor, but he realized that for all the talks he'd shared with Lacey, he never actually said the words to her.

"Lacey Hollis, there is no place I'd rather be, than right here with you. Walking out on you the first time was the worst decision I ever made and I never plan on doing it again. I thought I wanted my life to be a certain way…but then you came along…I've never felt so lucky. I can't possibly imagine my life without you. I'm in love with you."

The smile that broke out over her face was worth everything in the world to him. He had plans for them, the kind of things he used to scoff about, that he couldn't wait to experience with her. He didn't want to control her life or future, but build it up together, support her in whatever she needed. It was love he felt, the forever kind of love. The kind he never thought he would be capable of or even wanted to attempt. It was because he hadn't met her, though. She was the only one.

"Oh my god, Asher," she said, happy tears in her voice. "I love you, too."

Epilogue

One Year Later

She walked into a bar wearing a tight, black and gold dress and five-inch strappy heels. Her hips swished provocatively as she breezed through the hotel lobby straight toward the bar. Men turned their heads and gaped at this vixen strutting across the tile like it was her personal runway, but she didn't pay them any mind. She was on a mission. She had a job to do. It had been a while since she had done anything like this. Anticipation rushed through her, giving her courage, making her feeling deliciously excited.

She swept into the hotel bar and her kohl-lined eyes scanned the patrons for her target. The yellow lights along the walls were dimmed, soft piano music coming from the back. It had a very noir feel. There were a few businessmen scattered around, they looked up at her when she walked in, but her eyes were on the man seated in one of the high-backed leather chairs. Tousled, curly blonde hair, a grey expensive looking suit; he was her mark.

Lacey took a deep breath and headed forward to meet him. She walked right up to him next to the bar, but didn't meet his eye. Instead she addressed the bartender.

"I'll have a seltzer, *s'il vous plaît*," she ordered. The bartender nodded and poured her a glass, sliding it to her across the bar.

"Funny, I would have pegged you for a gin and tonic girl," the man next to her remarked in his lilting, English accent.

"I don't drink while I'm working." She shifted to face him, tossing her blonde curls over her shoulder. She noticed the half emptied glass of scotch in front of him. "I see that you have no problem with drinking on the job, Agent Knight."

"Well," he smirked, "as I'm sure you've heard Agent Hollis, I don't play by the rules."

She took a sip of her drink, trying to ignore the flirtatious look in his eye. "I have a message for you."

"Let's hear it then, love."

She shook her head. "Not here. See those men over there?" Lacey pointed to a trio of black suits huddled into a booth. "Russian mafia. We should go upstairs to my room."

"If you insist," he shrugged, throwing back the rest of the drink. He slipped his jacket off the back of the barstool and followed her out of the hotel bar.

He couldn't help but notice the tempting way her hips swung back and forth, in time with the clacking of her heels across the marbled tile. His cock twitched inside his pants at the thought of those hips rotating against his own.

"Ahem." The soft noise of her clearing her throat brought him out of his lust filled thoughts. They had reached the lifts. The doors slid open and he followed her in, nodding to the couple that exited. She pressed the floor to the penthouse and the elevator took them up.

He watched her fidget nervously, her teeth worrying her perfect pink lips. If it weren't for the cameras in the lifts, he would

258

push her up against the wall and take her right there. But he could wait. Just a few more minutes and they would be inside the room, and she would be his.

They got off the elevator and she opened the door with her silver key card. The room was dark inside, except for a few candles that had been left around the room.

"So, what's the mysterious secret message, love?"

Asher had no warning as she pounced and plastered her lips against his. Her arms circled his neck squeezing him close, melding her body fully against him. Without hesitation his own arms encircled her waist, fingers pressing into those hips he had been fantasizing about just moments ago. Just as he was beginning to enjoy himself, she ripped away and hurried across the room.

"I'm sorry, I don't know what came over me." She gasped, her chest heaving from the force of her kiss.

Asher smirked, slinking toward her. "No point in fighting it."

"But we're in enemy agencies. We can't!"

Lacey loved the drama. He gripped her by the elbow and hauled her against him. "No one ever has to know."

He kissed her again, swallowing any of her further attempts at protest.

They stumbled over to the bed, kissing and ripping at each other's clothes. Agent Hollis let out a heady moan as they fell back against the sheets and Asher began sucking at her throat, her legs wrapped around him. His hands trailed up her leg and —

A cell phone rang loudly from the nightstand. The wedding march ringtone.

"That will be Chloe," Lacey groaned, pushing Asher off of her and rolling over to grab her phone. "What's up, Chlo?"

It was the night before Chloe and Delaney's wedding. Her best friend had decided to elope a week ago and their group rushed off to Paris for the wedding and celebration. Lacey still couldn't get over how quickly it all had happened. She never imagined Chloe would be the first of them to tie the knot, but she'd been wrong about a lot of her expectations in life.

Lacey massaged her temple and shot her boyfriend an apologetic look as she listened to the nerve-racked woman on the other line.

"Don't worry, I'll take care of it. It's almost midnight, you need your rest," she cajoled. "I promise everything will be perfect."

Lacey hung up and tossed the phone back. Asher was stretched out on the bed beside her. "Trouble in paradise?"

"A little," Lacey sighed. "The airline called. Luggage is still missing, including her wedding dress. And the bakery called to say that their orders got switched and they may not have the cake ready in time for tomorrow."

"I guess that means you'll be working that out for the rest of the night."

Lacey nodded. "Sorry Agent Knight, another time I suppose."

She leaned forward and nipped his lips. Asher smiled. "Another time, Agent Hollis."

When Asher woke the next morning, Lacey was already awake, and on the phone with airlines and bakeries, trying to sort out her friend's wedding. He smiled as she paced around the room in her underwear and half curled hair. She looked messy and frantic and absolutely adorable.

"What about cupcakes? Cute cupcakes with shimmering frosting? Oh, and those little pearl things. Can you have those ready by five?" She said into the phone.

Asher walked up to her and pulled her in for a good morning kiss on the cheek. She smiled at him and continued her phone conversation, trying to understand the French baker. He left her and walked into the bathroom to shave and start getting ready. Once her call was finished, Lacey joined him in the bathroom.

"Okay, so the cake problem is sorted out. And the airport

should have the luggage delivered by three, which gives the future Mrs. Delaney Sawyer just enough time to slip into her dress and sprint down the aisle." Lacey let out a large breath. She scooped up her toothbrush and applied some toothpaste.

Asher chuckled. He stood behind her, studying her reflection in the mirror, noting the faint scar above her brow. It had been almost a year since the accident, but he had never forgotten the feeling of almost losing the amazing woman standing in front of him. Each day they were together, he was grateful that the powers-that-be gave him a second chance.

Lacey finished brushing her teeth and turned around to face him. Wrapping her arms around him. "Sorry we were interrupted last night."

"No need to be sorry, love," he said. "Once the wedding is over, we can enjoy some time to ourselves." He lowered his lips to hers to steal a minty kiss. "We still have a few extra days in Paris."

"Plenty of time for Agent Hollis and Agent Knight to get into trouble," she smirked.

Asher chuckled and stole her lips once again, groaning when a knock at the door interrupted.

"Can't we get a bloody moment?"

Lacey slipped on a robe and went to answer the door. "It isn't our day, it's Chloe and Delaney's."

She opened the door to reveal the smirking groom. "Talking about me?" Lacey rolled her eyes and let him in. "Mind if I steal the boss man for a little while?"

"Not at all," she said. "I'll go check on the bride."

Lacey grabbed her things to go get ready in Chloe's room.

"Well, well, well, this is a pleasant surprise."

Lacey turned, recognizing the mischievous voice of Jaime Knight.

"Good morning, Jaime."

His playful brown eyes raked down her robe-clad form. "It

certainly is."

Lacey wrinkled her nose at his flirting and rolled her eyes. "Don't make me hurt you before noon."

The youngest Knight laughed. "In a poor mood because you were interrupted last night, Agent Hollis?" Lacey's mouth dropped open and her face turned cherry-red. "Old building, thin walls," he explained.

"Damn it, Jaime!"

Jaime was another reason Asher had been lamenting the interruption of their alone time. His youngest brother had been staying at his apartment for the past month. Lacey was still fuzzy on the details, but Asher was hesitant to leave him to his own devices for too long, and the only time they had been alone was on the rare night Asher would stay over at her place.

They'd been more or less obligated to invite Jaime along to the Paris excursion, even though he had yet to meet any of her friends and didn't know anyone besides her, Asher, Delaney, and Gabriel.

He laughed gleefully and returned to his room before Lacey could enact any violence. Her next mission—okay, poor choice of words—but her next goal was figuring out what was going on with Jaime night.

Delaney and Chloe were married in a small ceremony along the Champs de Mars. The sun shimmered over the group in the cloudless sky, with the Eiffel Tower glittering behind. All of their friends were there including Willa and Lacey as bridesmaids, while Gabriel and Asher served as groomsmen. Tristen circled during the brief ceremony, snapping pictures. Chloe's gorgeous dress had arrived just in time, and she was an absolutely beautiful bride.

The cupcakes arrived at the restaurant where they had their

reception dinner without difficulty. Lacey had pulled everything off without a single flaw, feeling breathless and giddy by the time she sat down and enjoyed her first glass of champagne.

After dinner, Asher spun her effortlessly around the small wooden dance floor. It reminded her of their first week together, at Duncan and Aleksa's wedding. So much had changed since then. Lacey and Aleksa had the opportunity after all to become better friends. Lacey had even spent a few weekends in New York while Duncan spent time in Chicago.

Lacey remained in her apartment and Asher in his. There were questions about why they hadn't moved in together yet, but any time someone was nosy enough to ask they'd just smile at one another and say they'd get there eventually.

Even after a year of being together, neither of them felt any need to change a thing. Lacey found she liked retaining some sort of independence while still being in a relationship, and Asher found that he felt the same way. They just liked being together. Simple as that.

Lacey glanced across the dance floor and saw Delaney and Chloe swaying together, Delaney whispering in his bride's ear. Chloe gave him a secret smile and pressed a kiss to his lips. Tristan snapped a discreet picture of his sister and new brother-in-law, a dark look clouding his face. Asher turned them and Lacey's found the reason for Tristen's sour expression. Willa, her now ice blonde hair, and Jaime who was pestering her from across the table.

"Oh no, your brother is attacking Willa," Lacey said. "I should go save her."

She tried to move, but Asher held on tight, pulling her to the other end of the dance floor. "Willa is a big girl, she can handle my brother," he said. "In fact, I'd quite like to see her put him in his place."

Lacey laughed, letting herself be pulled away to continue their dance. Asher held her close, feathering kisses along her ear. She looked up at the newlyweds once again and smiled at Chloe across the room.

"Do you think that would be us one day?"

Asher pulled back to look where she was gazing. "Do you want to get married?"

She looked up into his sea colored eyes, happy to see there wasn't a single sign of nerves. It wasn't a proposal, just a question. "Someday."

Asher smiled and pressed a lingering kiss to her lips.

Someday was the only promise either of them ever needed.

Acknowledgements

Kady Weatherford. I bet you didn't expect to see your name first, huh? You are the one who convinced me to run with this idea when I first shared it during the height of our fan-fiction writing days. Thanks for being an excellent beta reader and source of encouragement when I was first stretching my writing muscles.

Thank you to Ashley, Alex, Becky, Leah, and Miranda, the ones I refer to as my "Sisterwives." Near, far, wherever you are, I will always love you. I think I mixed up songs there. Anyways, you girls are the best ever, willing to discuss fictional things at all hours of the day or night, and I can't imagine not knowing you. Thank you for reading and supporting my various writings over the years--especially this one.

To my mom, Diane. I wouldn't be here without your love. Nor would I have written this type of book if you hadn't let me watch *Pretty Woman* as a young child. So, thanks for that, too.

To my dad, Tom. Damn, I wish you were here to see this.

Even though maybe it would be awkward to read a romantic book that includes sex scenes written by your daughter? Either way I think you would be proud of me for following my dreams, like you always told me to do. I'll never forget that. Fuck cancer!

To Hanna, for being a fantastic editor and catching all my errors. Thank you for the generosity of your time and your hard work. This book sounds way better thanks to your efforts.

Thank you Brandon, the best big brother from another mother. I'm so glad to have you as a touchstone to my childhood, someone who saw all my embarrassing teen moments and stuck around. Thanks for always kicking my ass into gear and not letting me even feel too sorry for myself for too long. My life wouldn't be the same without you.

Of course, thank you to my love, Kyle. You give me a romance novel type of love everyday, only better, because it's real. Your support, patience, and thoughtfulness is truly out of this world.

I could never close this out without passing the biggest of thank you's to each and every KC-er out there who ever left me a comment, kudo, like, fave, follow, etc. This happened because of you. The time spent in the fandom was truly an amazing experience and I met people from all around the country and globe I would not otherwise know. I wrote the original fan-fiction almost a decade ago and I still get messages about it asking where it is, when it will be published, can I please email you a copy or put it back online. This love is the kind that fills my heart and soul. And I'm so glad you guys are willing to wait for me, no matter how long it takes.

Wondering how Aleksa and Duncan made it to their happily ever after? Stay tuned for the next installment of the *Call On Me* series from Katie Edward!

To stay up to date with the latest news about Katie and her writing follow:
Instagram: @romance_is_punk
Facebook: /katieedwardauthor

www.KatieEdward.com

Valley Lily Press

www.ingramcontent.com/pod-product-compliance
Lightning Source LLC
Chambersburg PA
CBHW021230250626
47155CB00008B/2941